A Note on the Author

Allan Gaw studied medicine at Glasgow and trained as a pathologist. Having worked in the NHS and universities in the UK and the US, he took early retirement and now devotes his time to writing.

His non-fiction publications include textbooks and articles on topics as diverse as the thalidomide story, the medical challenges of space travel and the medico-legal consequences of the Hillsborough disaster. His poetry collections, *Love & Other Diseases* and *The Sounds Men Make*, are published by Seahorse Publications.

The Shadows and the Dust is the fourth novel in the Dr Jack Cuthbert series. You can read more about Allan and his work at his website: researchet.wordpress.com.

Also by Allan Gaw

FICTION
The Silent House of Sleep
The Moon's More Feeble Fire
To the Shades Descend

NON-FICTION
Born in Scandal
Trial By Fire
On Moral Grounds (with M. H. Burns)
Testing the Waters
Tales From an Oxford Bench
The Business of Discovery
Our Speaker Today
Abstract Expressions

POETRY
Love & Other Diseases
The Sounds Men Make

Praise for the Dr Jack Cuthbert mystery series

The Silent House of Sleep

WINNER OF THE BLOODY SCOTLAND
CRIME DEBUT PRIZE (2024)

'This murder mystery makes for compelling reading . . .
Cuthbert himself is a finely conceived and drawn character'
Allan Massie, *The Scotsman*

'The first in Allan Gaw's Dr Jack Cuthbert mysteries . . .
has a gritty historical edge'
Rosemary Goring, *The Herald*

'Heartbreaking and harrowing in equal measure.
Dr Jack Cuthbert is a brilliant, damaged genius you'll
want to follow to hell and back'
Pauline McLean, BBC Arts Correspondent

'The central character perfectly expresses the damage of both
the period and his environment, and the author's pathology
background was skilfully deployed'
Tariq Ashkanani

'An outstanding whodunit with a difference . . . a beautifully paced
account of the forensic examination of the victims of a
double murder by Scottish pathologist Dr Jack Cuthbert'
Ken Lussey, Undiscovered Scotland

'One of the most exciting debut novels in years'
Alistair Braidwood, Scots Whay Hae

'Deliciously dark, vividly visceral, heartbreakingly harrowing'
Sharon Bairden

'The novel's evocative historical setting adds to the sense of intrigue'
Historical Novel Society

'Vivid descriptions, rich characters and engaging plot'
LoveReading

'Dr Jack Cuthbert is a compelling and comprehensive character in a beautifully crafted world'
CrimeBookGirl

'A vivid and well researched story of the life of LGBT people of the time, as well as the medical procedures . . . a tightly knitted, twisty and solid mystery'
Scrapping & Playing

'I couldn't put it down . . . Jack is a wonderful character'
Lyndas_bookreviews

The Moon's More Feeble Fire

'Deeply immersive, it is beautifully plotted and written . . . the twists and turns are exquisite and the false summits artfully done'
Undiscovered Scotland

'Cuthbert is a brilliant creation – part Sherlock, part Watson – a brilliant mind but also a compassionate and skilled doctor who cares deeply for the victims he encounters but also for the living'
Alistair Braidwood, Scots Whay Hae

To the Shades Descend

'Switching between reactionary medical school and Jewish radicals, razor gangs and wary coppers, Gaw evokes a vibrant, bustling Glasgow . . . *To the Shades Descend* excels for its well-researched setting and appealing protagonist'
Alastair Mabbot, *The Herald*

'This is much more than a crime procedural. It is an opportunity to explore the religious and political sectarianism of Scotland's largest city and the conditions endured by its poor, issues that are arguably still current today . . . The narrative is pacey without feeling rushed and the characterisation is finely drawn'
Historical Novels Society

THE SHADOWS AND THE DUST

A DR JACK CUTHBERT MYSTERY

ALLAN GAW

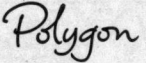

This revised paperback edition first published in Great Britain in 2026
by Polygon, an imprint of Birlinn Ltd. Previously published
by SA Press in 2024.

Birlinn Ltd
West Newington House
10 Newington Road
Edinburgh
EH9 1QS

www.polygonbooks.co.uk

1

Copyright © Allan Gaw, 2026

The right of Allan Gaw to be identified as the author of this
work has been asserted by him in accordance with the
Copyright, Designs and Patents Act 1988.

All rights reserved.

This is a work of fiction. Names, characters, businesses, places,
events and incidents are either the products of the author's
imagination or used in a fictitious manner. Any resemblance to
actual persons, living or dead, or actual events is purely coincidental.

The narrative takes place in the 1930s and contains language
and prevailing attitudes of the time which some readers may find offensive.
The publishers wish to reassure that such instances are there for reasons
of historical social context.

No part of this book may be used or reproduced in any manner for the
purpose of training artificial intelligence technologies or systems. This work
is reserved from text and data mining (Article 4(3) Directive (EU) 2019/790).

ISBN 978 1 84697 724 4
eBook ISBN 978 1 78885 803 8

British Library Cataloguing-in-Publication Data
A catalogue record for this book is available on request
from the British Library.

Typeset by Initial Typesetting Services, Edinburgh.

Printed and bound in Great Britain by CPI Group (UK) Ltd, Croydon CR0 4YY

For Elodie

damna tamen celeres reparant caelestia lunae:
  nos ubi decidimus
quo pius Aeneas, quo dives Tullus et Ancus,
  pulvis et umbra sumus

Yet the swiftly changing moons repair their losses in the sky.
We, when we have descended whither righteous Aeneas,
whither rich Tullus and Ancus have gone,
are but dust and shadow.

Horace, *Odes*, Book IV, 7
Trans. C. E. Bennett, 1914

Prologue

London: 14 September 1931

Something dark was moving in the wood. An urgent gust of wind rattled through the high branches. As some of the younger trees yielded to its force, their trunks bent, releasing a plaintive groan that might have been mistaken for a prayer. Or perhaps a warning.

The hooded figure froze, breathless in the moment, until the night settled again and recovered its silence. A wavering torch beam sought the right place and then, just as quickly, was extinguished when a light in a distant window flared.

Cloaked again in the darkness, the figure unshouldered its heavy burden and knelt. Slowly, it began to spread and part the undergrowth, clearing the way to the earth beneath. With a trowel and some effort, the topsoil was scraped back deeply enough to accommodate the package that lay by the figure's side. Tightly wrapped in cloth and trussed in twine, it could have been a bundle of clothes, or the carcass of something small – perhaps a lamb? A secret treasure, parcelled up to disguise its shape. It was none of those things, and it was all of them.

A hand reached out to break off some of the surrounding ferns and place them in the freshly dug hole. They were arranged with care to form a soft pillow of greenery. Only then was the package placed on top. Creases in the wrapping were smoothed, and from a small bag cut flowers were taken and placed around the folds of the cloth.

Not a word was spoken in the moonless gloom. The wind had now dropped, and the only sounds to accompany this ritual were the whispering rustle in the surrounding bushes and the harsh cry of a raven.

High above, the reluctant clouds were being prised apart by the wind. There was only a sliver of moon that night, but there was enough light to reveal the shape of the bundle. In the moment before the clouds passed over again, the moonlight fell on the folds of clean white cloth, the flowers and the glint of a buckle. Handfuls of rich black earth were thrown into the shallow trench, finally concealing two small feet in white socks and polished leather shoes.

Overhead, the clouds folded back over the moon and the figure was lost again to the darkness. Out of sight, out of mind.

Chapter 1

London: 7 September 1931

The long summer days were just a memory now. Although there was still some warmth in the air, the light was a watery silver, and Jack Cuthbert knew autumn was not far away.

He checked the clock. It was still early but sleep eluded him. The warmth of the bed was comforting but its emptiness was not. He stretched across to find where he had lain and stroked the sheets still warm from his body.

He reached out to the pillow, still dented by his head, and as he did, he caught a single hair and picked it up delicately between finger and thumb. He was used to handling evidence and this was evidence of a sort. A single golden hair that was the merest shadow of his presence.

It was the last night of their holiday together and it had ended too soon. He held the hair to catch the light and then put it to his lips. Such an insignificant remnant of their summer, but he took it and placed it carefully between the pages of a small book of poems on his bedside table. He recalled the summer sun and their time with each other. He closed his eyes, allowing the memories to linger.

*

Whether he had fallen asleep again, he wasn't sure, but when he looked at the clock, he knew he had to get up. He threw the linen sheets from his body and felt the morning chill on his naked skin. He swung his long legs over the side of the bed and sat up, trying to clear his head and gain some equilibrium.

When he stood, he stretched and caught sight of himself in the cheval mirror. He was six foot five, lean and heavily muscled with thick black hair, and he looked more like an ancient gladiator than anyone's idea of a doctor. But this morning his melancholy made him feel his age.

He had waited so long in his life to find the kind of fulfilment the summer had brought and now to lose it again was almost too much to bear. Nothing had gone wrong, he reminded himself; on the contrary, everything had been perfect. It was just that now he had to return to reality, to his role in life, and likewise Jaeger to his. They had found in each other a depth of feeling that neither expected, but they also knew that what they felt had to be hidden.

It was not over; indeed Cuthbert hoped quietly that it might never be over, but it had to be discreet and interrupted, to allow them both to pursue their other, more ordinary lives. In this house, though, they could be together, for the only other person who would know did not care.

Madame Smith had been in Cuthbert's employ for more than five years, and in that time she had grown to be his confidante as well as his housekeeper. She knew Cuthbert as no one else did – he had no secrets from her, and she passed no judgement.

When he and Jaeger had been in Italy the previous month, Cuthbert had felt free, showing him the sights of Rome, teasing him about his scandalous ignorance of the classics, walking and talking with him endlessly.

Every night had been spent in each other's arms, and Jaeger had taught Cuthbert just how beautiful love could be. Now, both men had to return to their work. It had been Cuthbert's first summer holiday since he had taken up his position as head of the forensic medicine department at St Thomas's, and he resolved now that it would not be his last. For too long, he had neglected his own happiness.

Cuthbert could already hear movement downstairs, where Madame Smith was preparing breakfast. He bathed quickly, shaved and dressed in the clothes she had laid out for him in his dressing room, and went downstairs to meet the day.

'*Bon matin,* monsieur. It is a beautiful day, is it not?'

'Good morning to you, madame. Indeed it is, but this holiday has made me lazy. I should have risen half an hour ago.'

She studied him and detected the hint of sadness in his eyes and understood the reason. 'Herr Jaeger, I believe, had to leave very early to catch his train. I'm afraid he left before even I had risen. He must think we are a very slovenly household not even to provide him with breakfast.'

Cuthbert smiled at her and realised what she was doing – quietly and discreetly acknowledging his friend's overnight stay while sympathising with him at his departure.

'I do hope we will see more of him, monsieur.'

She did not wait for an answer as she swept from the breakfast room to the kitchen. She returned with a tray of fresh coffee and warm brioches. She arranged the breakfast on the table in silence, giving Cuthbert a chance to speak, which he finally did.

'I need to thank you, madame, for your kindness and your understanding. But I fear I have placed you in a difficult position, perhaps even imposed upon you. I fully understand if you find the arrangements . . .' He searched for a word that would fit his meaning, but found none and opted for 'indelicate'.

Madame Smith was standing behind him, and she smiled before smoothing the black fabric of his jacket across his broad shoulders.

'Monsieur, you are troubled this morning because he has left for a while, but only to return to his work, as you will also be doing. He has to travel and there must always be times when you are apart. But when he comes back, I will be able to see your eyes light up again. And for that joy, I would give a great deal. I could not be happier that you have found someone to share at least a part of your life with. And, no, you have not imposed upon me in any way whatsoever. Never think that. Now, I suggest you eat rather than speak if you do not wish to be known in that hospital of yours as *le traînard*, or, how do you say, the laggard.'

He reached out, and she gave him her hand. He brought it to his lips and kissed it with the gentleness of a feather brushing her skin.

*

He walked from his home on Gordon Square more briskly than usual that morning. He found the pavements of London already strewn with the first of the fallen leaves from the towering plane trees that lined his route. He still made time, however, to buy a box of matches as he did every morning from the wounded ex-serviceman on the corner of High Holborn.

Cuthbert did not smoke and had no need for the matches, but the crippled man had a great need for his coppers. The man never looked up and merely touched the peak of his cap with one finger when he heard the pennies dropping into the small tobacco tin on the pavement before him. Cuthbert knew there were thousands like him, and they had been all but forgotten by a world that had moved on.

When he arrived at the hospital, it occurred to him that he had never been away for such a long time since he had started working there. He had rarely taken any days off and, apart from occasional trips to other departments and institutions and his enforced sojourn in Glasgow because of the bombing earlier in the year, he had spent every other day either here, at the university or at Scotland Yard.

The department of pathology, whose forensic medicine division he headed up, was one of the finest in the country in large part because of his tireless efforts to make it so, and he had built an unimpeachable personal reputation as a police surgeon and expert witness in the metropolis. Although he enjoyed his teaching of both medical and law students, it was his work with Scotland Yard that gave him his greatest satisfaction.

Despite the words of his mentor still ringing in his ears after fifteen years, he still found it difficult to conform to Professor Littlejohn's idea of a specialist. 'The cobbler should stick to his last,' the great man had always told him, especially when he saw his interest deviating from the strictly pathological issues at hand. 'Remember, Dr Cuthbert,' he would counsel, 'we are here to provide the evidence, but how that evidence is used is up to others. We must be neutral at all times in our deliberations, and the specialist in forensic medicine is not, and never should see himself as, a detective.'

Cuthbert, however, had come to see that what he did, and the contributions he made to any case, often went beyond the merely neutral. Even at his autopsy table, he needed to be as much a detective as any officer in the field. His job was certainly to uncover evidence, but he also felt he had a role in piecing that evidence together to recover the truth of what had happened. Of course, he was also insightful enough to know that this might all be just a convenient delusion he allowed himself in order to continue doing what he enjoyed.

*

When he entered the department, Simon Morgenthal, Cuthbert's assistant, was already working at the bench. He had been holding the fort while his mentor was on holiday, and Cuthbert had gone off confident that all would be taken care of.

Everyone in the department had been delighted when Cuthbert had announced that he would be going away for pleasure for a month during the summer, but not because they wished to see the back of him. On the contrary, he was fiercely admired and respected by everyone who worked there, not least of all by Morgenthal. His staff simply saw that a holiday was long overdue and that he badly needed a break, especially after everything that had happened to him this year.

Morgenthal had taken charge before when Cuthbert had gone to Glasgow and had managed successfully to demonstrate that the place did not fall apart while in his care. As such, Cuthbert was more than comfortable to hand him the reins for a second time.

Morgenthal was working on one of the many chemical assays that were performed in the laboratory area of the department and was giving some instructions to one of the technicians when Cuthbert appeared at his back.

'Still telling everyone what to do, Dr Morgenthal?'

'Sir, what a pleasure to have you back. How are you? How was the trip? You certainly seem to have caught the sun. Was it insufferably warm? I do hear that Italy at this time of year can be quite a trial. I've never been one myself for the heat, but Sarah is always on at me to spread my wings a little and take to the continent. And . . . and I'm talking too much again. My apologies, sir. Welcome back.'

'It's good to be back. The whole of Italy was so disappointingly quiet in comparison.'

Cuthbert's office was accessed through a door off the laboratory area, and he found it as he had left it: tidy, ordered and spartan. Cuthbert was not one for fussy ornamentation or the bric-à-brac that often filled other people's offices. For him, this was a place of work, a sanctuary for reasoned thought and insightful discussion. He required no distractions to those ends.

On his desk, the departmental secretary had ordered his mail by date of receipt, and he sat down to make a start on it as soon as he had hung up his coat and hat. He worked through the piles of envelopes quickly and efficiently. By the morning coffee break he was up to date with his correspondence, and he invited Morgenthal to join him so he could receive a briefing on what had happened in the department during his absence.

His assistant brought a typed report of all the cases that had been dealt with in the department during the previous four weeks. Clear summaries were provided alongside a table showing case details, analyses performed and conclusions reached.

'You've been busy, Simon. And you've done an excellent job.'

'Not on my own, sir. The staff are the excellent ones, and it was all teamwork.'

'But every team needs a leader, and you are showing yourself to be just that. I am starting to regret my absence. With all this experience, I don't doubt I will be losing you soon.'

'Sir?'

'It's almost time for you to leave the nest, young man. You

can't stay here for ever, in my shadow. You must find another department to run . . . to cast a shadow of your own.'

'But—'

'Please don't misunderstand me, Simon. I don't want you to leave, but I would be doing you a grave disservice if I held you back. If you should wish to apply for any senior appointment, just know that you can be assured of the finest recommendation from me.'

Mixed emotions swirled within Morgenthal; he felt nowhere near ready to leave the department at St Thomas's and Cuthbert's invaluable mentorship. Everything he knew about forensic medicine and science, he had learned at the side of this man, and any confidence he had in the job he had found because of him. But now to be told that he was not only doing a good job, but a job good enough to make him eligible for a significant promotion, was overwhelming.

There was no one whose approval he craved more than Cuthbert's, and here, in this moment, he had been granted it. He could not find words to say what he was feeling for he truly did not know how he felt. All he could do was nod in acknowledgement.

Cuthbert for his part did know how the young man was feeling. He had experienced exactly the same maelstrom of confusion at the hands of his own mentor when he was encouraged to think about moving on.

'Please don't worry. There is no rush and there is still so much to do here, but I wanted you to know that I expect rather great things of you. And, of course, it will give me no little pleasure to be able to say, "Oh yes, I taught the great Simon Morgenthal everything he knows." Now, shall I get us both that coffee?'

'Please, sir. Allow me.'

*

Over that first week back, Cuthbert was afforded a relatively light workload due to the vagaries of crime statistics. He had often pondered if there was any science to the prediction of murder rates throughout the year but had long since given up trying to second-guess what, if anything, determined them.

He was glad of the slow start, however, for it allowed him to prepare his lectures for the autumn term and to oversee the research work that Morgenthal was doing. His assistant's work was largely chemical in basis, and he had been developing and evaluating novel assay systems for different blood components. Cuthbert knew that the future of forensic science would be molecular rather than anatomical and strongly encouraged Morgenthal in this line of investigation.

In his second week back, he was standing at the bench discussing the results from Morgenthal's latest run of experiments, which his assistant had graphed out neatly for Cuthbert to review, when his office telephone rang.

'Dr Cuthbert? Sergeant Baker, sir. Good to have you back. I wonder if you could join us on site. We have a body, sir. I'm afraid it looks like a child.'

Cuthbert sighed and took the details. He told Sergeant Baker to expect him within the hour. Morgenthal asked if he was needed, but Cuthbert assured him that he would be better employed completing his assays. At this stage, there was certainly no need for both of them to endure whatever awaited him with Sergeant Baker.

He collected his bag and checked its contents. The stout case contained his notepads, pens, gloves, an apron, sample containers and bags, identification labels and ties, trowels and brushes, a thermometer and a testing kit for soil acidity.

Everything was in order, but, before he left, he added a large soft cloth that he knew he might also need.

*

The gates of St Gregory's were already open when Cuthbert's taxi arrived. The driver took him up the long curving gravel driveway and stopped outside the imposing Victorian building.

'Shall I wait, guvnor?'

'No, thank you – I expect I'll be here for a while.'

Already, Cuthbert had spotted the figure of Sergeant Baker striding towards the cab from the woodland. Cuthbert got out, paid the driver through the taxi window and hailed the sergeant.

'Good morning, sir. I'm sorry to drag you across London like this, but–'

'But that's our job, isn't it? It's good to see you again, sergeant. If only it was in pleasanter circumstances for once. But this does look a little better than some of the places you've dragged me to.'

Cuthbert looked up at the red-brick three-storey building and then out over the expanse of lawn to the wooded areas beyond. 'What exactly is this place, sergeant?'

'Church of England orphanage, sir. Been here for years. The house used to belong to some rich family who left it to the Church around the turn of the century and since then they've used it as an institution. There's the main house, a few cottages and a pretty big estate. Twenty-five acres or thereabouts.'

Cuthbert scanned the scene and looked back at the building. It was ugly in the way that architecture of the mid-Victorian period could often be. The design was fussy, lacking style or symmetry, and it looked to Cuthbert as if it was in sore need of repair.

In one of the large bay windows, his eye caught some

movement. A figure dressed in blue and white was watching him. He could not make out any details as the person had moved back from the glass and was now standing in the shade of the room. He fixed his gaze on the window, but there was no further movement and he wondered for a moment if he had imagined it.

'And what do you have for me, sergeant? I expect it's more than the view.'

'Indeed, sir. Please come this way.'

Baker led the pathologist across the grass towards the woods, and as they approached, Cuthbert could see two uniformed officers only yards away under the canopy of the trees. He had expected to be led deep into the trees and through the undergrowth, but if this was where the body had been discovered, someone had done a very inexpert job at hiding it.

Baker glanced at Cuthbert's boots and asked if he wished to change before going in. Everyone who had met him knew about Cuthbert's boots. He prided himself in always keeping them immaculately polished to a high mirror finish. It had, in truth, become something of a compulsion with the pathologist and he no longer tried to conquer it.

Cuthbert looked down at his shining black Oxfords and felt calmed by the gleam on the leather. But they would certainly not come out of the woods the same way they went in, so he reluctantly donned the regulation wellingtons Baker had brought with him.

'These should fit you, sir – at least, they're the biggest we have at the Yard. I can look after your boots for you.'

'Thank you, sergeant, but there's no need. I can stow them in my bag. Safer that way, I think. Do lead on.'

The morning was bright, but as soon as they went into the wooded area they found themselves in dappled gloom. As Cuthbert's eyes adjusted to the dim light, he could see that between the uniformed officers there was some disturbance of the soil. The rest of the ground was scattered with leaf mould, small broken branches and occasional ferns. Here, however, there was a patch of bare soil that looked recently dug over. At the end, nearest the constable on the right, some of the soil had been pushed back, and just visible were the feet of a young child wearing shoes.

Cuthbert thanked the sergeant and asked him to create a wide cordon around the area and to ensure no one entered. He asked the constables if they had touched or disturbed anything, and both knew that if they had they would soon be looking for other employment, such was the reputation of this pathologist.

'How was the grave disturbed?'

'The groundsman, sir. A Mr Dickson Barnaby. He lives on the estate in one of the cottages and he found the grave. He thought it might have been a badger burrowing, so he kicked some of the soil away to check and that's when he saw the shoes. Called us right away. This was about seven o'clock this morning.'

'Fine, sergeant, I'll take it from here. I don't suppose I have to tell you this might be a slow process.'

'We've done too many of these for me to hurry you, sir. I know how important it is to get it right at this stage if we're to find out what happened later. You take all the time you need, and I'll organise everything else.'

Cuthbert smiled and nodded at Baker, glad to be back working with this particular officer. They had indeed been through many cases together, and Cuthbert's respect for the man had only grown with the years.

From his bag, Cuthbert took his notebook and pen and started to record his observations. He would spend some time looking before he ever touched anything, knowing full well that as soon as he did, he would potentially be silencing anything the evidence was trying to tell him.

The feet protruding from the soil looked to be those of a child of about three to six years of age. There were neat ankle socks, and the shoes were brown leather, rather scuffed, with a buckle strap across the instep. The soil over the rest of the body was dark and loose and had only recently been turned. Cuthbert checked the area surrounding the shallow grave but found nothing unusual.

After noting all this, he began tentatively to remove the soil from the body. Only a few inches below the surface his small trowel scraped against fabric that appeared to be wrapped around the body. It looked like white cotton, although it was heavily stained by the sandy soil. It became clear that the child's head and body were tightly shrouded in the fabric and poking from the folds were fronds of plants. He did not immediately recognise these but, as he bent to look more closely, he could smell them. There was rosemary, and what he took to be a fern of some sort. There were others that he could not identify, but they all appeared as if they might be wildflowers. He looked about again. There were clumps of fern nearby, but there were no flowering plants in the wood that he could see.

As he brushed the soil away from under the small, shrouded corpse he saw that it had been laid on other plants that were still green, and the head was supported on a mat of fresh fern leaves.

The state of the plants, combined with the loose appearance of the overlying soil, told Cuthbert this was certainly not an old grave. If it had been dug in the last forty-eight hours, that might be the limit of it. Of course, that did not necessarily mean the child had died in the last two days. He would only know that when he was able to examine the body in the mortuary – a task he was already dreading.

*

While Cuthbert was working at the grave, Baker was making a start on his questioning of the orphanage staff. As he had mentioned to Cuthbert, he had already spoken briefly to Barnaby, the groundsman who had found the body, but had told him he would require a fuller statement later. First, however, the sergeant wanted to speak to whomever was in charge of the orphanage, to get some measure of the place. He had been informed that he would need to speak with the mother superior as it was an order of Anglican nuns who ran St Gregory's.

He rang the heavy bell pull on the house porch and waited for someone to answer the door. He did not have to wait long. The large door with its ornate stained-glass panel was heaved opened by a small woman who looked excited to welcome him in. He held out his warrant card and said, 'Detective Sergeant Baker, miss. I need to speak with the mother superior.'

'Oh, we know who you are, sergeant. Come in, come in. This is a terrible thing, is it not? And I haven't even introduced myself. Sister Hilda – I'm one of the sisters here at St Gregory's. I take care of the little ones. Please come into the reception room, and if you'll just wait, I'll go and tell the reverend mother you are here. Oh, what a to-do, and today of all days as well.'

'Sister, what do you mean by that?'

'Just that we are preparing for our visit from our parish priest, Reverend Henshall. Everything's already at sixes and sevens, and now this.'

But before Sister Hilda could rush off to the mother superior's office, they both heard the slow squeaking of rubber-soled shoes on polished linoleum coming towards them.

The mother superior almost glided along the passage.

She would have been unremarkable if it had not been for her calling. An otherwise average woman leading an average life. But here in the order she had put her years to a very different use. For the service of her God and for the sake of the other sisters in her charge, she had put aside every natural feeling. She had been elected by those sisters on three consecutive occasions as their leader, and she discharged her duties with fairness, if not warmth.

Her blue gown was tied at the waist by a thick black rope made of silk, which bore three heavy knots on the free-hanging ends. These symbolised her three sacred vows: poverty, chastity and obedience. As she passed the large wooden crucifix hanging on the wall, her hand came to her chest and the wooden cross she wore around her neck. She touched it and then clasped her hands again beneath the blue scapular she wore over her gown. Her wimple and tight-fitting coif of white cotton were topped with a simple white veil which hung to her shoulders.

'Welcome to St Gregory's, sergeant. That will be all, Sister Hilda – please return to your duties.'

The small woman composed herself, clasped her hands and bowed her head solemnly towards the mother superior, then scuttled away, keen to share the news of the detective's arrival with anyone who would listen.

'Thank you for seeing me, sister . . . my apologies, reverend mother.'

'Please do not concern yourself with our titles, sergeant. But rather like your profession, I imagine, there are those who think such things matter.'

The sergeant listened as she spoke, trying to place her accent, which was certainly not from London. He also observed her closely. When she finished speaking, she stood in silence, only intending to speak further when she was spoken to, only intending to answer exactly the question she was asked. There was nothing unnecessary in anything she did. Everything was measured, calm, the sergeant thought, even her breathing.

'I'm sure you will be aware by now, reverend mother, that this morning we uncovered human remains in the grounds. We will need to speak with everyone who works here, but I thought it would be useful if I could first orientate myself. Could you tell me a little about St Gregory's?'

She sat in the chair by the window and placed her hands in her lap. 'Won't you sit down, sergeant? Here in the light.'

Baker took out his notebook and sat down opposite her.

'We are members of the Order of the Divine Fellowship. Our Mother House is in Northumberland, but we have outposts throughout the country. Here at St Gregory's, we are a small community dedicated to the care of the orphans in our charge. We have a small domestic staff: a cook, a cleaner and a laundress. As for those in holy orders, apart from myself we have two sisters – Sister Margery and Sister Hilda, whom you have already met. We also have a novice sister, Mary Frances.'

'Yes, Sister Hilda seemed quite upset by the events. I understand you are preparing for a visit from the local parish priest.'

'Sister Hilda is rather talkative. We can do nothing else but bring the weaknesses of our human nature with us when we take the veil. Here in the convent, where people are trying to give their best to God, it is perhaps unsurprising that the Devil makes it his business to be active and ever present.'

'And the children?'

'We have some sixty-two children aged between three and twelve years of age in our care. Any younger orphans are cared for in St Anselm's, another of our homes; and older children are housed and taught useful skills in St Barnabas'. We fulfil the middle years, but I like to think the most important.'

'Are any of your charges unaccounted for, reverend mother?'

'So it is a child, then. No, sergeant. We in holy orders may be criticised for many things, but losing our children is not one of them. All are safe.'

Baker was taking careful notes of everything she said and wondered how much she knew about what had been discovered.

'How did you find out about the body?'

'Mr Barnaby came to inform me immediately after Lauds, our first morning prayers. It was I who instructed him to telephone the police. He made the call from my office just after seven o'clock this morning.'

'And what did he tell you?'

'Exactly what he told you, I'm sure. That he had discovered something quite dreadful near the edge of the wood and that he feared it may be a dead body, possibly a young child.'

'Do you and the other sisters all live in the building?'

'Indeed. Our cells are here, as are our communal and worship areas, along with the children's dormitories, playrooms and dining hall.'

'And have you seen anything unusual in the last week or so? Anything out of the ordinary, strangers in the grounds?'

'Our lives here are contemplative and inward-looking when they are not attending to the worldly needs of the children. I expect much that goes on in the world passes us by.'

The sergeant thanked her for her time but made it clear that he would need to return to interview the other staff and sisters and that he may well have further questions for her. She simply bowed her head in silent acknowledgement, rose and walked him to the door.

'If I may make one request, sergeant. When you identify the poor child, may we know the name, so we may more usefully pray for his eternal soul?'

It was Baker who nodded in silence this time, unsure of committing himself to any such request.

*

Outside, Cuthbert was already packing up his things, and had left the graveside for the edge of the wood. Sergeant Baker was coming back across the grass as the pathologist was changing out of the police wellingtons and into his boots. Before Cuthbert put them on, he could not help giving them a buff with the large, soft cloth he had wrapped them in.

'Do you need anything, sir?'

'No, sergeant, I think I've done just about all I can for the time being. I need the remains lifted and transported to St Thomas's. With all the usual precautions, of course.'

Baker, who knew Cuthbert's requirements well, would make sure that the grave contents were first photographed and then removed intact and in their entirety, before being taken to his department.

Cuthbert was brushing some soil from his trousers where he had been kneeling at the graveside and casually asked, 'Are you a family man, sergeant?'

Baker did not answer immediately. Cuthbert saw him swallow before he made to answer and regretted his rudeness.

'Sergeant, please forgive my ill manners. Your private life is none of my business.'

'No, it's not that, sir. It's just that I'd like to be. We want a family, but we've been trying so long that it doesn't look like it will ever happen. Just not meant to be, I suppose. No one's fault – just the way of things, sir.'

'Forgive me. I really had no right to ask.'

'Really, sir, it's no matter. What about you? Do you have any little ones, sir?'

'I'm afraid not, sergeant. How wonderful it must be to be a father, though. But, like you, I'm not sure it's meant to be, either.'

'Doesn't make it any easier though, does it, sir? I mean, look at the little mite lying there alone in the ground. What kind of person could possibly do such a thing?'

'That, sergeant, is exactly what we're going to find out.'

Chapter 2

London: 17 September 1931

The small mound under the white sheet on the mortuary slab was the body of the child. Cuthbert closed his eyes tight and took a deep breath as he entered the dissection room. He had performed many post mortem examinations on children, and they had never become any easier over the years.

He remembered his first – a girl who had drowned in a canal in Edinburgh – and Professor Littlejohn, his superior at the time, had stood beside him throughout as he examined the lifeless infant. He had been unable to hide his distress then, and he was no better now. He approached the slab and in a quick movement uncovered the small corpse.

His first task was to examine the shroud wrapping the body and then any clothes the child was wearing. The white cotton was tied about the body with thick string. Cuthbert slit these ties and slowly unwrapped the corpse. While doing so, he took careful note of the position of each plant frond within the folds. Finally, he had to cut the material to free the body, which he now saw was that of a small boy with his hands folded in a cross over his chest.

The child was dressed in short white socks, a white cotton

shirt, short blue trousers and a thin, dark blue knitted cardigan. He looked through the pockets of the trousers and the cardigan but found nothing. He carefully cut off the clothes, bagged and labelled them for further examination. Importantly, as he removed the child's cotton underwear, he noted small labels hand-sewn into his vest and pants with the name 'M. Saunders'. There were no such labels on the shirt, cardigan or trousers, but Cuthbert made a note, nonetheless.

The boy was even smaller than Cuthbert remembered from the grave. His small naked form was almost lost on the adult slab, but Cuthbert had to be meticulous if he was going to give this child both an identity and a cause of death. He began as always with close observation.

First, he looked for any marks or abnormalities that might help with identifying the boy, but he found none. The boy had no birthmarks or deformities that would be distinctive.

Next, he inspected the body for clues as to the time of death. The skin was somewhat discoloured by marbling, an effect that was caused by changes in the network of surface veins on the body. There was also some greenish discolouration of the skin over the lower right abdomen where the appendix would be found beneath. This was an indicator of the early stages of putrefaction, which routinely began in the gut. Taken together, these suggested that death had occurred at least three to five days before, but the exact time was impossible to determine, as so many other variables needed to be taken into account.

The ambient temperature and humidity were important as were the body's clothing and exposure to air. This child had been found fully clothed and wrapped tightly in a shroud in very dry soil that Cuthbert had tested and found to be lime-rich and alkaline. All of these would have slowed his decomposition. The temperature was also unseasonably cool for the time of year and, unlike the heat of high summer, would again have slowed the process. There were no signs of insect invasion of the body, which might have given further clues as to the time of death, but given the circumstances of his interment, these might not have been expected. The aromatic herbs placed around the body would most likely have initially deterred some insect species.

There was little to go on, and the best that Cuthbert could conclude was that the earliest he could have died was three days ago, but it could easily have been more than a week, perhaps even ten days. The grave had been freshly dug and the plants within it were far from withered, again suggesting that the burial had been recent, perhaps within the last twenty-four to forty-eight hours, but the child had probably been dead for some time before he was buried.

*

Cuthbert hoped he would fare better trying to determine the cause of death. He studied every inch of the boy's body, looking for any physical signs of trauma or violence. He was relieved to find none on his first pass. There were no head wounds, and the boy's trunk and limbs were largely unmarked. There were some recent scrapes on one knee and some healed scratches on the back of one hand and forearm as well as several old bruises on the shins, but all of these were consistent with the activity of a healthy young child scratching and bumping himself at play.

Cuthbert knew he must also check whether the child had been subject to any kind of sexual violence. He looked carefully and was even more relieved to find nothing that would indicate any interference of that kind. He did note the pattern of post mortem staining on the skin that was a tell-tale sign of how the body had been positioned at the time of death and shortly afterwards. Through gravity, the blood would always sink to the lowest levels, and where it settled there would be a mottled reddish-purple staining of the skin. The child had been on his back in the grave, but the pattern of staining was not at all consistent with that as the position of death. The discolouration was asymmetrical and more prominent on the left-hand side of the boy's lower back and buttock and the feet.

Cuthbert concluded that the child had died in a crouched or seated position, perhaps leaning more to his left side, and then the body had been moved and laid in the grave.

Cuthbert examined the child's eyes, ears and airways. When he looked in the mouth there was some blood and what appeared to be a ragged tear on the tongue consistent with a self-inflicted bite. He had seen such a sign many times and knew that it might be a clue to how the child had died. He felt inside the boy's mouth and found that all twenty of the child's deciduous – or baby – teeth had erupted and were fully present. This suggested that he was at least three years old and, because he had not yet lost any of his front teeth, was likely to be younger than six or seven.

Cuthbert arranged for X-rays to be taken of all the boy's bones and with particular reference to the hands and wrists. He required the full skeletal survey to assess any new or old healed fractures that might either help identify the child or hint at any abuse. And he needed the X-rays of the hands and wrists to perform the necessary scoring to work out the boy's bone age.

As the bones grow and develop, they calcify at different rates and from different centres of ossification. By examining the pattern of these in the wrist bones and those of the hand, a reasonably reliable age can be assigned to any child older than three years. When he did the scoring later, he was confident that the child on the slab was four years old.

The rest of the surface examination revealed nothing else, and Cuthbert prepared to make the initial incision for the internal examination. He was used to extracting and handling the organs of adults, but holding the boy's heart in the palm of his hand, he was reminded just how fragile this little body was.

When he dissected the stomach, he was careful to remove it intact in order to examine its contents. When he opened it in one of the large enamel dishes, he was surprised to find it empty, but what surprised him even more was the smell. He did not know what it was, but he immediately remembered the great camphor-wood box that his grandfather had in his house. As a child, he would imagine it to be a great treasure chest and would delight in opening it and inhaling the sharp, chilling smell that his nanny told him was so good at keeping the dreaded moths at bay. Now, as he bent to smell the boy's stomach lining, he could recognise almost the same odour. His mind was already trying to make a connection between the findings, trying to join the dots to make some sort of a coherent picture.

He also studied the boy's brain in more detail than he might normally, for he was already working on the premise that the boy might have bitten his tongue while suffering a convulsion. The most likely place to find any pathology that might cause that would be the nervous system. But the outward appearance of the brain was entirely normal. There was no swelling, no scarring from old injuries, no inflammation of the lining as would be seen in meningitis and no signs of any other inflammation of the brain matter itself.

With any post mortem examination, there was always the chance that the cause of death would be unforthcoming and the death ultimately unexplained. However, Cuthbert always regarded this as a failure on his part and would not yield easily to such a negative conclusion. He continued to work on the boy's body, collecting samples of tissue, blood and cerebrospinal fluid. He tried to sample urine from the boy's bladder but found it to be empty, which added weight to his idea that he was dealing with a convulsive death. He knew that urinary incontinence often accompanied any kind of seizure. There was, however, an inconsistency. None of the child's clothes were stained with urine, which pointed to him having been dressed in fresh clothes, perhaps after his death.

When he had finished the examination, he carefully reconstituted the child's body and stitched him back together. Often, large untidy stitches were used to close the body cavities that had been opened, but Cuthbert took almost as much care stitching the boy in death as he would have done if he had been repairing a laceration in life. When it was complete, he smoothed the boy's hair and covered him respectfully with the sheet.

At his desk he went through his notes to write up the report. The bitten tongue, empty bladder and absence of any other obvious anatomical cause of death all pointed to the child having suffered a seizure. The cause of the seizure, however, remained unclear.

Cuthbert knew the list of contenders was lengthy and difficult to differentiate. The child had no outward physical evidence of neurological disease and exhibited no signs of any of the common febrile illnesses that might lead to convulsions. But there was that odd smell in his stomach. Could he have ingested some sort of poison, for many of those could also cause seizures?

Most poisons leave other marks on the body and the internal organs; here, there was nothing save the odour. Some of the most common poisons could be detected in the blood, and Cuthbert would have his assistant set up the necessary assays in the morning. But, of course, they could only look for something if they knew what it was, and at this moment he had no idea. He opted to hold back his report until all the additional analyses were complete.

*

The next morning, he gave Morgenthal a copy of his preliminary assessment and discussed with him his thoughts on the case. Cuthbert was an experienced pathologist, but he was more than willing to admit he did not know everything. Enlightenment was not the sole reserve of seniority, but of anyone who had done the necessary study.

'Have you ever come across anything like this, Simon? It looks as if we might be dealing with a toxin, but it's nothing run of the mill.'

Morgenthal read the report carefully and asked if he might smell the sample of stomach lining that Cuthbert had taken. He unscrewed the glass jar and wafted the scent towards his nose with care, rather than sniffing the contents directly.

'It's unmistakably something quite volatile. It rather reminds me of cough mixture or perhaps rosemary. But I see from your report, sir, that the stomach was empty of contents. Could the child have vomited before death?'

'That's what I thought too, and I can only presume that's the explanation, but what is that smell? It must have been something the child ingested, but no foodstuff smells like that. And whatever it was, it likely killed the laddie. Can you run some analyses on the body fluids and see if you can come up with anything?'

Morgenthal agreed to get started immediately, but before he left Cuthbert, he thought he had better ask, 'What is it I'm looking for, sir?'

Cuthbert, screwing the top back on the specimen jar, shrugged.

'The answer, Simon.'

Morgenthal took the problem back to his bench in the laboratory along with Cuthbert's post mortem examination notes. There were quite literally thousands of poisons that if eaten, drunk, injected or inhaled could result in death. Not only could he not test for them all, but there was also no distinguishing chemical test that could be used to specifically identify many noxious agents. So he had to narrow the search.

First, there was the route by which this poison entered the child's body. There were no needle marks, no changes to the tissues of the lungs that might be expected if the poison had been inhaled, and the only clue was in the stomach and that peculiar smell. Thus he concluded he was dealing with a poison that most likely was ingested.

Next, he could reasonably rule out all those poisons that caused corrosive changes to the tissue of the lips, mouth and stomach, such as acids and caustic liquids. Even the many poisons that routinely produced marked irritation of the stomach lining were unlikely here, as Cuthbert had observed no such changes at the post mortem examination.

Given the way the child's corpse had been adorned by herbs, might they be dealing with one of the many highly toxic plant species? Most gardens and certainly most wild areas had many pretty but ultimately fatal flowers and plants if they were eaten either whole or in part. The complex chemicals within plants were collectively known as alkaloids, and although there were some specific tests for these, many still eluded precise chemical evaluation.

He thought it best to begin with a broad-brush approach to check for the presence of potentially toxic alkaloids. However, he also knew that Cuthbert would expect him to test for the commonest poisons used in homicide, as well as those responsible for most accidental poisonings. He first set up the apparatus to perform the preliminary but lengthy Dragendorff

Process. This was an elaborate and labour-intensive system that would enable him to process the boy's tissue samples and separate out any alkaloids using a variety of solvents. This would allow him specifically to exclude such common poisonous plants as monk's hood, deadly nightshade and foxglove.

In addition, he made the necessary preparations to perform the specific laboratory analyses for arsenic, strychnine, chloral hydrate, opiates, cocaine and chloroform. All these were unlikely candidates, but collectively they accounted for a large percentage of poisonings. He could hear Cuthbert's words of diagnostic wisdom as he was drawing up his plan. 'Remember, Simon,' he would counsel, 'when you hear the sound of hooves, it is more likely to be a horse than a zebra.'

The analyses took almost two days to complete. Only when he had written up his report, making sure every detail of the methods was documented along with his findings, was he ready to present them to Cuthbert.

'I certainly focused on the horses, sir, rather than the zebras, but I'm afraid I drew a blank with the common poisons. I knew arsenic would likely have led to irritant changes in the stomach which were absent, and the Marsh Test for it was indeed negative. That also ruled out antimony as the poison. I also checked for strychnine, although there was no evidence of any tetanic spasms and no abnormal residual stiffness to the body, and as expected that was also negative. There was also no specific evidence of chloral hydrate in the lining of the stomach, and nor was there any chloroform in the tissues.'

'Did you use the Nicloux Method for the chloroform? I always found it to be more reliable than Harcourt's.'

'Indeed I did, sir. Although the stomach had a distinctive smell, it was certainly not that of prussic acid or opium. However, I have run samples with the Marquis Reagent and there was no colour change consistent with the presence of opium, morphine or laudanum. I did not check further for prussic acid given the time since death.'

'Yes, that was wise. We'd be unlikely to recover anything after about twenty-four hours. And as you say there was nothing to indicate it at all in the smell. But we're left with the smell that we did both detect. Any thoughts?'

Morgenthal turned to the next section of his report and proceeded to explain his approach. 'Given the nature of the burial – the herbs, I mean – I was working on the hypothesis that some plant-based poison may have been used. I ran a Dragendorff and tried various solvents to extract any alkaloids present. There was nothing in the fractions that should have contained the alkaloids from aconite, digitalis or belladonna, and I also confirmed by this method that there was indeed no strychnine or morphine in the boy's body.'

'A very thorough and very time-consuming job, Simon. We certainly now know a lot of things that didn't kill the lad. In the meantime, I need to bring our colleagues at the Yard up to date with the findings. I just wish we had some better answers for them.'

*

After the brisk walk to Scotland Yard along the Victoria Embankment, Cuthbert arrived at the building overlooking the Thames. His first visit to the Metropolitan Police Headquarters had now been a good five years ago, but with the ever-changing rotation of uniformed constables on the reception desk, he still found he had to introduce himself and state his business before he would be admitted.

Today was no different and neither was Cuthbert's level of impatience. He was aware of how intimidating his physical presence could be and when he employed one of his thunderous scowls, he knew that no young lad in a uniform was going to give him too much trouble.

'Dr Cuthbert to see Chief Inspector Mowbray.'

'I beg your pardon, sir, I didn't catch that.'

'Then I suggest you open your ears and listen next time, laddie. This might be a Scottish accent, but I can assure you I am speaking English, and I am speaking it clearly.'

The constable cowered in the shadow of the man and quickly admitted him. Cuthbert bounded up the stairs three at a time and entered the C.I.D. duty room on the second floor. The desk sergeant there knew him well enough and waved him through without any preliminaries. When Cuthbert arrived to join the others around the pinboard at the far end of the duty room, he could see Sergeant Baker was disturbed. He was staring at the post mortem photograph of the child's face that had been pinned on the board.

'What possible motive would there be to kill a four-year-old child, sir?'

'And likely an orphan, at that. Orphans are always an inconvenience to somebody.' Mowbray, too, was staring at the picture of the child as he spoke. His arms were folded tight, almost holding himself together, and Cuthbert suddenly thought he knew what Mowbray was thinking. He chose not to contradict the chief inspector, but rather to shift the subject onto a more profitable line of inquiry.

'What has puzzled me most about this case is the way the child was positioned in the grave. Most burials in shallow graves are hurried, almost haphazard affairs, but not this one. He was laid carefully in the ground, his arms folded across his chest and wrapped in a clean shroud. There was even a pillow of ferns placed under his head and the grave filled with herbs. What does that tell us?'

Mowbray was still staring at the board, and the sergeant

could see he had not been listening to anything the pathologist had said, if he had even noticed him arriving. He also sensed the deep anger Mowbray was feeling and, like Cuthbert, tried to refocus the discussion by taking up the question and offering his opinion.

'To me, there seems to be an absence of malicious intent, sir. Perhaps we are dealing with an accidental killing and the perpetrator was trying his best to lay the child to rest.'

'Or we're dealing with a crackpot that thinks a pillow makes up for murder. Are we any closer to a cause of death, doctor?'

Mowbray had turned away from the board and was now firmly back in the room and taking charge. His brows were still knitted, but whatever had been going through his mind had passed and now he was directing any residual anger at the team.

'It is taking longer than expected,' said Cuthbert. 'It is still our working hypothesis that the child was poisoned, but as yet we do not know the cause. We have ruled out a number of common poisons, but we are clearly dealing here with something rather out of the ordinary.

'We know the child was moved after death and the pattern of post mortem staining would indicate that he died sitting or perhaps propped up in some way. The repositioning in the grave would only have been possible if rigor mortis had subsided and that would mean an interval of approximately twenty-four to thirty-six hours after death.

'The physical findings at post mortem suggest that the death occurred a minimum of three days before he was examined, but it could be as much as seven. The alkalinity of the soil and its dryness would also slow decomposition. I would estimate, given the state of the plants in the grave and freshness of the soil disturbance, that the body was probably in the ground for less than two to three days. Taken together, this gives us a presumptive date of death of around the seventh to the fourteenth of September. Unfortunately, I can be no more precise than that.'

'Right. So what you're telling me is you don't really know when he died or how he died. And on top of that none of us know why he died. It does make me wonder what the fuck we're doing here sometimes. What about the child's identity? Do we at least have a name for the lad? Baker, have Missing Persons got their finger out yet?'

'Nothing yet, sir. But Dr Cuthbert found a name stitched into some of the clothing. It's not certain, but he could be an M. Saunders. We're following that up to see if we can track down any family in the South London area.'

Mowbray shook his head and marched off to his office at the far end of the duty room, leaving Cuthbert and the sergeant at the board.

'I'm sorry about that, sir. Something's spooked him about this case. I'm sure he wasn't criticising your work.'

'Please don't worry, sergeant. After all, everything he said is true. I have been unable to provide you with the most basic forensic information in this case. All I can do is redouble my efforts. I will leave the chief inspector to your care and return to the hospital. Obviously, I'll be back in touch as soon as I know anything concrete. In the meantime, tread carefully with him. I suspect he has some personal issues with this case, but neither of us has the right to pry.'

'I understand, sir. It's always a bad lot when it's a little one.'

Cuthbert glanced at the photograph of the small dead face on the board and nodded before leaving.

*

As he often did when he needed to think, he walked back to his department at St Thomas's by a circuitous route. Instead of walking westwards along the Victoria Embankment and across

Westminster Bridge, he turned left on leaving the Yard and walked in the opposite direction.

He followed the curve of the Thames and found a bench by the ancient obelisk that everyone called Cleopatra's Needle. He sat close to one of the large bronze sphinxes that had been installed on either side of the obelisk when it had been re-erected in London, and looked out across the wide brown river.

He found the flow of the water and the rush of the river traffic a good distraction from his thoughts. When his mind was full, he never sought silence in order to clear it. Rather, he tried to find a different set of stimuli that could rush in and wipe things clear. Sitting on the bench with the autumn sun on his face, he was forced to let go of the thoughts about the child in his grave, of Mowbray and his dark memories, and even of what was going on at the laboratory bench in his department. Instead, heavy coal barges and lighters ferrying cargoes of all sorts filled his view. There was constant movement on the river and the mighty Thames itself was shifting and rolling seawards beneath them.

He looked up at the sphinxes. Why had they been positioned looking at the carved obelisk? Surely, he thought, if they were guardians, they would have been better placed looking outwards.

The obelisk itself was a remarkable palimpsest of history. There was the grain of the prehistoric granite, overlaid by the deep carving of ancient hieroglyphs, and much more recently the random pockmarks of the shrapnel from a stray German bomb that had exploded nearby during the war. And yet, it was still standing, adored, if not protected, by its modern-day sphinxes.

As he looked at the sculpted face of the sphinx closest to him, he recalled the famous riddle that had so perplexed the ancients. 'What walks on four legs in the morning, two legs in the afternoon and three legs in the evening?' The mighty but ultimately doomed Oedipus had been the only one to see that the answer was man – crawling on all fours as an infant, walking on two legs as an adult, and hobbling with a cane as an old man. The image reawakened his thoughts of the young child.

He felt he could now focus on the case, and he walked quickly on towards Waterloo Bridge, crossed the river to the South Bank and made his way back towards Westminster and the hospital.

*

By the time he had arrived, he was ready to re-evaluate everything they had done in the laboratory. He went over all his notes but kept coming back to the grave flowers.

'Simon, would you come in for a moment? I have an idea.'

Morgenthal went to Cuthbert's office and was preparing himself for further laborious and ultimately fruitless laboratory analyses, but Cuthbert had a different approach.

'I think your instinct was right. The way the boy was buried was very distinctive, and the use of plants must have some significance. Is it possible, do you think, that any of those specific species were also used to kill him? I'm afraid I only recognised some sprigs of rosemary, and I think some ferns, but there were several other plants in his shroud, some with distinctive flowers. We have them all, and perhaps before they are too far gone, we should get some help identifying them. Could you take that on?'

Morgenthal was far from an expert in botany, but he was excited by the prospect of pursuing this problem from a different angle. He was unsure where he would begin, but he knew the answer Cuthbert was waiting for. 'Leave it with me, sir.'

Morgenthal collected all the grave flowers and plants from the evidence store where they had been labelled and placed. He could begin with books, but he thought it might be faster if he could work with someone, unlike himself, who knew the difference between a rose and a daffodil without having to consult a textbook. He made a call to the Department of Botany at University College and after explaining his mission was put through to Dr Davenport.

'Janet Davenport.'

'Oh, I thought you would be a man.' There was a silence on the other end of the phone, which Morgenthal realised he had caused with his clumsiness. 'I'm so sorry, Dr Davenport, I didn't mean that the way it sounded.'

The silence persisted, and Morgenthal knew he was in danger of causing further offence. But before he could correct things, she took the initiative.

'I really am rather busy. Who are you and what do you want?'

'Again, my apologies. I've been nothing but rude. My name is Dr Simon Morgenthal, pathologist at St Thomas's. We are working a case that would benefit greatly from some botanical expertise.'

'The nature of your request?'

The clipped voice still sounded irritated and impatient, and Morgenthal was becoming dry-mouthed.

'Well, we were hoping to get some help with identifying some plant materials that were found at a crime scene. It is a possible murder investigation.'

'What state are the plants in?'

'They are stems and fronds from different species that we believe to have been cut fewer than ten days ago.'

'Bring everything you have and also details of the soil at the scene. Room 283.'

The receiver clicked as she hung up abruptly. Morgenthal was left holding the dead receiver. Might he be able to make a better impression in person than he had on the phone? He could only hope.

He packed the bagged and labelled material into a case and took it by taxi to the U.C.L. buildings on Gower Street. He found Dr Davenport's room without difficulty but hesitated before he knocked. He was unsure of what to expect, as the woman had said so little on the phone that he had no impression of her age. He knocked lightly on the office door and was immediately told to enter.

'Morgenthal, I presume. I thought you would be older, so that makes two of us who suffer from prejudice.'

'I'm so sorry about earlier, Dr Davenport. It was such a stupid thing to say. Please allow me to start again.'

The young woman was in her late twenties, almost the same age as Morgenthal, and was wearing a white laboratory coat. Her office was untidy with teetering piles of papers on top of stacks of books. Her desk had wire baskets that were overflowing with correspondence and proofs of manuscripts and behind her on the wall was a notice board covered with pinned pieces of paper with handwriting that no one perhaps other than herself could read.

She watched the man survey her domain and enjoyed the look on his face. This wasn't what he expected either, she thought.

'So have you brought them? Good, let's get to work.'

She led Morgenthal into the laboratory, which was an altogether tidier environment, pristine in its order and cleanliness. She took the case from him and opened it without asking and laid the plants in their large envelopes on the bench. After putting on gloves, she carefully extracted each plant from its wrapper and laid it on a sheet of clean blotting paper.

There were eight different species, although two of them, which had small yellow flowers, looked very similar.

'So this crime scene would have been in South London, close to a forest area, but not a completely wild space. I'm thinking a large garden with its own wooded areas. Given that it is such a location, I would suggest that the soil was on the alkaline side of neutral, and I would also suggest that the plants were cut no more than four to five days ago.'

Morgenthal's face could not hide his pleasure, but she was not looking for praise, just confirmation.

'Well? Is that correct, so far?'

'Yes, indeed, Dr Davenport. Is it possible to identify the plants? Would they have grown locally?'

'Yes, they are all now local species, although some are not originally native to the British Isles. Those Roman invaders had a lot to answer for, botanically speaking. This is one they brought over – rosemary, *Salvia rosmarinus*, the culinary herb. And this is another – common sage, *Salvia officinalis*, with its purple flowers still intact. Here we have a frond of royal fern, *Osmunda regalis*, and this one with the small yellow button flowers is common tansy, *Tanacetum vulgare*. The one that looks similar over here is tansy ragwort. They often get confused, and that's a pity because one is much more poisonous than the other, at least to humans.'

Morgenthal, who had been making notes and quickly writing down everything she said, stopped her and asked for clarification. 'Which are you referring to, Dr Davenport?'

'Here, this one is the common tansy. If eaten, it will likely make you very sick. In fact if you take enough, it will kill you. This other one, the tansy ragwort, is mainly poisonous to horses. They normally avoid it because of the taste, but sometimes they get it in their winter feed. It gets harvested along with the grass, you see, and ends up in the hay. But by all accounts, it's relatively harmless to people. The *Tanacetum* does have a very distinctive smell though. I do not wish to damage your evidence, but if you choose to, you could crush one of those little yellow flowers between finger and thumb and you'll see what I mean. People say it smells like mothballs.'

Morgenthal immediately took one of the small flowers and crushed it as she had told him to do. He smelt his fingers. That was it: that was the smell in the boy's stomach.

'Would any of the other plants be potentially toxic to humans, doctor?'

'Well, as I'm sure you know, everything is toxic if you eat enough of it, but, no, you would be hard pushed to kill someone with any of these. In addition to the ones I've already mentioned, we've also got Timothy grass, *Phleum pratense*, meadowsweet, *Filipendula ulmaria*, which is commonly eaten, and this pink one is red campion, *Silene dioica*, which was used to treat snake bites. So are you looking for a poisonous plant that might have killed the person?'

'A child. I'm afraid it was a young boy, Dr Davenport. And, yes, we think he may have been poisoned. Not by these specific plants, but these were all found in his grave, and we thought that whoever poisoned the child may have also used some of the same plants to adorn his body.'

Dr Davenport looked again at the plants on the bench before her and straightened them on the white blotting paper. They were almost pretty, she thought, but she now had to imagine them in the grave of an innocent young child, and the thought chilled her.

'That's dreadful. I'm sorry you have to deal with such things, Dr Morgenthal. If I can be of any further help, in any way, please do not hesitate to call again. Let me put these specimens away for you; I can see now how important they are.'

She handled the plants with care and laid further clean sheets of blotting paper on each before returning them to the correct envelopes. Finally, she took her pen and very neatly on the corner of each envelope wrote the common and botanical names of the plant within.

'There, they should be easily transported back to your department now.'

'I can't thank you enough, Dr Davenport. And I must apologise again for my clumsiness earlier. I'm really an oaf at times.'

'As are all men, Dr Morgenthal. But I'm also sometimes oversensitive. Working here, I meet rather a lot of people who think I must be the technician or even the tea lady rather than the lecturer. It can be rather grating after a while.'

Morgenthal knew a little about prejudice from his own experience and sympathised with her. He was preparing to go, when he thought he should ask something. 'Dr Davenport, would you like to be kept informed of the progress of the case? You have, after all, provided an invaluable contribution.'

'I didn't know if that would be allowed. But yes, that would be most considerate, Dr Morgenthal. And as I said, if you require any further botanical input, even from a woman, just get in touch.'

Morgenthal saw that this time she was smiling, and he smiled back, shook her hand and thanked her again before leaving.

*

At St Thomas's he made straight for Cuthbert's office to tell him of the new findings.

'Common tansy. That does ring a bell from somewhere, Simon.'

'Yes, there is only a single case reported in any detail in

Glaister and that was an adult female who recovered. With a child and with the right dose, however, it can be fatal. The expected symptoms would be convulsions, shock and cessation of respiration. And, importantly, the only post mortem findings reported are a distinctive smell of the plant in the stomach. Nothing else. Everything fits with this being a fatal poisoning with *Tanacetum*. The oil extracts are often made into infusions and used by herbalists for a variety of purposes. Everything from the treatment of worms and rheumatism to its use as an ecbolic, sir.'

'They use it to produce abortions? Do you think the child could have taken it accidentally?'

'Given the dose he would have had to ingest, and given the strongly aromatic smell of any concoction containing tansy, I would doubt it, sir. I think he was deliberately given this to drink. Whether the intention was murder, or some botched attempt at medication, remains to be seen.'

'I agree, Simon. Good work. Let's get all this written up and we can hand it over to Sergeant Baker. There are many questions that will need to be asked at the orphanage. First and foremost, to my mind, is who has any knowledge of herbs.'

*

Cuthbert was aware of his responsibilities to mentor his assistant but was also aware that the day-to-day work sometimes got in the way. During his first year in the department, Morgenthal received regular formal teaching and was supervised in everything he did, but since then Cuthbert had become increasingly confident in the young man's abilities and, more importantly, in his self-awareness of what he did and did not know.

He preferred junior staff who were worried about their abilities rather than those who displayed any misplaced arrogance. Much of what Morgenthal learned was self-taught from his reading, but it was ordered and put into context through his discussions with Cuthbert. And these discussions often turned into invaluable impromptu tutorials.

Lately, Cuthbert knew he had been neglecting his responsibilities, but every now and then he remembered with a jolt his role as trainer, and he would corner the unfortunate young man and grill him on some aspect of forensic science or another. That afternoon as he was re-reading his assistant's toxicology report was one such jolt.

'Dr Morgenthal, I think it's time for a tutorial.'

'Sir?'

'I have been lax of late in my attention to your training, so let me exercise that brain of yours. Given what you've been up to this last week, it seems only appropriate we should discuss toxicology. So . . .'

And with that Cuthbert assumed his severe face, and although Morgenthal knew by now he was essentially play-acting, he still found the dark, towering man most intimidating.

'Dr Morgenthal, why do we call it toxicology?'

The young man had not expected this as an opening question and was somewhat thrown, but he should have known that Cuthbert would seize on any opportunity to discuss the precise meanings of words, especially if those words had their origins amongst the ruins of Ancient Greece or Rome.

'From the Ancient Greek, sir? *Toxikós* meaning "poison" and *lógos* meaning "study" or "subject matter", thus we have the study of poisons.'

'Really, and that's your answer, is it? A common mistake, but not one that any self-respecting pathologist should make. Despite popular misconceptions, *toxikós* does not mean "poison" in Ancient Greek, but as an adjective it means "of the bow", or as a noun, "bowman" or "archer". It became linked to the notion of poisons by the more correct form, *toxikós pharmakon*, which was a poison smeared on an arrowhead. With time, that became shortened simply to *toxikós*, but it retained the same meaning. So we might say that toxicology is really the study of arrow poisons. I expect you think that is all pedantry, but words do matter, and we should never forget where they came from.'

Morgenthal made a mental note and wondered who might ever ask him such a question again.

'And from one apparently simple question to another, how would you define a poison, Simon?'

Morgenthal felt he was on safer ground here, for this was a common question in medical jurisprudence, and it was one designed to expose any superficiality of one's reading. There was much debate, both medical and legal, as to the answer. He opted for the most widely accepted definition and quoted it word for word before going on to qualify it.

'Letheby would define it as follows, sir: "Anything which otherwise than by the agency of heat or electricity is capable of destroying life, either by chemical action on the tissues of the living body, or by physiological action from absorption into the living system." However, it must be added that even this widely held definition is open to criticism and may not encompass every agent we might classify as a poison. In legal circles, a rather simpler and perhaps more pragmatic, if consequentialist, definition is used: "Any substance which, if applied to the body, or administered internally, has been applied or administered with the intention to kill or do harm."'

Morgenthal put a heavy stress on the word 'intention' and Cuthbert smiled and nodded. Morgenthal might be a little lacking in his knowledge of the classical languages, but there were no shortcomings in his grasp of forensic medicine.

Cuthbert took himself back to his desk and the case notes. He had always tried to view the corpses on his slabs as people and to treat them with every respect. But he had also tried to view them as strangers, to separate himself from them as much as possible, for he had to be dispassionate if he was to do his job well. Sometimes it was easy to separate himself from the bodies he dissected because they were so different from him and the life he had led. However, this was a mere four-year-old boy who had barely started to live before he had died. Everyone had been a young child like that, a blank sheet with everything still ahead of them, and Cuthbert could not help but remember a day when he had been almost the same age as this child.

Chapter 3

Edinburgh: 11 October 1898

That day was at the farthest point of his memory. Its edges were blurred, and he could see only the vaguest of images. There were no voices, no sounds at all in those colourless images from the past.

He remembered feeling cold, but the morning was bright. He was standing in a forest of people outside the old church. His grandfather was holding his hand tight, keeping him close. Some men were carrying the long wooden box high on their shoulders, and he remembered one stumbling on the uneven ground as he approached, only to regain his footing quickly. There was a large black hole in the ground and a great white stone at its head. There were words carved beautifully into the marble and there was one he recognised. It was his mother's name: Alexandra.

He could feel his grandfather's hand trembling as they stood at the open graveside. They both watched, one with sadness, one with curiosity, as the box was lowered in. There was a woman there, standing close by him, wearing a long black veil, and he thought she looked terribly sad. She dabbed at her eyes beneath her veil with a handkerchief. He did not know the others.

His grandfather seemed to talk to everyone, and some would bend down to stroke Jack's cheek or pat his shoulder before they went. Throughout it all, he said nothing, but dutifully went and stood where he was told. He did not understand that this was his father's funeral and now, thinking back, he was unsure if at the time he even knew his father had died. But here William Cuthbert was being laid to rest beside his wife, who had died only four years before him.

He had not seen his father for a week and although he knew he had left him again, he did not understand this was for the last time. It was to the nursery of the big house he had come that morning. He appeared unexpectedly in the doorway after breakfast, and Jack had been startled by his long shadow.

'Come sit by me, laddie.'

The boy laid aside the picture book in the nursery and ran to his father. The tall man towered above the child, who held up his arms pleading to be lifted. But William Cuthbert took one of the boy's hands and led him over to the window seat. He sat and encouraged the boy to sit at his side rather than on his lap.

'Look out there. Can you see the birds flying south? They're going away to find somewhere warmer for the winter. Don't you wish we could do that too?'

The boy was more interested in the heavy rose gold watch chain slung across his father's waistcoat. He ran his fingers over the links and found his way to the watch in his pocket. He loved that watch, but his father would never tolerate him touching it. This time though he surprised him, and he took it out, pressed the release to open the case and handed it to the boy.

'This will be yours when I'm gone, Jack. Do you know how to tell your time?'

The boy traced the lines of the hands as he had been taught by his nanny and announced that it was ten o'clock.

'Very good, laddie. But you were always a quick one. You don't just have your mother's eyes; you also have her wits.'

He stared out of the window while the boy held the watch, feeling the weight of it in his small hands. The great wedge of flying geese was almost out of sight, and he turned back to the boy. His small son's fascination with the timepiece almost made him smile. He held out his hand to stroke his hair but stopped himself in case he should disturb his concentration. Very quietly he rose, hoping to slip away, but the boy felt him move and clung to him.

'No, no, none of that. I just have to go away for a little.'

'South, like the birds, Papa?'

'Something like that, Jack. You need to be good now and always do as Nanny tells you.'

The boy held out the watch to return it, but his father looked at it in his son's hands and then left. Jack was still offering the watch back as his father opened the nursery door and walked away down the upper hallway. The boy was confused and called after his father through his tears, but William Cuthbert did not look back.

*

Now, he was back in the nursery, still in his black mourning clothes and his nanny was coaxing him to eat. Aunt Helena had slipped away from the gathering downstairs and found the nursery. She appeared tall in the doorway, as his father had done the week before, and she studied the boy sitting on the floor playing with his toys. The nanny rose and curtsied. Without acknowledging her, Helena motioned her to leave them.

'Hello, Jack. Do you remember me, boy?'

He looked up at the veiled face and when she saw his eyes, she raised the sheer black silk and smiled at him. Whether she expected him to come to her she was unsure, but he remained where he was.

'Your father was my brother, you know, and I am your Aunt Helena. We are family and I would like you to come and live with me now.'

The boy's nanny was listening from behind the screen that separated her own bed from the child's in the nursery, and she was concerned by what she was hearing. She had no say in what was to become of the boy, now orphaned, but she knew that plans were already in place for him to live with his grandfather. She did not want the boy confused and she felt she had to protect him. She deliberately rustled her skirts and came back into the room. She bobbed a curtsy again but spoke firmly. 'Begging your pardon, ma'am, but Master Jack needs to have his nap now. His father was always most particular about it.'

'Indeed. Jack, remember what I said. I'll come back soon to take you with me, and we'll get away from this big old house and all its sadness.'

The boy's nanny was frowning at her now and moving towards the child, who reached out for the comfort of her hand. Helena lowered her veil again. She tilted her head slightly and looked the nanny over from top to toe, thinking she would have to go. She left without further words or sign of affection, and the boy went to the nursery window.

People in black were walking away from the house and downstairs his grandfather was seeing the last of the guests out. Soon the door would be closed and there would be quiet again. He lifted his eyes and sat watching the sky, trying to find the birds his father had pointed out, and when they were nowhere to be seen, he dropped his face into his hands and sobbed.

'Young Master Jack, come away over here and see what I've got for you.'

His nanny felt deeply for the young boy and her heart was heavy at the thought of him now alone. She was unsure how much he understood, but it was not her place to decide what and when he should be told. All she could offer were distractions, and she held out a new picture book.

'Shall we read this one together? It's a very old story from long ago and far away. Look, here's a picture – what do you think of that?'

She pointed to the engraving of a large wooden horse that looked to be on wheels and was being pulled by many men. Their ropes were straining at the great weight, and they were trying to draw it through the gates of a mighty fortress. She knew how to get his attention and all she hoped for was to provide him with a few moments of solace where he might forget about everything he had lost. He went to her and climbed onto her lap and lost himself in her embrace.

'So let's begin . . . *Once upon a time, in the far-off land of Troy, there lived a king with many sons . . .*'

*

The next day, Jack's nanny was packing bags. She pulled the large leather case from under her bed in the corner of the nursery and began emptying the clothes from her chest of drawers into it. She left him alone in the nursery, looking at his picture books, while she went to find another slightly smaller case which she proceeded to pack with his clothes.

He came over to watch her folding his vests and shirts, and then wrapping his boots in linen before putting them in the case. There were his play clothes and his caps as well as all the undergarments and stockings he had. She said nothing to the boy as she busied herself with the preparations, but she could see that he was watching her. Without looking over, she said cheerily, 'We're going on an adventure, Master Jack. And we're to take everything with us.'

'What sort of adventure? Are we to sail on a ship, Nanna?'

'No, but we're going on a journey in a carriage to the other side of Edinburgh. We're going to live with your grandfather. He's to look after you now, but don't you worry, I'm coming too. And I think the nursery there will be even more splendid than this one. He has a bigger garden too. I hear he has squirrels that we can watch and chase. Now won't that be fun?'

The small boy looked suspicious of her good humour and began to wonder why they were going somewhere else to live. How would his father know where to find him when he came home from his many journeys? He was suddenly quite sure that he did not want to leave. He sat down on the floor and said so and told his nanny why. She stopped her packing and sat beside him on the nursery floor and invited him on to her lap.

'I know, Jack. It all seems like a terrible upheaval, but, you'll see, it's really all for the best. We can't stay here now that your papa has gone away.'

'But when he comes back, we won't be here.'

'My little darling, your papa can't come back, not from where he's gone this time. But before he went away, he made sure that you and I could go and live with your grandfather. Oh, what a time we'll have in that wonderful house. You've been to see him, haven't you? You know what a magical place it is. He even has a stuffed bear in the hallway. Do you remember that? A great big, growling black bear, but it can't hurt you. You can even stroke its fur – something you could never do if it was alive. So, you see, a stuffed bear is so much more useful than a living one.'

The boy's eyes were widening at the memory, and he was oblivious to his nanny's tactics of distraction which never failed to take him somewhere else, somewhere safer and more exciting than the shattered family he inhabited.

'Come on, Jack! There's no time to lose. We've still got all your books to pack, and I just don't know how we're going to fit your bed into the suitcase. Perhaps if we both sit on it, we'll be able to get the lid shut.'

The boy giggled and teased her for being 'a big silly' because the bed would never fit and, besides, Grandpapa had lots of beds. She laughed with him and held him close to her. She had been his nanny since he had been born and the two were as close as any mother and child.

*

The next morning, Jack was standing in the hallway dressed in his travelling clothes, beside the pile of suitcases. His nanny was putting a long cape on over her uniform and tying a large satin ribbon underneath her chin to hold her bonnet in place. The carriages sent by his grandfather had already arrived and his man, Osbourne, was sizing up the luggage to work out how best to transport it.

'Miss, we can put all the big trunks in the second carriage, but I think you'll need to take the smaller cases in the brougham with you. If you want it all to go in one trip, that is.'

'Thank you, sir, that'll be quite all right. Master Jack and I don't take up much room, do we, my little shilling? Come on, let's help Mr Osbourne with the bags. The sooner we get them loaded, the sooner we can be off on our adventure. I do hope there'll be squirrels.'

There was much activity in the hallway as the largest of the trunks were lifted shoulder high by the footman and tied on to the back of the second carriage. The dark green brougham carriage in front had four large spoked wheels, the rear two taller than the boy. The brass work was glittering and the two glass lamps on either side of the open driver's seat had been polished to a high sheen.

Jack had to be lifted by Osbourne for he could not reach the step even when it was folded down. The chestnut mare harnessed to the carriage stood stock still while the passengers and the smaller bags were loaded, but as soon as Osbourne took his seat, released the brake and flicked his whip, the carriage lurched forward.

The horse picked up speed and trotted briskly over the street cobbles. Jack stood rather than sat in the carriage, peering out of the window at the sights beyond. The roads became busier with traffic as Osbourne navigated the slow-moving flat-bed delivery carts, hand-drawn barrows, jangling open-topped trams, smoky horseless carriages and Hansom cabs.

There was bustle everywhere Jack looked, and he drank it all in. His nanny did not even try to make him sit safely down, knowing that excitement might be the best medicine for the boy. At last, they turned onto the wide Princes Street where the elegant shops were, and he saw the castle perched on its great rock overlooking the city. There were news boys shouting to hawk their papers, street sweepers collecting the manure from the roads, a line of uniformed girls in red capes and straw hats snaking along the pavement behind their school mistress, a man roasting chestnuts, a barrel organ and even, joy of joys, a real live monkey.

But they were all gone in a flash as the horse clipped along the wide boulevard, with Osbourne making sure he didn't get the carriage wheels caught in the tram lines. Quieter roads of elegance and black railings replaced the bustle and then there were long roads lined by trees and fields. Jack could see the shining river and small clusters of houses and parkland. Soon, they were turning off the road altogether through ornate gates that were closed behind them.

The Dalrymple Estate swept down a long gradual slope towards the Forth, with views of the Fife hills to the north and Arthur's Seat back in the city. As the carriage rolled up the driveway, Jack could see the house in the distance but kept his eyes peeled for the promised squirrels amongst the trees. All too soon, he was being lifted down from the carriage in the capable arms of Osbourne, and at the front door of the great house his grandfather was waiting.

He stood dressed, as he always was, in a black frock coat and grey silk cravat. But today he also wore a black armband in mourning for his son-in-law. The white hair on his head was long and because of its thickness gave him the appearance of a lion. His white mutton-chop whiskers completed the picture, but, despite his somewhat fierce appearance, Jack had never been frightened of him. The old man had always had the softest of spots for the boy, for when he looked into his eyes, he saw again his beloved daughter, Alexandra. That morning was no different and he smiled a rare smile as the boy ran to him up the stone steps.

'Grandpapa, do you have squirrels?'

Old John Dalrymple looked over at the nanny, who dropped her eyes and tried to hide her blushes. 'Well, laddie, I'm not sure what you've been told, but, yes, I do have squirrels, and I think they will be more than pleased to find someone new to feed them. But first we need to get you and your things upstairs. Your room is all ready, and you might even find a little present waiting for you on your new bed.'

Jack turned to his nanny and shouted to her that he was right – he knew his grandfather would have beds. Osbourne unloaded the bags, and the nanny followed the boy into the house after bobbing a curtsy to the old man.

'And what do I call you, Nanny?'

'Violet, sir. Thank you for allowing us both to come here.

I think this is the best possible place for the young master. You have such a lovely home.'

'It was lovely once, Miss Violet, but it hasn't been so for many years. But now that there is a child in the house again, I have high hopes. Please, don't let me keep you. I am sure you have much to do, and you must both be tired after all your packing and travelling.'

'Nothing tires that little laddie, sir. But I must go and find him to make sure he's not getting himself lost.'

In the ornate marble hallway of the house, she found him standing looking up at the snarling jaws of the stuffed bear. When he saw her, he giggled and impersonated the beast. She feigned her terror, and they both laughed and ran upstairs to the nursery. Dalrymple watched them from the shadow of the doorway and smiled for the second time that morning. He could not help remembering hearing the very same giggles from another child some twenty-five years before.

*

The nursery was bright, with high, south-facing windows. Everywhere was painted white wood and there was a large toy chest and bookshelves all waiting to be filled with everything his nanny had brought from his father's house. There were pictures on the walls; not the kind of reproductions on paper that had hung in his old nursery, but framed oils that his grandfather had thought appropriate for the child.

There was a storm-tossed galleon, St George slaying his dragon and, largest of all, a sumptuous yet fantastical vision of Ancient Rome in its heyday. The small boy stood before this painting that was larger than him and traced the marble columns and billowing banners with his eyes. He then followed the line of the great triumphal procession that was parading past the temples of the forum.

His nanny was already unpacking and was delighted to discover that, for the first time in her career, she would have her own separate but adjoining room. The boy's bed was already made with fresh linen and, as promised, on the counterpane there was a large flat box wrapped in a blue ribbon to welcome him.

'Master Jack, have you seen what's over here?'

He turned to the bed and was more surprised by its size. It would be his first full-sized bed, and he ran and jumped upon it. Only when he had bounced on the mattress did he notice the box, and he stopped to look at his nanny who nodded, giving him permission to open it. Inside, he found one of the largest books he had ever seen. It was bound in rich red leather with gold tooling. He stroked the soft leather cover and traced the outline of the large letters.

'What does it say, Nanna?'

'Let's sound it out, the way I taught you. Now what does this first letter sound?'

'Ah.'

'And the next . . . and then this one . . .'

And so she went on patiently until the boy had assembled the sounds into the word 'Atlas'.

'But what does it mean, Nanna? What's an atlas?'

'Well, let's look inside to find out, and you can tell me what you think it is.'

The boy struggled to open the cover, but she helped him. He found he needed both hands to turn the large pages but was delighted by the colourful pictures inside. He recognised them as maps and tried to read the names, but many were longer than he could manage.

On and on he turned the pages, finding blue oceans and countries coloured in pink and blue and yellow and green. Some had mountains and rivers marked, and the names of all the cities. There were also pictures of what the animals looked like in these far-off lands. There were elephants and tigers, brightly coloured parrots and strange insects. There were even growling black bears just like the one his grandfather had in the hallway.

'It's a book of the whole world, Nanna! Grandpapa has given me the whole wide world and everything in it.'

'Yes, my little shilling, I think he has.'

*

It took most of the next week for the pair to familiarise themselves with the house, for it was so much larger than anything they were used to. Nowhere had been marked as off-limits for their adventures, and they spent the afternoons exploring the rooms with all their finery and wonderful paintings.

Jack enjoyed the pictures most of all and always urged his nanny to sit with him in front of the larger oils and to imagine what was happening in them. They also roamed the gardens playing in the autumn leaves and collecting different kinds to make into pictures.

They even managed to find the squirrels, or, more correctly, the squirrels found them, for as predicted they saw a new source of food in the young boy. He was delighted when the small, red-coated animals with their tufted ears and luxuriant tails would come close, tentatively sniffing the air and eyeing him to gauge his level of threat.

His nanny taught him to be very still and to lay his hand with the nuts flat almost on the ground. The braver squirrels darted to his hand to snatch a nut and he would squeal with joy, but his nanny would put her finger to her lips to remind him to be quiet in case he frightened them all away.

In time, the timid red squirrels gained their nerve and

would feed from his hand, taking a nut and even sitting on their haunches to feed on it, clasped in their forepaws, right beside him. In that moment, he could think of nothing else in the world that might make him happier.

As they were walking back to the house, Jack spotted something white in the grass. He bent to pick it up before his nanny could discourage him. It was hard and smooth and was complicated to look at with ridges and holes. He held it up to his nanny. 'Is it a seashell, Nanna?'

'No, Master Jack, it's a bone from an animal. It looks like a bird's skull, but I'm not sure.'

'What's a skull?'

She knew from experience that the best way to deal with his endless questions was to answer them all as fully as she could. He knew when he was being fobbed off and would only keep on until he got the real answer. And so she proceeded to explain that all animals had a skeleton made of bone, even little boys, and that when they died, their souls would go to heaven to live with God, but their bodies would stay here on Earth and they would change. In time, the flesh would disappear, and all that would be left would be the bones, like the one he had in his hand.

'So the bird is dead, but a bit of it, the inside part, is still here.'

'That's right. You can feel the bones inside your own body. That's why your head is hard. And feel your knees — that's the bones inside your legs. You're just full of bones, aren't you? And I know something else about bones . . .'

'What's that?'

'They tickle!'

He ran from her giggling as she chased him into the house. In the hallway, he darted away across the black-and-white tiled floor and rushed into a room he had never been in before — his grandfather's study. Although they had not been expressly forbidden from entering this part of the house, his nanny had never thought it appropriate in case they should disturb old Mr Dalrymple.

When she saw where Jack had gone, she slowed and prepared herself for any rebuke she might receive, but she was relieved to find the room empty. When she went in, she found the boy, as always, transfixed by the largest painting in the room.

It was a full-length, almost life-sized portrait of a young woman, and it hung in its heavy gold frame above the white marble fireplace. The woman was standing in the portrait, dressed perhaps for a ball in a sumptuous blue velvet dress the colour of her eyes. Her skin was pale to the point of translucence, and on the table beside her was a loose bouquet of old roses. Her hair was as black as the boy's and she had his eyes. The nanny stood watching the boy looking up at the painting and could see he had been transported in his imagination into the picture. He looked as if he were standing beside the young woman, perhaps even holding her delicate hand and smelling the rich perfume of the flowers.

'Who is the lady, Nanna?'

'I think this is your mummy, Master Jack.'

'She's dead, isn't she? Will she have bones?'

'She's in heaven now, and that's all you need to think about.'

'But where are her bones, Nanna?'

'We all leave our bones in our graves, Master Jack, and that's where they rest for ever. Now, have you seen what else is in this room?'

His gaze was finally pulled away from the portrait and over to his nanny and then to the space behind her. Row upon row of books lined the other walls of the room, for this was also his grandfather's library.

Even as a four-year-old still learning his letters, Jack knew the value and the wonder of books. He cherished the picture books he had brought from home, and the large leather-bound atlas from his grandfather had already given him such joy. But now he could see that the old man had every book in the world in this room. His eyes widened, and he was drawn to the shelves as much by the smell of the leather and the paper as the sight of the gold lettering on the spines. He reached out to touch a set of dark green leather volumes only to be stayed by his nanny.

'Now, Master Jack, we must only look and never touch without asking. Remember, these are your grandfather's precious things.'

He drew back obediently but froze when he heard his grandfather's voice.

'I see you have found my treasures, young man.' Dalrymple was standing in the open doorway and nodded at Violet to assure her that all was well. He put his paper down and went over to the boy. 'So, tell me, Jack, can you read?'

The boy was convinced he had committed a serious crime and could not speak. He stood with his mouth open and his eyes filled with tears.

'It's all right, my boy. Grandpapa is not angry with you. But I can see you like books. Why is that?'

His grandfather's face was soft, and there was a warmth in his eyes that showed Jack he truly had done nothing wrong. He looked at the books again.

'They're so pretty. And they have pictures and stories. And when Nanna reads to me, it's like dreaming.'

'It is indeed exactly like that, my boy. Do you know your letters, young man?'

'I know the sounds, but sometimes the words are too big.'

'Don't you worry about that. They get smaller as you get

taller. Here, let me show you my favourite book in the whole world.'

The old man scanned the shelves to find a slim, dark blue volume. He took it down and called the boy over to him and hoisted him up on to his lap. He opened the cover and the boy marvelled at the rich creamy paper and the ornate lettering. There were no pictures, but the words themselves made beautiful patterns on the pages.

'What is it, Grandpapa?'

'This, my boy, is a book of poems. And I think it is the most wonderful book of poems ever written. And do you know who wrote it? No? Well, let me tell you. It was the beautiful lady in the painting, my darling daughter, Alexandra, and your mother.'

The boy looked again at the pages and realised the letters were handwritten in perfect, swirling copperplate. He could read none of the words, but he needed to reach out and touch the page and to feel the paper she had once held.

'One day, you will be able to read these wonderful poems and your mother will be able to speak with you again. That's the real miracle of books, my boy – they ensure that no one who writes ever really dies. We can still hear them speak to us long after they have gone.'

The nanny could see the old man was losing himself in his thoughts and she worried that the boy might be tiring him.

'Master Jack, it's time to leave your grandfather to his study. Come now, quickly, we need to go back to the nursery and plan our next voyage across the Pacific Ocean.'

The old man closed the book and released the boy from his embrace. He nodded at Violet again and they both understood each other. She curtsied and led the boy away.

*

All his life it would be the familiarity of certain smells that would transport him instantly back to his grandfather's house – and none more so than cigar smoke. His grandfather only indulged in this particular vice after dinner, but his cigars of choice were sweet and expensive.

Jack loved to watch him lighting the great log of rolled tobacco with the spill he would take from the fireplace. The cloud of blue smoke that would first envelope the man and then fill the room became for the boy the very essence of his grandpapa. He would already have had supper with Nanny in the nursery and would be bathing and readying for bed while the old man ate alone at the overlong dining table. When he retired to his study to smoke his cigar, Jack, in his nightgown, was allowed to come in briefly to say goodnight.

Inevitably, the boy would stretch the few minutes to twenty or more by asking his grandfather questions about all the books he had on his shelves. He did so because he wanted to know about the library and all it contained, but he also wanted to savour his grandfather's smoke. The old man knew that no child ever wanted to go to bed when there was still excitement to be had, and he indulged him but never for too long. Nanny would always be on hand to tap the fob watch hanging on her breast and remind them both that little boys need their sleep. Dutifully, Jack would go, holding her hand and taking one last delicious breath of the sweet air in the study.

*

That night, he was in his bed in the nursery but unusually there was a light beneath his door. And he could hear voices. He crept from his bed and opened the door to find all the landing and hall lights on.

In his bare feet, he padded across the carpet and peeked through the wooden balustrade to see who was speaking.

Standing in the hall below were his grandfather and a woman. He couldn't at first make out who she was but when she spoke, then shouted, he recognised her voice.

'You have no right, Mr Dalrymple, no right whatsoever.'

'I would ask you to lower your voice while you are in my home.'

'This isn't a home; it's a mausoleum, and it's no place to bring up a child. He is only four years old, and he needs to be with his family.'

'And what, pray tell, am I? I am his grandfather and I consider this matter closed. Good evening, madam.'

More was said before she left, but they were moving as they spoke, and Jack could not make it out. Soon after, he heard the heavy front door being closed only to be followed by the thick, weighty silence he had become accustomed to in the house.

He knew he should not be out of bed, and he crept back into the nursery as quietly as he could and lay in bed wondering why Aunt Helena was shouting at his grandpapa. He also knew that shouting was something grown-ups didn't like to talk about, so he quietly put it away with the other little sadnesses and confusions that he had to keep out of sight. With tired eyes, he reached out to stroke the red leather of the atlas lying on his bedside table. He fell asleep again with his hand still on it.

Chapter 4

London: 21 September 1931

Given Sister Hilda's agitation when she spoke about the impending visit of their parish priest, Sergeant Baker was expecting a much more forbidding figure. However, when he called on Reverend Henshall, he was greeted at the rectory door by a pleasant, smiling young man.

'I was half expecting you, sergeant. I'm Teddy Henshall. Please do come in. Tea?'

'I won't, if you don't mind, sir. I just need to ask you a few questions, and I don't want to keep you from your work.'

Henshall led Baker through into his sitting room-cum-study. The timbered ceilings were low in the old cottage, but the place had a cosy rather than a claustrophobic feel.

'Please, take the weight off your feet, sergeant. I'm sure in your job there's a lot of traipsing about. Here, let me move these for you.'

The vicar took an untidy pile of papers from the armchair by the fire and all but forced the sergeant into it. Baker relented and made himself comfortable. He had already been taking mental notes of the man and his home. He reckoned him to be in his late thirties and, judging by the state of the place, a bachelor. No housekeeper had answered the door, and he was naturally suspicious of the man's disposition. Few people, in Baker's experience, were that pleased to see a policeman arrive at their doorstep. He decided to begin gently.

'Thank you, sir. Might I ask how long you have been affiliated with St Gregory's?'

'Affiliated. That's a very grand term for it. I'm just the local parish priest and it falls within my remit to provide them with spiritual support. I go once a week to serve communion to the sisters, and as for my support, I'm sure Sister Eglantyne would tell you that I was entirely superfluous to their needs.'

'Sister Eglantyne?'

'Oh, I think we're supposed to call her mother superior these days, but when I first met her, she was just plain Sister Eglantyne and it's rather stuck. To tell you a little secret, she doesn't like me and because of that I rather deliberately forget to address her properly. She does have a bee in her bonnet about titles. In fact, if you could get that bonnet off, I suspect you'd find a whole hive of the blighters.'

'So no love lost between you?'

'That's it in a nutshell. Are you sure I can't get you some tea? I'm parched and I was just putting the kettle on before you arrived. No? Well, I hope you won't mind if I just make a brew.'

He jumped from the chair and made his way through to the kitchen at the rear of the cottage. He was a thin man, and his clothes appeared a little too big for him. His glasses were horn-rimmed and thick, and judging by the cuts on his neck and cheek, he was still learning how to master the art of shaving. Baker could hear him in the kitchen, rattling crockery and teaspoons and pouring water. He called from the kitchen, 'Please go on, Sergeant Baker. How else can I help you?'

Baker called back that he was happy to wait.

A moment later, Henshall appeared in the doorway with a tea tray. 'I brought you a cup just in case you change your mind. I'll let it brew and then I'll be mother. Such a silly expression, but there you are. Now, where were we?'

Baker checked his notebook and went on to ask about the staff of the orphanage.

'The Order of the Divine Fellowship. An order from the North East, and Sister Eglantyne – I mean, the mother superior – is from that neck of the woods, I believe. The order has been running the orphanage here since it was founded – 1902, if I remember rightly, so coming up to thirty years. They're what you would expect from a group of Anglican nuns. Mixed bunch, but I rather think they all have their hearts in the right place. The children are well cared for, and that's the main thing in my book. I can forgive them their little vanities as long as they do their jobs well.'

'Vanities, sir? Seems an odd expression when referring to nuns.'

'Oh, do you think they stop being women and thinking like women when they get togged up in those habits? Let me disabuse you of that notion. No, they are very aware of the pecking order, and the little privileges that go along with rank. A holy order is almost military in its hierarchy. And that's another reason they don't like me. As well as being altogether too modern for them, I don't fit into their scheme of things, and I have a habit of pulling rank sometimes. I confess it's just to see the look on their faces. At times, I really am a very bad vicar.'

He poured the tea and without asking again poured a cup for Baker, who took it just to please him.

'In your time as parish priest here, have there been any deaths at the orphanage, sir?'

'Goodness, what a question. Let me think. Only one, about two years ago. She was a little girl, about two or three, who became very ill suddenly one weekend. I believe she had a high fever and suffered a convulsion. The doctor was called, of course, but by the time he arrived, I'm afraid there was nothing to be done. I think the cause of death was given as scarlet fever. A couple of the other children came down with it too, but they all recovered. The little mite is buried in the churchyard. Sister Hilda still puts flowers on the grave, you know. I expect you've met Sister Hilda. She's the one who is most concerned with the very small children. She took it very hard when we lost that little girl. Cake?'

'No, thank you, sir. I just have a few more questions.'

Baker was able to flesh out more of the details of how the orphanage was run and how little the vicar had to do with it all. His visits were confined to regular short communion services for the sisters, and he had no formal role in the management of the orphanage other than expecting to see the older children in his congregation every Sunday.

'The nuns are very good in that department. The spiritual wellbeing of the children is understandably high in their priorities, but they do care for them. I would go so far as to say love them, and that's all one can really ask, isn't it?'

'Would you mind if I looked around the church, sir?'

'Not at all. Open all hours, that's my motto. If you need anything, just shout. You know where I am.'

Baker took his leave after taking a perfunctory sip of the vicar's tea. The rectory and the church had once been part of the same large estate that the orphanage now occupied. From the churchyard, the roof of the large house was visible over the trees. The church itself was much older than the house, and Baker expected that the house had been built on its land rather than the other way round.

The churchyard bore witness to at least three centuries of graves. The oldest were nearest to the church, and as Baker walked down the gentle slope, he found he was walking forward through time. Some rather more ornate Victorian gravestones gave way to modern, more modest affairs, and in one corner there was the smallest headstone that marked the grave of the little girl who had died in the orphanage.

Carved in the stone was 'Isobel Steadman 1926–1929'. And as the vicar had indicated, there was indeed a posy of simple wildflowers on the grave. Baker looked around and noticed the distinctive headstone of a war grave. He walked over to pay his respects and to read the inscription on the white Portland stone. There was a carved regimental insignia of a dragon and a simple cross. Between these were the words:

> 19632 LANCE CPL.
> R. D. BARNABY
> ROYAL BERKSHIRE REGIMENT
> 26TH OCTOBER 1917

That was two weeks after Passchendaele. He knew the date only too well because his elder brother had died on the twelfth. He was buried out there, but Lance Corporal Barnaby must have been wounded and sent home only to die here. That was the only way his grave would be on English soil.

Baker bowed his head as he always did when confronted by one of the fallen, and silently he thanked whatever powers there were that he had come home unscathed. His moment of silent reflection was broken by a sound behind him. He turned to see an older man, probably in his sixties, bending to clear some growth from one of the graves. He recognised him immediately as Dickson Barnaby, the groundsman of St Gregory's. As he remembered the man's name, he made the connection with the grave he was still standing beside. He hailed the man and walked over.

'Mr Barnaby, Detective Sergeant Baker. What a stroke of luck – I was just coming back to see you.'

'Oh, no bother, sergeant. I won't be long here. Just trying to get some of the weeds off of our Tilly.'

Baker read the simple headstone. It was the grave of Matilda Barnaby, aged 23, and she had died only a year ago. He could see the man was working hard to pull the long-rooted weeds from the grave. There were no flowers here and it looked untended, apart from the effort that Mr Barnaby was now putting in.

'Just want to tidy it up a bit for our girl, sergeant. There . . . that'll do for the time being. I can come back later and finish it off. Should never have got in this state.'

'Is this your daughter's grave, Mr Barnaby?'

'That it is, sir. We lost her twelve months ago now, but it seems like yesterday somehow that I was standing here putting her in the ground. At least she's with God now and I hope with Robert, her brother. He's over yonder.'

Baker could not comprehend having to tend the grave of one child, let alone two, and he stood in silence, allowing the man to finish his task.

'All right, that's me. Do you want to walk back with me, or would you like to ask them questions here in the church?'

Baker led him across the churchyard to a bench beneath the large rowan tree, close to one of the more ostentatious Victorian memorials.

'It's a fine spot, Mr Barnaby.'

'That it is. Just a pity it's a boneyard. Now, what is it you need to ask me?'

Although Dickson Barnaby had a lot to be angry about, he appeared not to have a shred of bitterness in his soul. He took off his cap, loosed his neckerchief and tilted his sunburnt face up to the sky. He breathed in the autumn air, smelling the last of the life in the trees. Baker watched his face, deeply lined but placid, and wished he didn't have to break the moment and bring the man back into the present. But he had a job to do.

'Mr Barnaby, can you tell me more about that morning when you found the grave in the woods?'

'I'm always out early doing my rounds. You can get a lot more done before the day starts for everyone else. We've had a problem with badgers in the woods, see. They do a lot of damage, those beasts – digging up the bulbs and the like. Anyway, I saw the freshly turned earth and I thought it must be one of their setts. I went over and kicked the soil and that's when I saw the feet. It gave me quite a turn, I can tell you. I didn't touch a thing, just stepped right back.

'At first, I wasn't sure if my eyes had been playing tricks, so I went a bit closer. But there was no mistake. I turned tail and went up to the main house. When I arrived, there was some singing coming from the chapel and I knew the sisters must be doing what they do in the morning before the children rise. This must have been about seven or thereabouts. I waited and caught the mother superior when she was coming out. She took me straight to her office and even dialled the number for me, but she said I should speak.'

'Has there ever been anything like this here before, Mr Barnaby?'

'No, never anything of the sort. This is a very quiet part of the world, and that's one of the reasons me and the wife love it here. But the very idea of it still sends a shiver through me. The children play in those woods and the thought that one of the little ones could have found it – well, it makes the blood run cold.'

'What does Mrs Barnaby do here?'

'Eliza just keeps house now. She was a cook at the main house, but this last year, what with Tilly, it's just been too much for her. She's a changed woman. We live in Briar Cottage over by, in the grounds. We've been here nigh on twenty years, worked hard and brought up our two. And, of course, they'll always be here now, so we can't be going anywhere else, can we?'

'I'll need to speak with Mrs Barnaby too. Would she be in this afternoon?'

'You'll usually find her in the house or in her garden. But can I ask you one thing? When you talk with her, could you not mention that I was here tidying Tilly's grave? I'm sorry to ask, but it's just that she's still not coping with that loss, and, well, it's difficult.'

'Of course, sir. I understand, mum's the word.'

Barnaby retied his neckerchief, straightened his cap and rose from the bench somewhat wearily. He stretched by arching his back and grimaced at the twinge of pain in his lower back. 'Not getting any younger, sergeant, but I must get on. No rest for the wicked when it comes to keeping this place under control.' He shook the sergeant's hand and asked him to do everything he could to find out about the child in the grave. 'He was somebody's little lad. And we all need to know where our children are.'

The man walked off down the slope, then through the back gate of the churchyard and across the lawns towards St Gregory's. Baker took another look at the Barnaby graves and shook his head, wondering just how big a price sometimes had to be paid to be a father.

*

Next on his list of interviews were the other nuns at the orphanage. Sisters Hilda and Margery and the novice sister,

Mary Frances, were all expecting him as he had telephoned the day before to arrange the meeting. And, as before, it was Sister Hilda who met him at the door of the orphanage.

'Here we are again, Sergeant Baker. My, what a to-do, right enough. Do come in. We're all waiting for you in the reception room.'

When Baker entered the room just off the hallway, the other two sisters were standing with their heads bowed. Sister Hilda joined them, and the trio waited in silence for permission to speak.

'Thank you for agreeing to see me, sisters. I only have a few questions, but I would like to talk with you individually, if I may.'

The novice raised her head and looked at the others in alarm. Sister Hilda patted her arm and mouthed something soothing, while Sister Margery sighed.

Baker asked, 'Will that be a problem?'

Sister Hilda smiled and assured him that it was one of their rules that no sister would ever be alone in a room with any man other than the parish priest. However, the mother superior had anticipated this, and special permission had been granted in these exceptional circumstances.

'The reverend mother did stipulate, however, that the interview-room door should be left ajar. I do hope that is acceptable.'

Baker was discomfited by the implication that he was thought to be a threat, but he could also see that these were far from conventional interviews. For the time being he was happy to go along with their requirements, but if any of these sisters should end up at the Yard, they would have to accept rather different treatment. No doors were left ajar there.

'Shall we start with you, Sister Hilda?'

The other two went out quietly and left the door wide

open. Baker suggested they sit by the window and Sister Hilda was happy to comply. Baker had realised by now that this middle-aged woman had two competing personas that she had managed to meld. On the one hand was the chatty, if not gossipy, woman and on the other there was the silent, obedient nun. He wondered, as he sat down, which one he would have to contend with today. He didn't have to wonder for long.

'I can't tell you what an upset all this is. We've been keeping everything that's happened from the children, naturally, but even the little ones sense when something's not right. There's been a terrible atmosphere in the orphanage since that morning. Do you know yet who the body belongs to?'

'I'm sorry, I really can't divulge any details of the investigation. But perhaps I could ask you some questions.'

'Oh, of course. I'm sorry, my mind's just getting away with itself. So much to think about, to worry about. We've been praying for you, you know. We all need God's help, and your job must be so very difficult. That's right, isn't it?'

'Thank you, but again perhaps I could ask the questions, and we might get through this a little quicker.'

Sister Hilda composed herself and remembered her vows, as she had to do several times every day. She nodded in silence.

'How long have you been here at St Gregory's, sister?'

'Fifteen years. I was twenty-five when I started my novitiate, twenty-eight when I took my vows, and I was posted here soon after.'

She was about to tell him how much she had enjoyed her time at the orphanage, to share stories of all the children in her care over the years, but she could see by his face that the question had been answered.

'Has there been anything out of the ordinary in the last week or two? Anyone in the grounds that you didn't recognise?'

'Not that I can think of. I spend almost all my time in the main house with the very young children, apart from our play hour every day and our visit to the church every Sunday. In the house, there's been nothing unusual. No new staff or children. No visits from anyone apart from Reverend Henshall, to my knowledge.'

'And what of the children in your care? Could any have gone missing?'

She looked aghast at the suggestion but recovered enough to answer politely, 'No.' He recorded her answer but also made a note to check the records to confirm.

'Sister, does the name M. Saunders mean anything to you?'

'Was that the name of the child? Sorry, I know you can't tell me. No, I can't say I know of any Saunders. It's certainly not the name of any of our children at present and I don't recall anyone over the years with that surname. I'm afraid I'm being no help at all.'

'On the contrary, even a negative can help exclude things. One last thing: does anyone here have any specialist knowledge of herbs?'

She brightened suddenly on finding something she could answer. 'Sister Mary Frances is our expert in that department. We have a kitchen garden that used to double as a herbarium. When I first came, one of the older sisters used to grow a whole range of medicinal herbs. It rather fell into disrepair, but now Mary Frances has taken a keen interest. It's undergone quite the resurrection. I'm sure she'd be happy to show you it.'

'I'll certainly be sure to ask her. Thank you, Sister Hilda – you've been most helpful.'

As she rose to leave, he remembered he had meant to ask her about the little girl's grave in the churchyard. When he did, she stopped on her way to the door. After a moment she turned round, and he could see her eyes were wet and she was already sobbing. He went to her, helped her back to the seat and then waited for her to answer his question.

'It was my fault, all my fault. Little Isa was so ill, and I didn't realise. I waited too long to call Dr Jones and when he came, she was already gone. I'll never forgive myself. I let that little one down so badly.'

'But it was scarlet fever, as I understand it. There was nothing you could have done, that anyone could have done.'

'I've prayed for that little girl, and I've prayed for my own forgiveness. But I know I'll answer for it all one day. Please may I go now?'

He helped her to the door this time and outside he could see Novice Sister Mary Frances waiting her turn. When she saw Sister Hilda in tears, she blanched and looked at the sergeant with nothing short of terror. He tried to calm the situation by encouraging Sister Hilda to explain, but she was still reliving that night two years before when the girl had died in her arms.

'If you don't mind waiting just a few minutes more, sister, I'll be right with you. Now, Sister Hilda, why don't you go and get yourself some water and stop dwelling on the past? What's done is done.'

The nun nodded, but she knew he had never lost a child. She went off to the back kitchen. Sister Mary Frances was still standing outside the reception room awaiting her interrogation, and Baker could tell this was going to be like pulling teeth. He smiled broadly though, trying to put her at ease, and invited her in to sit down.

'I'm sorry about all that. Sister Hilda was feeling a little emotional. Now, this won't take long – I only have a few questions.'

After clarifying how long she had been at the orphanage and whether she had noticed anything out of the ordinary in the past week or so, he turned to the matter of the herbarium. She lit up when he mentioned the garden and was clearly not expecting to discuss something so close to her heart. From her tense monosyllabic demeanour, she became almost animated. She spoke at length about how she had found the old garden thoroughly neglected but that over the last two years she had cleared the weeds, relaid the beds and replaced some of the old woody plants with new varieties.

'And it's all been so enjoyable. When I work in the garden, I feel I am so much closer to God. Nurturing the plants is just like nurturing the children here. They each need care and sustenance, but they also need love if they are to grow up and grow strong.'

'Why do you grow the herbs, sister?'

'We eat them, we use them to make teas and of course we use many of them for their medicinal properties.'

'And do you know much about that?'

'Well, I'm certainly learning. We have some wonderful old books here in our library and Sister Justine taught me so much. Sadly, she passed away at the beginning of the year, but she had such a knowledge of the herbs.'

Baker took careful note of all this and pressed on. 'Would you ever use the herbs to treat the children?'

'Yes, for simple things like tummy upsets or coughs and colds. A soothing tea made of peppermint or chamomile and fennel can be most effective at easing a little one's tummy ache and a syrup made with thyme can help a tickly cough.'

Baker was about to close his notebook when he thought he would ask one more question.

'Tell me, sister, what makes someone like yourself want to become a nun?'

'Oh, that's a difficult question. I'm sure no two people are exactly alike in that respect, but for me it was a realisation that

I needed to live a life in service of my God. They say it's a calling, and for me, quite literally, it was. I was in my garden at home, and I felt something draw me to the plants. It wasn't a voice or anything like that, just a feeling, but an almost overpowering feeling, a beckoning if you like. As I stood there in the sunshine, I realised that I needed to devote my life to His works, to nurture His creations. So when I heard of the Order of Divine Fellowship and its work with children, I knew that had to be it, for what greater creation is there in all the world than children?'

Baker could see the excitement in her eyes as she told her story. However, he was still unable to reconcile the thoughts of a young woman willing to forego a life with a family of her own for a life in an institution like this. But that, he reminded himself, was not the point of his being there. As Novice Sister Mary Frances was leaving, Sister Hilda was back, hovering outside the room, her eyes now dry.

'I'm sorry to disturb you again, Sergeant Baker, but Sister Margery is busy with the children. The school-age children have just come back from their classes and Sister Margery has to supervise their homework. Would it be possible to postpone her interview?'

'Yes, of course. I need to go and speak with Mrs Barnaby. Perhaps after that I could come back and conclude things here with Sister Margery. I expect I can be back in about an hour. In the meantime, perhaps you would be good enough to direct me to the cottage. I understand it's nearby in the grounds.'

*

Sister Hilda gave him clear instructions, and only five minutes later he was standing in front of Briar Cottage on the other side of the wooded area. It was small but built of the same red brick as the main house and had doubtless been put up at the same time, perhaps as a gardener's or stableman's house.

True to its name, the portico of the cottage's front door was swathed in briar and many pink roses were still blooming between the prickly stems. The front garden was full of far less ornamental plants. There were grasses of various kinds and small low bushes that looked to be arranged for function rather than appearance. He knocked on the door but there was no answer.

Baker looked for Mrs Barnaby in the large back garden, where he thought she might be working. That was a larger version of the front garden with rows of vegetables and several fruit trees. There were none of the usual flowers he might have expected to see, but there was colour. Some of the plants had small yellow, blue and pink flowers, but from their positions, he concluded they were grown not for show but for utility.

Mrs Barnaby was nowhere to be found, and no formal appointment had been made, so Baker wrote a quick note and posted it through the letterbox saying that he would call the following morning at ten o'clock and he hoped to speak with her then.

Knowing he was too early now for Sister Margery, he took the long way back to the main house around the perimeter of the wooded area.

As he was trying to estimate the distance between the cottage and the house, he was aware of someone watching him. He looked across the lawn and saw the blue-and-white figure of the mother superior. He raised his hand to acknowledge her, but she did not move. Baker assumed she had not seen him, and he walked quickly towards her. Almost as he reached her, she turned to go. He thought the behaviour odd and called to her as she was only a short distance away. This time she could not feign ignorance of his presence and she stopped and turned slowly towards him. She nodded in his direction and was about to leave again when he said, 'Mother superior, I need to ask you something.'

She waited for him to catch up with her and looked at him as calmly as before. 'How may I be of service, Sergeant Baker?'

'The Barnabys, reverend mother. What do you know of them?'

'I know a great deal. Do you have something specific in mind?'

'They seem to have had their fair share of tragedy. I was in the churchyard this morning and I saw the graves of both their children.'

'Indeed. Their son was killed serving his country. And their daughter, well . . .'

'She was very young. How did she die?'

'I don't know, but I will say she shouldn't be in that churchyard at all.'

'I'm sorry, why not?'

'She had no right to a burial in that sacred ground – none of them did.'

'Are you saying there is some irregularity about the burials?'

'Oh, you had better ask Reverend Henshall about that. It is not my place to criticise a parish priest. Now, I believe Sister Margery will be ready for you now, Sergeant Baker. I would take it as a kindness if you did not keep her any longer than you have to. The children's dinners must be served soon. I'm sure you understand.'

*

Sister Margery was the eldest of all the nuns and, as far as Sergeant Baker was concerned, the only one to have a foot in the real world.

'We have been visited by evil here at St Gregory's and we all need to do everything in our power to make sure that whoever has done this terrible thing is brought to justice. Now, how can I help?'

She answered everything he asked plainly and simply, and all the time Baker could see she was horrified by what had happened. And unlike the others she was able to look beyond the confines of the orphanage walls and appreciate the enormity of what had been discovered in their grounds. He asked her all his routine questions including his catch-all about having seen anything unusual in the previous week or two.

'You say anything or anyone unusual, and nothing immediately springs to mind except the lights. At night here, the grounds are usually in complete darkness save for the lights in Briar Cottage and the light from the windows here in the main house. I am usually the one to check that all the downstairs windows have been closed before retiring, and as I was drawing the curtains on that window over there, I saw a flash of light in the woods. I thought at first that I'd caught a reflection from the lamp in the room on the glass, but I looked again and there it was. It was a bright white light, and it was moving. It could easily have been a torch.'

'When was this exactly, sister?'

'I was doing my rounds about half past nine, and it was exactly a week ago today, so that would have been Monday the fourteenth of September. I remember because Mr Gandhi had arrived in London from India that weekend for the conference. There were pictures in the morning paper on the Monday, and we had been discussing it over supper, just before I made my rounds.'

Baker was a little surprised that the nuns took such an interest in outside events and even that they had access to the newspapers.

'We're not a closed order. How could we be? We have over sixty children to look after. There is a deeply spiritual side to our lives here at St Gregory's, of course, but we have to fit it around the care of these wonderful boys and girls. Our order believes that the way to God's grace is through good works. We are a practical bunch, you see, and we're not the kind of nuns to sit around in silent contemplation. You've met Sister Hilda, so you should already know that.'

Baker smiled and asked her to contact him if she should remember anything else that might be important. He gave her a card with the phone number of the C.I.D. duty desk at Scotland Yard, and she carefully put it away in the pocket beneath her scapular.

It was now late Monday afternoon, and he could hear much scraping of chairs as the children assembled in the dining hall. He would get nothing else useful done, so he decided to call it a day and go home.

*

Home for Sergeant Baker was also south of the River Thames, in Waterloo. He lived with his wife Enid, close to her mother. His own family was from Clapham, but when they married, he moved all of three miles closer to the river and felt he had crossed into another country. Such was the way of things in London – the biggest city on Earth, but really it was an amalgam of hundreds of small villages, all with their own high streets, parks and peculiarities.

He had lived in Waterloo for eight years, where the couple rented a modest brick terrace house on Roupell Street. Baker drove from St Gregory's in the black Wolseley car that he had the use of from the Yard and parked outside his house at number 17.

The street of late-Georgian terraced houses was already a century old when they moved in. The house itself was really too big for them, but they thought when they got married that they would soon be needing the space, for Enid was already three months pregnant.

Those first weeks were some of the happiest in his life. The war was well and truly over, and he had just moved from uniform to C.I.D. as a detective constable. Now they had a place of their own and a baby on the way. He remembered how Enid was so busy building her new nest, she couldn't stop smiling.

It wasn't until she started bleeding that night that they knew anything was wrong. The doctor told him in the parlour that she had nearly died and that they would have to think carefully about another pregnancy. For over a year they kept the door closed on the room they had been painting as a nursery. But with a new spring came new hope and new thoughts of a family. They had decided to try again, but this time Enid only managed to carry the child for a few weeks.

There was a longer gap next time, waiting for the right moment, waiting for their future together to begin, but again it didn't work. Each time chipped away a little more of their hope, and after eight years and five miscarriages, they had just about come to terms with each other being all the family they would ever have.

The narrow front door was right on the street and topped with an arch of the same dark brown brick that formed the facade, over a leaded light. He turned the key in the lock and as he entered the hallway, his wife called from the kitchen.

'That you, Walter?'

'Well, if it's not, you're in trouble. How's tricks, darling?'

'All tickety-boo. I wasn't expecting you for another hour or so. Dinner won't be till six, so you can take that hungry look off your face. What brings you back home so prompt?'

As a rule, Baker did not discuss his investigations with his wife, and he certainly did not want to share the details of this one with her. She found it hard to look at women pushing prams or to watch children playing in a park, and even talking about children, especially very young ones, made her quiet and withdrawn. He wanted only happiness for her and had been shielding her from everything that might affect her for as long as he could remember now.

'Oh, just this case. One minute they want you here and the next it's over there. One of the places I had to be got cancelled at the last minute and I thought, wait a minute, there's a good-looking woman waiting for me on Roupell Street in her ravishing pinny. So, I thought to myself, I should get straight home and remind her just how dashed good-looking her husband is.'

'Get off me! You'll make me spill this gravy. Why don't you go and do something useful with yourself, Walter Baker? There's a coal scuttle through there that's not going to fill itself, so jump to it, my lad.'

'Yes, sir. Right away, sir. Three bags full, sir.'

'Just the one bag'll do nicely, thank you.'

She was still smiling at his antics as she watched him through the back kitchen window. He was shovelling coal from their bunker into the brass scuttle, and she thought he was still as handsome as the day she met him.

Over dinner, he was talking again about the day and let slip that he had been to a lovely spot over lunchtime.

'Where was that, love?'

'Oh, by a church. There was a bench, and it had a lovely view out over the trees. You know when the sun is just right and the sky is just right and everything about just falls into line? Well, it was one of those rare moments.'

'Sounds lovely. You must take me sometime.'

'Yes, we should get out and about a bit, especially as I've got the car every other weekend now.'

'We could go to the park or the Crystal Palace in Sydenham. We could even go to the beach at Southend. That would be nice.'

'Yes, we should. Let's make a date.'

But no date would ever be made because all those places would be teeming with young families out for the day, and Enid would only come home with the stark reminder of everything she could never have.

That night in bed, he lay awake for hours unable to sleep. In his years in C.I.D., he had had to deal with a lot, but like Cuthbert he had never got used to the deaths of children. Although he told himself he avoided children for the sake of his wife, the truth was he found it just as hard as her to watch a mother with her baby or a father with his toddler.

Now, to have to deal with a young boy someone had just discarded in the wood like some piece of rubbish, he felt it was so unfair. Even to walk around the orphanage and see those innocent faces running along after the nuns, he was filled with the deepest sadness. Any of those children might have been his, and he and Enid would have given them so much love. But there they were, being looked after by strangers.

What sin had he and his wife committed that this was their punishment, a life without children? What sin had all those children committed that they should have a life without parents? And what of that little boy in his lonely grave? What possible sin could he have committed that he should have no life at all?

Chapter 5

London: 22 September 1931

After a difficult night, Baker woke with a start. His bed was empty, and he heard his wife already downstairs in the kitchen. His mind suddenly filled with his tasks for the day.

He had to go to the Yard first thing to check on what progress, if any, Missing Persons had made looking into four-year-old boys and more specifically anyone called Saunders. He then had to go back to St Gregory's to speak with Mrs Barnaby. And on top of that, he had to have everything straight with the statements from the orphanage to present them in summary at the afternoon's case conference.

He had already seen how angry this case was making his boss, and he did not want to make it any worse with shoddy work. He had learned long ago that good detective work was not about great leaps of deductive logic, but hard plod. It was about doing a huge number of little things well. Individually, they were all easy, but keeping them all up in the air at the same time was the real juggling trick. He washed quickly and shaved but then took some time to carefully trim the moustache he had been growing all year.

'Walter, you'll be late! And I'm not letting you out this

door until you've had some breakfast inside you, so get your skates on.'

The shout up the stairs from the kitchen was firm but good-natured, and he knew Enid would have prepared his eggs just the way he liked them and the toast would already be buttered.

'There you are, slowcoach. What's got into you today? Coming home early yesterday and now going in almost late today – going part-time, are we?'

'Can't a man eat his toast in peace? Come here and give us a big wet kiss, Mrs Baker.'

'Get on with you! C'mon, out of my kitchen when you've finished that cuppa and go and catch some criminals. I don't know! The streets of London aren't safe these days, and do you know why? I'll tell you why – because all the coppers are having a lie-in.'

He left, still eating the crust of his toast, and made her squeal as he squeezed her backside as he passed.

*

He drove the short distance across the river to Scotland Yard and went straight to the Missing Persons department. His opposite number there was Detective Sergeant Fred Howard and he found him with the morning paper open on his desk.

'Hard at it, I see, Freddy. Don't let me stop you reading your horoscope, mate, but I was wondering if you had anything for me.'

'Don't you be so bloody pass-remarkable. We always check the papers to see if there's any leads. And as for your question, the short answer is no. But it wasn't much to go on, was it? Small boy, maybe four, maybe local, maybe called Saunders. Well, we've got a few four-year-old lads who've been reported missing, but none as long ago as seven to ten days before he was found. And there's no Saunders of any age on the files at the moment.'

'Well, thanks for trying. I'll let you get back to that advice column. "Dear Aunt Flossie, please tell me what to do. All the other coppers say my truncheon is very small. Are they just being mean? Or do you think I should—"'

'Will you just fuck off back to homicide, Walter? And see if you can't get yourself killed while you're up there.'

'See ya, Fred!'

'Not if I see you first, mate.'

*

The drive out to St Gregory's was a pleasant one. It was the kind of autumn day that they wrote poems about – bright blue skies and trees everywhere still arrayed in orange, red and gold before the winds later in the month would lay them bare for winter.

As he drove up the driveway, he saw that Sister Hilda and Novice Sister Mary Frances were on the lawn with about a dozen of the smallest children. They were running and screaming with joy in the sunshine. He smiled at the delight in their eyes as they escaped from the clutches of the sisters and ran around them, grabbing the skirts of their habits as they went. He also noted that the faces of the sisters were filled with the very same delight, and he was forced to conclude that the children of this orphanage were safe and happy. But then, of course, he remembered why he was there, and much darker thoughts blocked out the sunlight.

He parked beside the main house and walked across the lawn, past the playing group and round the wood to Briar Cottage. This time there was an older woman in the front garden, bent over, clearing one of the beds of old growth.

'Mrs Barnaby? Detective Sergeant Baker. I dropped by to

speak with you yesterday and left a note. I hope you can spare me a few minutes to answer some questions.'

'Of course. I'm sorry I missed you yesterday. Truth is, I'm always here. Except when I'm not. Just popped over to the High Street to get some bits and pieces. Couldn't have been gone more than fifteen minutes.'

'Not to worry, madam. Might I come in?'

She rushed to open the gate, inviting him into the garden. The flower bed where she had been working was all but clear. Only some dried stalks remained amongst the scattered yellow petals.

'Watch your clothes on those damned briars. I'm always at Dickson to chop them back, but what is it they say about the cobbler's children? Well, it's just the same with the groundsman's garden. Come in and I'll get the kettle on. I'm sure you'll take a cuppa.'

She led him into the parlour, and he took in the room while she was in the kitchen preparing the tea. Mrs Barnaby was clearly fond of roses, for they were everywhere in the room. Not the flowers themselves but their patterns on the cushions, the curtains, and even the wallpaper. There was also a large jug on the table by the window full of wildflowers and grasses. It was an unconventional bouquet but not unattractive. Mrs Barnaby saw Baker studying it closely when she came back with the tea.

'Them's just some of the flowers from hereabouts. Nothing special, but I think they look just as good as shop-bought. The garden is one of my little passions.'

The cups and saucers also had roses on them, and Baker took the one proffered. He continued to look about the room as Mrs Barnaby was sugaring her tea and cutting thin slices of sponge cake. On the mantelpiece, there was a studio photograph of a young man in uniform, the kind he himself had sent home to his own mother. Beside it were odd, twisted objects that looked as if they had been made from straw.

'What are those, madam?'

'You mean my corn dollies? Just a bit of superstition. I'm from Suffolk. I was brought up on a farm. We were churched, but we were also aware of the old ways. We always made the dollies at harvest time, so old mother corn would have somewhere to live out the winter. All sounds like nonsense now, I'm sure, but we all used to believe it. Now what was it you wanted to ask me?'

He confirmed how long they had lived on the St Gregory estate and that she had indeed been a cook at the orphanage until a year ago.

'You must have got to know the sisters well.'

'Oh, I wouldn't say that. They're quite a tight-knit group, but then I suppose they have to be. Don't get me wrong. Everyone was friendly enough, especially young Sister Mary Frances, but you could only ever get so far into their world before the barriers would come down.'

'So you got on well with the novice.'

'Yes, well, we had a lot in common – both gardeners with a love of herbs, you see. I grow a few here, but the real herb garden is at the main house. They have all sorts there. And she was always asking so many questions about how this one was used or that one. It's nice when someone takes an interest, isn't it?'

Baker probed her about the events a week before and asked her if she had been aware of any unusual activity in the woods, especially in the evenings.

'Can't say that I have, but then I'm not out in them woods much. I go to collect some flowers sometimes, and there's a patch of mushrooms that I make very good use of, but I certainly don't go out at night. It's really very quiet about here.

That's one of the attractions for us. Mr Barnaby and me, we both like our peace and quiet now that we're getting on a bit.'

'Is that your son, Mrs Barnaby? In the photograph?'

'Yes, that's my Robbie. Fine-looking young man, he was. Fourteen years next month, and it only seems like yesterday we got the letter. Were you out there too?'

He nodded but was annoyed with himself. Why had he brought the subject up? Quickly, he asked if he might have some more tea, and she was delighted to keep him and his conversation for another twenty minutes. He chatted with her about her life in St Gregory's, keeping it informal but taking mental notes of everything she said. He asked about the orphans and watched her eyes smile at the thought.

'Some of them are such little darlings. You couldn't help but want to take them in your arms and give them a little bit of love. No parents at all, most of them, and those that do have someone . . . well, let's just say they're not worth having if they leave their children in an orphanage. Don't get me wrong. This is a good place, and the sisters do everything they can for the poor little souls, but it's not the same, is it? How could it be? A child needs its mum. Who else can care for it the same?'

He thanked Mrs Barnaby for the tea and for her time and asked her to get in touch with him at the Yard should she remember anything else about the goings-on over the last days and weeks.

He walked back to the car. The lawn had now been left to recover from the earlier games, and the place was quiet save for the breeze in the trees and the songbirds chirping. It was picturesque and peaceful, but knowing what had occurred here, he was chilled by the place. Quiet, yes, he thought, almost as quiet as the grave.

*

In the car, Baker made some further notes of his conversation with Mrs Barnaby. He also started to read over his other notes from the interviews at St Gregory's, sifting through them trying to find some simple narrative that he could present at the case conference that afternoon at the Yard.

Without trying, he had formed opinions of all the interviewees as he always did, but he was careful not to let those first impressions cloud his judgement. Too many times before, he had become anchored in his thoughts about a witness far too early, only to discover later that he had been very wrong in his initial assessment.

He knew only too well that bad people often made a very good fist of appearing as if butter would never melt in their mouths. Similarly, good folks, perhaps because they were anxious about being questioned, sometimes came across as highly suspicious. The trick, he had learned, was not to take anything at face value. Collect the facts, order them and see how they might contribute to the bigger picture.

Because the child had been buried in a secluded, almost residential woodland, the most likely suspects had to be amongst those who lived on the estate. Perhaps one or more of the people he had interviewed had killed the boy. Perhaps one or more of them had buried him. Mowbray would be looking to him for suspects, but so far he had little to offer. An Anglican priest, a gaggle of nuns and an older couple didn't seem much to go on, but it was all he had to present at this stage.

*

The afternoon case conference got off to a shaky start when Mowbray failed to turn up. Cuthbert and Baker and Detective Constable Marshall were all gathered around the pinboard in the duty room ready to start at two o'clock as planned, but the chief inspector was nowhere to be seen.

Cuthbert paced in frustration. 'Well, gentlemen, I don't think we can start without our illustrious leader, so shall we perhaps find some coffee to while away the time? A crossword even? It's not as if any of us have anything else to do.'

Cuthbert was irritated at being kept waiting, especially as Mowbray was such a stickler for punctuality. Baker turned to the constable and asked, 'Have you seen the Pie today?' Marshall shook his head. 'No, sir. We thought he was out with you this morning at the orphanage.'

Cuthbert was about to exercise his seniority and start proceedings, even although he had no authority to do so here at the Yard. However, at that moment Mowbray arrived, hung up his hat and coat and without explanation called on Baker to bring him up to date with the investigation. Cuthbert barely hid his displeasure, but Mowbray ignored him as Baker talked the group through the case.

'A male child, approximately four years old, was found buried in a shallow grave in the woods on the St Gregory's Orphanage estate on the morning of sixteenth September. The grave had been recently dug and the state of the soil along with findings of relatively fresh plants within the grave suggest that the child had been buried only around twenty-four to forty-eight hours previously.

'We have a witness statement from one of the sisters who claims she was drawing the curtains in the main house and saw what she thought was a torchlight moving in the woods. That was on the evening of fourteenth September. If that was our perpetrator burying the child, it would fit with all the other evidence. Dr Cuthbert suggests that the time of death would have been anywhere between two to seven days before that.

'The child is as yet unidentified, but we are working on the hypothesis that his name was M. Saunders because of name labels sewn into his underwear. Missing Persons have so far drawn a blank both with the name and any small boys that match the age and time of disappearance. Constable Marshall is still searching for families called Saunders in the South London area, but it's not that uncommon a name, so I think we'll need more to go on.'

Cuthbert, whose irritation had subsided as he became once again engrossed in the detail of the case, raised his finger to make a point. 'If I may interrupt, sergeant, there is one other complication here. I am reasonably sure the boy suffered a convulsion prior to his death. That would likely have rendered him incontinent. However, none of his underclothes were stained, suggesting that he may have been changed before his burial. Given that the vest and pants we found him in may not be his, perhaps focusing all our attentions on looking for a Saunders family might be ultimately fruitless.'

Mowbray, listening in silence, nodded, half in agreement and half as a signal for Baker to proceed with his report.

'One of the more unusual aspects of this case is the way the body was interred. He was wrapped tightly in cloth, and various plants were placed on and around the body. This was almost ritualistic and doesn't point to a hurried disposal of the body, but rather a carefully planned burial. Interestingly, there were no Christian symbols in the grave, which may prompt us to consider some form of pagan rite. According to Dr Cuthbert's preliminary post mortem report, we do not yet have a cause of death other than strong circumstantial evidence of some form of poisoning.'

Again, Cuthbert interrupted to bring the new evidence to the fore. 'We now have a good idea what the poison was, chief inspector. The boy ingested a toxin from a wild plant. It's called tansy or, more correctly, *Tanacetum vulgare*.' Cuthbert had brought a drawing of the flower and now pinned this to the board.

Mowbray stood and looked at it closely. 'Tansy? Don't horses get sick when they eat that?'

'You're thinking of tansy ragwort, chief inspector. Despite the name and somewhat similar appearance, it's a quite different plant. The chemicals or alkaloids in ragwort, although potentially fatal to livestock, don't seem to be as poisonous to humans. However, if humans are given enough of the common tansy, the one in the drawing there, it would certainly lead to vomiting and diarrhoea, abdominal pain and shock, and it could well lead to convulsions.'

'Would that have been enough to kill the boy?'

'I'm afraid so, chief inspector. Not every child who suffers a convulsion will die, but unfortunately it can happen. During any seizure a person might have difficulty breathing. If the seizure is lengthy, that in itself might be life-threatening. Also, the child might have aspirated some vomit during the fit which would block his airway, again leading to asphyxia and death. And it's thought that a seizure in some people might precipitate a seriously abnormal heart rhythm, and again that could result in his demise. However, this little boy did not aspirate, because if he had, I would have found evidence of that at his post mortem. But as for any sort of respiratory or cardiac arrest, if they happened as a result of the seizure, they would leave no trace for me to find.'

'Poor little beggar. But the question that remains is whether he was killed deliberately or accidentally. I assume you can't shed any light on that, doctor.'

'Tansy is used as a herbal remedy, and might well be administered to children. It's thought to get rid of worms, but whether it's effective is anybody's guess. But where the herbalists use it most is in trying to induce an abortion. It's known to have marked effects on the womb, causing strong contractions that can lead to the loss of the child. So there are a number of possible scenarios for how the tansy ended up in his stomach, but one of them would have to be the deliberate and premeditated poisoning of the child. There is very little known about fatal doses, but I suspect we're dealing with a very strong concoction here. It would have been highly aromatic, and I doubt it could have been taken inadvertently by the child. I think he was given it.'

'So we have to assume that whoever killed the boy knew what he or she was doing. They must have known how to prepare the poison and probably how much to give. Baker, did you turn up anything that might shed light on that?'

Baker, who was still standing by the board, started to go through the witness statements he had taken and highlighted that there were herb gardens both at the main house and Briar Cottage.

'Also, there are a lot of wildflowers growing around the place. We could check if this tansy is amongst them. As for know-how, Novice Sister Mary Frances seems to take a keen interest in the herb garden and I suppose Sister Hilda, Sister Margery and—'

'Do none of these women have real names?' Mowbray looked as angry now as he had at the last case conference. 'Sister this, sister that. Get that sorted, Baker. I want first names, last names and dates and places of birth, and I want them all checked out. A nunnery is just the place if you're hiding from something. Young Marshall here can do some work for a change, instead of sitting picking his nose. Sit up straight, you lazy little bastard, and get it done today.'

The constable tensed and sat up from his only slightly slouched position and prayed that the attention might pass. He wasn't sure if he was expected to get up now and go and make the necessary phone calls or whether Mowbray would demand his presence for the rest of the conference. He was reasonably sure, however, that whatever he did, it would be wrong. He cast a plaintive look at Baker, who motioned him to stay put.

'Right away, sir. It'll be on your desk by the end of the day.'

Mowbray was in a thunderous mood. He was standing staring at the photograph of the boy on the board, his arms folded tight about him and breathing heavily. Cuthbert was becoming concerned by his behaviour which he thought was becoming erratic. Everyone knew he had a hot temper, but arriving late and lashing out were not at all his style.

When Mowbray dismissed the group, Cuthbert hung back. When Mowbray went to his office, Cuthbert followed. Without knocking, he opened the door, went in and sat opposite the chief inspector.

'All right, what's wrong?'

'What do you mean? Nothing's wrong. Or everything's wrong, depending on how you look at it.'

'I mean, what's wrong with you? You're obviously not your charming, personable self. So what's got under your skin? I've unburdened myself in this room before; now I think it's your turn.'

'Nothing like that. I just hate ones involving kids.'

'No, it's more than that, Jim. We've worked cases with child victims before. This is different. Is it the fact that it's an orphanage? Or is it the nuns that are getting to you? Lots of people find them off-putting?'

'Off-putting? That's a nice word for it. You're right: I don't like nuns. I *really* don't like nuns. Did it show? Bad experiences that you don't need to hear about.'

Mowbray's life before he joined the force was a mystery to most people because that's the way he wanted it. He had certainly never shared anything with Cuthbert, or anyone he had ever worked with for that matter. It was the past, as far as he was concerned, and was irrelevant to the here and now.

He had lost both parents through circumstances that were more than tragic, and he chose not to remember them, let alone talk about them. Unlike most of those in St Gregory's, he had not been left alone as a very small child, but he had been orphaned nevertheless, and he knew exactly how that felt. He knew what it was to be unwanted and to be nothing but an inconvenience.

The war had been his escape, and it was in the trenches that he found new family and new purpose. Terrible as it was, he still secretly thanked God for that war, for he wasn't sure he would still be here if he had not left London when he did.

His own time being cared for in an institution had been brief, but it had been formative. Like St Gregory's, it had been run by an order of sisters, but many of his fellow inmates were deeply troubled boys from broken and often violent homes. He remembered the fear, never knowing what was going to happen next, and never, ever feeling safe in the night. On top of that was the callous brutality of the nuns themselves, who would use the harshest corporal punishment to keep order. He had never forgiven what was left of his family for placing him there or the nuns for the way he was treated.

There was a lot going on behind Mowbray's eyes as he evaded his questions, but Cuthbert decided it would be best not to press him. If he wanted to tell him more, he would. Instead, he shifted the conversation. 'Well, I think you certainly put the fear of God into your new constable. I doubt he'll ever slouch again in your presence.'

'A firm hand is needed with the youngsters. You know that as well as I do.'

'Yes, as long as you don't scare them away altogether.'

'Too hard?'

'No, but close. Look, if you change your mind and feel

like getting it all off your chest, you know where I am. In the meantime, I'd better get back to the hospital.'

As he was about to leave, there was a knock on the door. Cuthbert opened it, much to the surprise of the W.P.C. who was standing waiting for permission to enter. Mowbray looked up and saw she had a note for him in her hand. He waved her in, took the folded paper and read it. He then shouted loudly after Cuthbert, who was already walking back through the duty room.

'Don't go anywhere just yet, Jack.'

Cuthbert was confused and came back into his office.

'Here, take a look at this.' Mowbray handed him the note, written in Sergeant Baker's hand. Cuthbert read it and sighed.

'I know. It just gets worse. Now it looks as if we've got another one in the same wood. Can you take a look?'

'Of course. I'll get Dr Morgenthal to accompany me. We'll need to sweep the whole area to find out what we're dealing with here. Let's hope there's only one more.'

Cuthbert called his assistant from the duty-room phone and instructed him to meet him at the Yard and bring the necessary fieldwork kit.

'This might be a long one, Simon, but we need to make a start this afternoon before we lose the light. Sergeant Baker will drive us both out to St Gregory's as soon as you get here.'

While he was waiting for Morgenthal to arrive, Cuthbert used the time to acquaint himself with the details. Baker was already at the case board, pinning up new information and rearranging what was already there.

'So what do we have, sergeant?'

'Looks very similar, sir. This time it was one of the nuns, Sister Margery, who called it in. Apparently, she was in the woods looking for a ball that had been kicked into the trees by one of the older children. She says she went over near the boundary wall and there was an odd, almost rectangular mark in the soil, with some plants growing that looked thinner and smaller than those around them. She poked the site with a stick and hit something hard. She cleared some of the soil away and found an object wrapped in cloth. She left it at that and phoned us right away. It could be something else entirely, but, given the way the little boy was swaddled in cloth, I fear the worst.'

'Well, we'll know soon enough. Do you have anyone on site already to preserve the scene?'

'Of course, sir. I've been in touch with the local bobbies and briefed them on exactly what and what not to do. It should be safe until we get there.'

*

When they arrived at St Gregory's, the grounds were empty and there were no signs of activity at the main house. Indeed, although it was still afternoon, the blinds were drawn. Cuthbert looked up at the window where he thought he had seen a figure before, but the curtains were closed. Baker was also taking in the state of the main house.

'I expect all the sisters will be well aware of what's going on, sergeant. It was one of them, after all, who found the new grave.'

The three walked across the lawn to the woods, but this time Cuthbert had to weave his way through the thick growth until he reached the stone wall on the far side. There, a uniformed constable was standing near where Sister Margery had found what she thought might be suspicious.

'Afternoon, constable. I'm Sergeant Baker from Scotland Yard, and these gentlemen are our police surgeons, Doctors Cuthbert and Morgenthal. You've done as I asked?'

'Yes, sir. Nothing has been touched and no one has been

allowed near the place. I've been here since I arrived, but there's been no one to keep away, if I'm honest.'

Cuthbert nodded and suggested to Sergeant Baker that the constable might be usefully employed setting up a rope cordon around the site.

'I know we don't know what we're dealing with yet, but better safe than sorry, don't you think, sergeant?'

Baker took the local constable and told him what to do and to expect some relief within the hour from other uniforms that would be arriving. Without approaching the possible gravesite, Cuthbert spent some time taking in the scene. The stone wall was old, certainly older than the main house, and was heavily covered in mosses. At the edge of the wood where the trees were thinner and there was more light, the undergrowth was generally greener and thicker than elsewhere. But where Sister Margery had been, the plants were somewhat stunted.

Cuthbert knew that bodies buried in the earth had variable effects on the plants that would repopulate the site. Usually, the decomposing body would suppress any plant growth above for the first year, but by three years it would be lusher than the surroundings. When he took a closer look, he could see where she had pushed back some of the overlying nettles and grasses and where the bare soil was showing through. He called Morgenthal to his side. 'What do you make of this, Simon?'

'There's an oblong area of about one square yard in total where the plants are thinner and less well-developed than nearby. It's not due to lack of light, so it might be the quality of the soil. But it is very defined, almost a perfect rectangle. And although it's difficult to see, I think the soil level is proud of the surroundings. If it is a grave, and it was dug within the last year, it's likely that the soil would not have resettled yet.'

'Yes, I think we need to clear this growth away as gently

as we can so as not to disturb whatever lies beneath. The sister who found this has already made a start for us. Let's go gently.'

The two pathologists started at either end of the grave and set about cutting the plants close to soil level rather than pulling them up by their roots. They laid all the cut plants to one side in a pile and proceeded to scrape the top layer of soil away.

Just as Cuthbert had done with the first grave, Morgenthal's trowel rubbed along a fabric layer a few inches below the surface, and he stopped abruptly. Now, using his fingers only, he gently brushed the sandy soil away and exposed what appeared to be cotton fabric tightly bound around a curving object.

'It looks very much like the last grave, Simon. Go gently, there might be important evidence tucked around and between those folds of cloth.'

After almost an hour of careful, almost archaeological, excavation, the length of the body was exposed. This time the feet were also wrapped in the shroud which had again been tied about the small body with coarse twine. Cuthbert studied what he was sure was the wrapped corpse of another child, but this time an even younger one. The body had also clearly been in the ground for a lot longer than the first. Certainly, this was long enough for new plants to cover the grave, but the smell of decomposition was markedly stronger and suggested months rather than weeks.

'Are there any plants in this grave, Simon?'

'Yes, sir. The body appears to be resting on some and there are some stalks in the windings of the shroud.'

'All right, we need everything photographed and taken back to the hospital. I'll perform the post mortem examination tomorrow morning, and I would like you to come back here.'

Morgenthal was a little puzzled by the request, but

Cuthbert soon made himself clear. 'I fear this wood may have more secrets to reveal. I need you to spend time looking for any other potential shallow grave sites. You know what you're looking for – patches of freshly turned earth, inconsistent soil levels and small areas of unusual plant growth.'

'Of course, sir. Perhaps I should start now.'

'No, the light's fading and it's already dull in here. Wait till the morning. If any other child is buried in these grounds, they will still be here tomorrow.'

Cuthbert looked about to find Sergeant Baker and when he spotted him, he gave him his instructions for the transport of the remains.

'So it is another child, sir?'

'I'm afraid so. I'll know a lot more when I've examined the body. But this is now a multiple crime scene. I've instructed Dr Morgenthal to continue the survey of the site first thing tomorrow morning. Can you facilitate that? If there are any other children here, I want them recovered as soon as possible.'

Cuthbert was breathing heavily, and Baker was unsure if he was angry or distressed. Of course, he could well be both.

'Consider it done, sir.'

*

The next morning, Morgenthal was on site by eight o'clock and he met Sergeant Baker at the rope cordon.

'Good morning, sir. Lovely morning, but a rum lot this, isn't it?'

'Good morning, sergeant. Yes, not the best way to start the day, but Dr Cuthbert wants this sorted, so I had better get on.'

'Perhaps this will help, sir.'

Baker handed Morgenthal a folded paper, which was a map of the grounds.

'I've already marked on it in red the positions of the two

graves. I thought it might help you to mark off the areas that you've searched. I know you and Dr Cuthbert like to do these things very methodically.'

'That's uncommonly helpful. Just the ticket. Right, I'd better get in there. I do very much hope I'm wasting my time. The last thing we need is another dead child.'

Using the map, Morgenthal set about orientating himself. He stood at the edge of the wood. He could see just beyond the tree line where the first grave had been found, and much further through the trees where he and Cuthbert had excavated the second, near the wall. He decided to mark a grid on the map and survey the area, square by square.

The light was certainly better than it had been the day before, but the sunlight still had a hard time penetrating the woodland. His eyes took a while to adjust to the gloom, but he was soon able to commence.

He was looking for all the tell-tale signs that Cuthbert had enumerated. The ground was very uneven, and in places was just a mesh of twisted surface tree roots, especially where the trees were at their densest. Those areas would be almost impossible to dig in and that made them very unlikely sites for another grave, so he focused his search where there were more open areas.

After some time, he found some disturbed earth, but it looked very freshly dug and appeared to be piled in front of a burrow. This was likely one of the badger setts that the groundsman had been trying to find. He swept the wood in a systematic way from west to east and, when he was at the furthest point from the other graves, he found another area of almost bare ground, apart from a very loose covering of annual weeds. The soil was mounded and there were no more mature plants growing on it.

He marked its position on the map and bent to investigate,

hearing Cuthbert's words always in his ears: 'Look first, look second and then look again, before touching anything.' It was a mantra he had learned to live by in his forensic practice.

The edges of the disturbed soil were sharp and straight and likely man-made, and the area was small but slightly larger than the grave he and Cuthbert had been excavating. He made notes of his observations, and only when he thought he had learned everything he could from simply looking, he began to scrape the soil back. Very gently at first, he removed the top inch or two of soil from the centre of the raised area. He continued a little more forcefully as the soil was in places more compacted and difficult to shift.

When he was about six inches below the surface his trowel hit something firm. It felt much like the cloth-wrapped corpse in the other grave, and he was reasonably sure he had found a third body. He chose to stop before going any further and report the findings to Sergeant Baker.

'Are you sure, doctor?'

'As sure as I can be at this stage. It seems to be just like the others. I think it would be best to leave it undisturbed until I complete the survey of the rest of the wood. Unfortunately, this might not be the last one we find.'

Baker nodded in agreement and made arrangements to extend the rope cordon to include the new grave.

By early afternoon, Morgenthal had finished searching the woodland and was relieved to find no further graves. He now returned to the one he had identified and began the painstaking process of uncovering the body.

As the wrapped corpse was slowly exposed, it became clear that this was again a child, but an older one. His nose told him this was a fresher interment than the one he and Cuthbert had worked on, but again there was evidence of the ritual of placing plants in the grave and in the windings of the shroud.

He took notes at every stage, but it was clear to him that they were now dealing with three burials most probably by the same hand.

'Sergeant, I've done all I can in uncovering the body. So it's the usual now: photography and transfer. Can you arrange that? I think I should head back to the department to see if Dr Cuthbert needs any help. And, of course, to tell him we have a third victim.'

'Right away, sir. We know the drill by now.'

Chapter 6

Edinburgh: 14 August 1902

By the fourth summer at his grandfather's house, Jack Cuthbert had all but tamed the squirrels in the gardens. They would happily eat the nuts from his palm and would even scamper on to his chest when he lay in the grass.

He would lie still, barely breathing, and leave nuts between the buttons of his jacket so he could watch them up close and listen to their curious squeaks as they ate. He was fascinated by the long tufts of red fur on their ears that almost made them look like little foxes. And then there were their magnificent tails that curved and swirled behind them as they moved and then settled into a sweeping S when they sat to eat the nuts that he had provided.

Many summer hours were spent alone in the garden with just the squirrels for company, and his nanny was becoming concerned. He was an intelligent child, and he had long since surpassed her both in reading and in understanding what he read. She had felt for some time that his schooling, which had been conducted at home with her help and later a governess who would arrive each morning, was doing little for him.

He was learning his three Rs, of course, but she could see he needed people if he was to grow. Old Mr Dalrymple was often at home but kept his distance from the boy. The warmth he had shown Jack when they first arrived had faded over the years. Perhaps, she thought, it was because with every passing day Jack had become more and more like his mother. He was a handsome child, but an introverted one, often lost in his own imagination. Something had to be done.

One evening after dinner, when the boy was still brought in to say goodnight to his grandfather, after sending Jack up to bed she lingered in the study.

'Miss Violet, is there something you wish to say?'

'Begging your pardon, sir, it's about Master Jack. I'm worried about him, sir.'

'He seems a perfectly healthy young chap to me. What's your concern?'

She explained how she had watched him becoming quieter and more withdrawn and how she thought he needed to be with other children, to play with them and be taught with them.

'I think he needs to go to school, sir. He has such a quick mind, and he reads everything, but there's so much more to growing up than books. I can only take him so far, and with all respect, sir, so can you.'

'But if I send him off to school, and boarding school at that, it does rather put you out of a job, does it not?'

'I'm aware of that, sir. But I think I have to put Master Jack's wellbeing first.'

'You really do care for the boy, don't you?'

'Like a son, sir.'

'Well, you've looked after him like a mother, so that's hardly surprising. Let me think about it and we can discuss this again. I see you have the boy's best interests at heart. I do want to do what's best and perhaps you're right.'

She curtsied and went up to the nursery, where Jack was waiting for her. He had been eavesdropping on their conversation and was now looking at her suspiciously.

'So you want to leave me, Nanna?'

'No, what could make you say that? I love you, shilling.'

'But you told Grandpapa that I should go away to school without you.'

He had been listening, and there was no use pretending she had said anything else.

'You are growing up, my darling, and it's time you learned about more of the world than you can be taught in this house. Wouldn't it be fun to play with other boys your own age? To chase them and play at being pirates on the high seas? You could learn to play rugby – you'd be so good at that because you're strong and fast. And then there's all those wonderful new things to learn that we can't teach you here.

'There are so many other books to read, ideas to understand, languages to learn. There's a whole world to explore, and it's out there – not in here in this house and garden. I want you to be happy, my darling, and if that means we have to part for a while, so you can get to know some new people and learn new things, then that's the way it should be. It certainly doesn't mean I love you any less. In fact, I love you so much that I know I must let you go a little. You have such an exciting life ahead of you at school, and one day you'll be able to tell me about all your new adventures.'

He came to her, and she folded him in her arms. Violet Cranston was no longer a young woman, and her life had been spent caring for the children of others. She had never married and any thoughts of what it might have been like to hold her own children in her arms were dispelled when she looked at Jack.

For the last eight years she had spent every day of her life with this boy, watching him grow from a little, motherless newborn to the fine young lad he was now. As she held him, the tears welled up in his eyes and spilled over onto his cheeks, and she felt her own about to do the same.

*

The next day, his grandfather was watching him on the lawn from his study window. The boy was following the swallows that were nesting in the eaves of the stables as they swooped and darted around the garden, scooping up flies as they went. Apparently always on the wing, blurring the air as they flew, they contrasted with the stillness of the child sitting cross-legged on the grass.

It was the stillness that troubled him and made him think that perhaps Violet was right. It was time this boy was running around breathless with excitement in the company of playmates his own age. He could provide the boy with all his material needs, but he could not hope to give him the kind of companionship and camaraderie that a boy his age needed.

He made the decision then and there to send him off to school that autumn. The choice of which school was easy, for he wanted to send him to his own alma mater, the exclusive Lauriston College. Built in extensive grounds near the city centre in Edinburgh, he was confident that the college would do well for the boy and help prepare him for life.

He turned from the window and went to his desk where he immediately penned the necessary letter to the college principal. By return of post, he received an acknowledgement and the offer of a place. The old man had expected nothing less. The Dalrymple name still carried much weight, especially in institutions that required patronage from rich men such as himself.

He left the letter on his desk and thought it best to discuss the matter first with Violet before informing the boy of his future. If she could help prepare him for the move, so much the better. He summoned her that evening when Jack was asleep.

'Do come in, Miss Violet. I have given some thought to your suggestion, and I'm pleased to say I have now arranged for the young man to attend Lauriston, my old school. He will be starting there in a fortnight's time, and I would like you to do everything you can to smooth the way.'

'Very good, sir. I will of course make my own arrangements and be out of the house as soon as I can. Might I have till the end of the week to find some new lodgings?'

'No, no, I think you misunderstand. You have been a mother to the boy these last eight years, and I am not about to lose you too. No, I wish you to stay in my employ. My initial thoughts are to send Jack as a weekly boarder. He will stay at the school during the week but will return to us at weekends. As he grows, that may change, but for the time being I want you here when he comes home and of course for the holidays. While he is at school, I would like you to take on other household duties, commensurate with your seniority of course, but I certainly do not wish you to leave. I hope such an arrangement might be acceptable to you, Miss Violet.'

She was finding it hard to contain her appreciation for the offer and Mr Dalrymple could see from her expression that she would indeed be pleased to stay as part of Jack's world.

'I can't thank you enough, sir.'

'Oh, I think if any thanks are in order, it is for me to thank you. You have helped turn that boy into a remarkable young man, but you are right: he needs more now than we can give him. I know he will enjoy Lauriston – I certainly did. But I do anticipate some resistance when I tell him. It will be quite a change for him. Perhaps you might be present? I know how much he cares for you, so if we are able to present a united front, it might make things easier all round.'

'Of course, sir. When will you let him know?'

'Tomorrow, after breakfast, I think. Bring him to my study then. The sooner, the better. Don't you agree?'

*

Over his porridge in the nursery the next morning, Jack's nanny was already starting to prepare the way. She was arranging his books on the shelves beside his bed, and she picked up one that he had been reading on his own about Alexander the Great.

'Is this one interesting, my shilling?'

'Oh yes, Nanna. He was a general who conquered the world. And he had a magnificent black horse called Bucephalus.'

'It must be lovely to read all these stories from so long ago. But how do we know they're all true, do you think?'

'Of course they're true, Nanna. People at the time wrote them all down.'

'But they didn't write them down in our words, did they? I expect they wrote the story of the great Alexander in his own language – would that have been Greek? So how do we know what they said?'

'Because people know how to read that language and they write it again in our language.'

'It must be good though to be able to read what they actually wrote, to be able to understand their strange words and letters. I mean, just imagine being able to learn that.'

'Can you teach me, Nanna?'

'Oh no, my dear, not even the governess can teach you that. You would have to go to a fine school to learn such things as that. And all the other things too.'

'What other things?'

'All the things that we know so little about in this house. You're always asking questions, and I used to be able to answer them, but not any more. You're much cleverer than me, Jack. What was that you asked the other day? Oh yes, "Why do we only see a rainbow after it rains?" And then there was that one about why ladybirds are red and how do the crickets chirp and even why your eyes are blue and mine are brown. There is so much for you to learn, but I've run out of answers.'

He became pensive and finished his porridge in silence while she somewhat distractedly finished arranging the books.

'You know, your grandpapa wants to speak to you this morning. I wonder if he's got an adventure planned for us. Eat up and we'll brush our teeth and go and see him, shall we?'

*

The carriage ride to Edinburgh was always exciting, but that afternoon the following week, Jack was preoccupied with his thoughts. Both Nanna and his grandpapa were in the carriage with him, but no one was speaking.

The boy was feeling anxious even though he now knew he would still see Nanna at the weekends. He had been brought up in such isolation that he was unsure of how he would get along with the other boys. And how would he manage with the schoolwork? So many of the others were likely to know much more than him. He would be the dunce of the class, he was sure.

His nanny sensed he was worried, and she felt for his hand and squeezed it in hers under her bag on the carriage seat so that Old Dalrymple would not see. Jack managed a smile, and she made a funny face in return that made him giggle.

The journey took almost three-quarters of an hour, but all too soon for the boy the carriage was rolling up the gravel driveway of the school. It was the first time he had set eyes on the place that would be his new home, and its towers and crenelations made it appear like some fantasy castle. He expected there to be cannon and a drawbridge over a moat, but the fantasy had only extended so far in the Victorian architect's imagination.

The building was three storeys of elaborate sandstone with ornate window traceries, and it was surmounted by a grand-looking flagpole from which flew the school flag – a green field emblazoned with a golden letter 'L'.

There were other carriages and even one or two motor cars in the driveway, all delivering the next generation of Lauriston Boys dressed in their bottle-green blazers, caps and short grey trousers. Cuthbert was holding his new cap in his lap and, as soon as the carriage came to a halt, he quickly donned it so that he would not stand out from the rest.

The Dalrymple carriage drew some admiring glances from the other parents and when Mr Dalrymple himself stepped down, there were whispers that soon became recognition and then remembrance of the family tale.

'And I suppose that must be the boy,' said one mother from the comfort of her furs. 'He certainly has her looks, don't you think?' said another.

But Jack was oblivious to the interest he was arousing. All he could concern himself with was making sure he created a good first impression. He wanted very badly to hug his nanna and lose himself in her arms, but instead he turned to her and held out his hand to shake hers. She, for her part, knew exactly what he was thinking, and she politely took his hand and curtsied to him.

Osbourne was already taking the boy's trunk down from the rear of the carriage, and his grandfather took him in and led him to the school's assembly hall where the reception of new boys was being held.

One of the older boys, who Jack later learned was Head Boy, read out a list of names. He called out four surnames at a time and his fellow prefects collected the new boys and escorted them to their dormitory rooms.

When Cuthbert's name was called, he didn't hear it, such was his wonder at looking around the great hall. It was oak-panelled and hung with grand oil paintings in ornate gilt frames. These were former headmasters in their colourful academic robes, all staring sternly down at the new intake to their institution. Many others had stood where he was now standing, including his grandfather almost sixty years before, and indeed the old man was reliving the moment in his own memories.

'Look sharp. Cuthbert, I'm still missing a Cuthbert.'

Jack looked up to see a tall prefect glaring down at him.

'Not a good start, Cuthbert. Pay attention and you'll get along much better. Now, join the others. We haven't got all day, you know.'

His grandfather patted his head and assured him that all would be well.

'Run along with you now. There's an adventure to begin.'

He joined the others, and the four small boys had to run to keep up with the prefect's long strides. They climbed the broad central staircase to the first floor and then followed the long main corridor to a second, rather more utilitarian stairwell that took them up to the dormitory rooms on the second floor.

'You four are in here. Your bags are already up, but you'll need to get unpacked. In one hour, you are to assemble in the hall for the introductory address from the principal. Do not be late and do not make me have to come back here to get you. No nonsense now. Are you listening to me, Cuthbert?'

Again, Jack was lost, looking about the room, taking

in every detail. The four short, iron-framed beds with their dark brown blankets and green coverlets, the small chests of drawers that doubled as bedside tables, the tall thin locker-style wardrobes and the lamps with green glass shades. There were two beds by the window and two on the opposite wall and the windows were open, filling the room with the scent as well as the chill of autumn.

'Cuthbert!'

Jack was startled to find he was again the object of the tall prefect's ire, who just shook his head and muttered something under his breath about the state of the young these days. Impatiently, he turned to go but shouted back, 'Remember, you lot, one hour!'

The boys began opening cupboards and pulling out drawers. Jack found his trunk and his bag piled by the bed in the corner on the back wall. The bed was not unlike the one he had in his grandfather's house, but the room was far from his nursery. There was no colour, no pictures, no books, no toys and, worst of all, no Nanna.

While he was taking in the emptiness of it all, he felt a firm hand on his shoulder. He turned to see one of the four boys looking him over.

'And who are you?'

'I'm Jack. Jack Cuthbert.'

'No first names here, you fool. You're just Cuthbert here, and I'm Abercrombie. What about your folks, Cuthbert? What does your father do?'

'I lost my father some years ago.'

'Lost? That was careless, wasn't it? What did your mother have to say about that?'

'I never knew my mother. She died when I was born.'

'Listen up, everyone! Cuthbert here killed his mother. And he's being rather cagey about his father. I wouldn't be at all surprised if he had a hand in the old man's disappearance too.'

Jack's face flushed as he felt the eyes of the others on him in the dormitory room. Cuthbert was the youngest of the four by at least six months, and Abercrombie was slightly taller than him. He was keen to accentuate the advantage by standing slightly on tiptoe as he was speaking.

One of the others, Jenner, who Cuthbert learned was already a good friend of Abercrombie, was snorting with laughter at the outburst. The other boy in the foursome was looking on unimpressed, and he pulled Cuthbert away.

'Don't listen to him, Cuthbert. He's just full of hot air. By the way, I'm Cruikshank.'

The smallest of the four boys, almost by a head, held up his hand. Jack took it and felt a surprisingly strong grip. Cruikshank shook his hand firmly and vigorously, doubtless the way he had been taught by a zealous father, and announced, 'I'm sure we're going to be good friends, aren't you?' Jack was not at all sure but thought it best to humour the small boy, who was now lugging a suitcase the size of himself from the floor onto the bed beside Jack's.

'We're neighbours now. I was supposed to be over there, but I can't possibly sleep beside a window. Far too draughty. I say, do you suffer much from draughts, Cuthbert?'

'I . . . I'm not sure.'

'Well, best to be over here near the radiator, that's my advice, especially when it gets cold. According to my father it can get very chilly.'

Jack watched him unpack the suitcase and saw that amongst everything else, he had brought a pot of marmalade and several bars of chocolate.

'Supplies. You can't be too careful in a place like this, Cuthbert. We don't know what they might feed us, and it's important to keep our strength up. Here, take this.'

Cruikshank held out one of the chocolate bars and Cuthbert accepted it with a broad smile. Perhaps, he thought, they might be good friends after all.

Abercrombie and Jenner were now standing on their beds by the windows, hurling pillows at one another. The bedsprings creaked alarmingly with each leap, but Cuthbert followed Cruikshank's lead and began to unpack, carefully putting all his clothes away and taking the small collection of books he had brought with him from home and arranging them on top of the bedside drawers beside the lamp. Beside Cruikshank's lamp was his prized pot of marmalade. Jack smiled; already the room was being transformed from the empty shell it had been when they entered.

'Come on, Cuthbert, let's go and explore. We've still got half an hour before the assembly.'

Cuthbert was happy to leave the other two still jumping up and down on their beds and follow Cruikshank out and down the hallway. There were five rooms on their landing and all the doors were open. In each, there were quartets of new boys all unpacking and beginning friendships, some of which would last a lifetime. In one room at the end, Cuthbert looked in and saw a boy sitting on his bed sobbing. He stopped and felt sorry for the stranger, but he was pulled away again by Cruikshank.

'My father told me there was always one. Best not to get too mixed up with the cry-baby.'

Cuthbert looked at Cruikshank and back at the small boy on the edge of his bed and pulled away himself this time to go in and sit with him.

'My name's Jack, but I think I'm only supposed to say it's Cuthbert. What's yours?'

The boy was embarrassed by the stranger sitting beside him,

but sensed he was no threat and through his sobs said, 'James Morton, but everyone calls me Jimmy.'

'Here, I think they'll call you Morton. It seems unfriendly, but it's just the way they do things at a school like this. That's Cruikshank. We're going to do a bit of exploring before assembly. Come with us, won't you?'

Cruikshank, who was standing in the doorway, was far from pleased by the invitation being extended. This was after all his party, and he was starting to feel just a little cross with Cuthbert.

'It's all right, but I need to unpack. You go on and maybe we can see each other later.'

'If you're sure. We'll tell you if we find anything exciting, won't we, Cruikshank?'

Cuthbert's new friend just snorted by way of reply and told him to hurry up. They were gone in a moment, but Morton had managed to find some space between his tears, and he turned to his trunk to start unpacking.

'Do you really have no parents, Cuthbert?'

'Not living ones.'

'No father to teach you all about the ropes in this place?'

'My grandfather is an Old Boy, but he didn't really tell me anything other than how much I would enjoy it.'

'I expect that explains it. You'll need to stick with me, Cuthbert. You can't go off like that befriending the cry-babies. It's just not done, if you want to get along. I know all the ropes, so if you're not sure what's what, just ask me. Right, this is the dining hall. I think we should inspect it. I want to make sure everything's in order in that department. You can't be too careful when it comes to food.'

'No, I expect you can't.'

Cuthbert was pulled into the hall where the long tables were laid out with benches on each side. Immediately, it reminded him of the drawing of a medieval banquet in one of his picture books from home.

Across the top of the room there was a long table at right angles to the others, where doubtless the king and his queen would sit with their most trusted nobles or, perhaps in this case, the principal and his senior masters. Like the assembly hall it was replete with large oil paintings, but these were of scenes from Scottish history. There were battles and castles, the thrust of claymores and dirks, and even disguised princes in rowboats. Cruikshank was much more interested in the state of the cutlery which had already been laid for the evening meal.

'Yes, it all looks to be in order. Not quite what I'm used to from home, but it is a school, after all. Right, where next? What would you like to see, the games hall or the library?'

'The library, please.'

'A bit of a bookworm are you, Cuthbert? Well, I think you'll like what they've got here.'

The two boys descended the main staircase and took a sharp left turn and pushed open the heavy carved oak doors to find themselves in the grandest room of the school.

From floor to high ceiling there were bookcases filled with volumes, the upper shelves accessed by ladders that ran around the room on a polished brass rail. On the pilasters between the shelves were brightly coloured images in scrolled cartouches that Cuthbert at first mistook for small paintings. As he looked more closely, he could see they were intricate mosaics made from hundreds upon hundreds of small pieces of coloured glass. They formed the images of the greats from the past and each was surmounted by the legend's name. Plato, Aristotle, Aeschylus and Euripides were on one wall with Cicero, Caesar, Virgil and Horace on another. Dante, Chaucer, Shakespeare and Erasmus occupied the third. And the last was reserved for the artists, da Vinci, Giotto, Michelangelo and Raphael.

Cuthbert scanned the names; some he had heard of, but most were new to him. The green leather-covered reading desks in the centre of the room all had their own lamps, and after stroking the leather, he started to walk over to the stacks to see what treasures were there.

'Come on, Cuthbert, we can't be late. You can come back and see the rest later. It's always here and it's always open.'

Cuthbert took a deep breath of the air in the room and filled his lungs with it as he hoped to fill his mind. What a place of wonders a library like this was.

The assembly hall was already bustling, and Cruikshank led Cuthbert to the seats at the front where the new boys were expected to sit. Behind them were ranked each year until the eldest pupils occupied the back two rows.

As they walked down the aisle, some of the older boys whistled at them and called them 'runts' and 'shorties'. Cruikshank drew close and whispered to him.

'Don't let them see you can hear them and don't ever show fear, no matter how frightened you might feel inside. They only keep at it with the ones who cry. That's what my father said.'

Abercrombie and Jenner were already in their seats and Cuthbert looked about for Morton, who was sitting on his own.

'Let's go over here,' said Cuthbert, and before Cruikshank could correct this latest lapse in judgement, Cuthbert had already seated himself next to Morton and was telling him about the library.

There was a sudden rush of feet at the back of the room as the most senior pupils arrived at the last possible moment before the entire assembly rose to welcome the principal, Dr Harrison. He walked through a side door held open for him by one of the masters, and he was wearing his Oxbridge robes of blue and red with his black mortarboard. He mounted the small dais and stood erect at the lectern. 'Let us give thanks.'

All the boys bowed their heads reverently and listened in silence to the short school prayer before coming in at the end with a loud and rousing 'Amen'.

'Be seated, boys. Another year begins for us here at Lauriston College. For some it will be their first; for others it will be their last. Let me address those two groups specifically.' He looked over the lectern and down at the first two rows of seats where Cuthbert and the other new boys were seated. 'You have a great adventure in learning ahead of you, and we at this distinguished school will serve as your guides and mentors in the years ahead. You have joined a great tradition going back almost one hundred years, when Sir Alfred Lauriston, our founder, first opened his new school. Only a total of six students were in that first class, but look about you at how we have grown over those decades. We will be with you every step of the way on your journey but never forget that only you can take those steps.'

As the principal spoke, the older boys were mouthing the familiar story of old Lauriston and his six students that they heard every year.

'And now to those of you about to embark on your final year at Lauriston. You are on the home stretch and the goalposts are in sight, but you must not falter at the final hurdle.'

'Do make up your mind, Harry. Which is it, a flat race, a game of football or the four-hundred-metre hurdles?'

The whisper from the back row was clear enough to reduce those around him to fits of giggles, but fortunately for the senior pupil not loud enough to make it to the dais. The principal was only aware of some inattentiveness in the rear, which oddly he had also observed in past years just at this point in his address. Undaunted, he pressed on. 'This year is the culmination of all your studies at the college and the results of your Leaving Certificate examinations will determine your next steps. Whatever you do, wherever you go, you will leave here as Lauriston Boys and will carry the flame forward. You will leave enriched in both mind and in character, and it is those that matter more than all else. Always remember your school motto as you make your way through life: *omnia mea mecum porto*, all that I own, I carry with me. We will now be upstanding to sing the school song. Mr Evans, if you would be so kind as to lead us.'

The Welsh music master stepped forward and with a proud tenor voice kept the rest of the school assembly in tune for all three verses of the college anthem, 'I Carry the Lord in My Heart'. None of the new boys knew the words, except Cruikshank, who sang out loudly beside Cuthbert, having been schooled over the summer by his father.

Everyone else in the front two rows just found the tune and hummed along as best they could. During the final verse, the principal made his exit through the same side door he had come in by, and that was the first and last time many of the boys would see him for most of the year.

The next day was the first day of school proper, and the new boys were instructed to wait in a line outside their classroom on the ground floor. Only when their master arrived would they be permitted to enter. There was much jostling and chatter, especially from those at the back of the line, but everything stopped as they heard footsteps approach. By the time the dark, cloaked figure was standing tall over them at the classroom door there was complete silence. With practised ease, their master ushered them into the room and instructed them where to sit. The small wooden desks with their inkwells filled and ready for the day were arranged in four columns and five rows. The room itself was bright and airy, with tall windows overlooking the lawns outside.

Cuthbert noticed that Cruikshank was less than happy at being seated beside the window at the back. After the initial scuffing of chairs on the wooden floors, the room was once again as silent as it was when they entered. The master took his seat at the head of the class, consulted his register and then stood by his blackboard looking at his new class over the gold-rimmed, half-moon spectacles that were perched somewhat precariously on the end of his nose. He was balding with a substantial grey moustache that he stroked and curled as he spoke.

'Good morning, gentlemen. I am Mr Robertson, and at all times you will address me as sir.'

He chalked his name upon the blackboard and then underneath wrote in even larger letters another word, 'Jampot', which was met by some barely suppressed giggles. 'And this is what you will doubtless call me behind my back, for generations of students have found it an irresistible appellation, such is their appreciation of my namesake's strawberry conserve.

'Gentlemen, do not think that I am unaware of this. However' – as he spoke, he took the chalk duster to the nickname – 'I choose to feign ignorance to spare all our blushes. Now, this morning we are here to learn Latin. Some people will tell you that Latin is a dead language. That no one speaks it, perhaps even that no one really knows any longer how it should be spoken. Gentlemen, do not be taken in by such deception, for not only is Latin spoken, you yourselves have been speaking it all your lives.'

As he enunciated his words, he walked up and down the aisles between the desks and held the twenty boys in the class rapt by the depth of his voice and the swirl of his long black academic gown. He now went back to his blackboard and, as he spoke, he chalked each of the Latin words he was about to use in large clear script.

'. . . e.g. (*exempli gratia*), here we are at nine a.m. (*ante meridiem*) in the year 1902 A.D. (*anno Domini*). In your busy *curriculum*, there is little time for anything *extra*, but there are always choices on the *agenda*. Now, how might we spend this first hour together? We may make a list of *pros* and *cons* to help us decide. What, we may ask, is the *maximum* to which we can put this time with the *minimum* of waste? Perhaps we should discuss it and reach a *consensus*. Perhaps we should abandon the classroom altogether and take a trip *via* the fine streets of Edinburgh to the great *stadium* at Tynecastle – built alas for a game played by ruffians. We may pass a grand *villa* on the way and then *alter* our route. In that great *arena*, we may watch our team play *versus* the visitors. The *onus* will be on our side to win, but if they draw, we will have the *status quo*.' As he spoke, the boys were hurriedly copying down his blackboard writing into their jotters. 'And these, gentlemen, are only a few of the everyday words that have come down to us unchanged. There are also many other Latin phrases used in English. Can anyone tell me one of those?'

Mr Robertson scanned his classroom of fresh new faces. He was now in his mid-sixties and had taught some of these boys' fathers and he suspected even one or two of their grandfathers in his earliest days as a Latin master.

Every September, the boys were new but in so many ways they were exactly the same. There were the shy ones, who might be concealing great talent or stark indifference, but only time would tell. There were the inattentive, who could be brought to heel as much by inspiration as the rod. There were also the intense ones like the boy in the second back row, whose piercing blue eyes had never left him since he walked into the room. He was dark and handsome, and Mr Robertson tried to place him. Might he be a Dalrymple?

'What about you, boy? Tell me your name.'

'Cuthbert, sir.'

'Ah, and can you think of any phrase that we might use today that is originally from the Latin?'

Jack hesitated and felt the eyes of the others on him, but he was also sure that he knew an answer. '*Post mortem*, sir.'

'Excellent, Cuthbert, and do you know what it means?'

'After death, sir.'

'Indeed. Everyone, write that one down too. Now, pray tell, where did you hear that somewhat ghoulish expression?'

'In a book, sir. A book about medicine.'

'Yes, the study of Latin will stand you in very good stead if you wish to pursue such studies in the years to come. Roughly one in every ten words we say or write is derived ultimately from Latin. Many more if we become lawyers or, in your case, Mr Cuthbert, a doctor. Learning this language and understanding it will not only aid you in your mastery of English, gentlemen, it will also open up to you new possibilities, previously undreamt of. You will be able to speak with the ancients, listen to the words they wrote two thousand years ago and marvel at their wit and their wisdom. Such a journey awaits you, and there is no time to lose. As the mighty Horace said, "*Dum loquimur, fugerit invida aetas: carpe diem, quam minimum credula postero.*" "While we speak cruel time is fleeing. Seize the day, believing as little as possible in the morrow." Now, gentlemen, let us begin with a verb.'

Abercrombie, who was seated on his right, was already looking askance at Cuthbert and scowling at him for being a show-off. He was particularly peeved at having to write down anything the orphan had said. In a deft move, he flicked his pen and spattered Cuthbert's jotter with dark blue ink.

Cuthbert remembered Cruikshank's advice about never showing that you were affected by anything anyone said or did to intimidate you. He calmly turned the page in his jotter and started writing on a fresh one.

*

Over the first few weeks of that new term at Lauriston, Cuthbert flourished. Despite his reservations, he found that he took to his new school with relish. Subjects like English and Mathematics that he had previously only skimmed with his governess opened up and invited him in. And completely new subjects like Science and Latin stirred in him a hunger for new knowledge that had always been there but had lain dormant and unfed.

Even the initial iciness between himself and Abercrombie was beginning to thaw, as the latter found in Cuthbert an invaluable resource to help him through the schoolwork. Quickly, everyone, including the masters, recognised that Cuthbert was academically gifted. He remembered everything he read, and he read a lot, often well beyond the reach of the syllabus.

Mr Robertson had come across boys like him before, but they were few and far between in his more than forty years of teaching. One morning he held Cuthbert back at the break.

'Mr Cuthbert.'

'Sir?'

'No need to be concerned; nothing is untoward. I simply wished to speak with you. Are you enjoying your Latin lessons?'

'Very much, sir.'

'Might I ask why?'

'Because it's like solving a puzzle, sir. Or decoding a secret message from the past.'

'Yes, indeed, Mr Cuthbert. It is exactly that. And it is also so much more, as you will discover in time. Now, run along, lest you miss your much-loved game of tag.'

The boy collected his book and jotter and ran from the classroom, and the master watched him go, wondering just how many puzzles this one might solve before he was finished.

Chapter 7

London: 23 September 1931

While Morgenthal had been working his way systematically through the grid squares on his map of the woodland at St Gregory's, Cuthbert was embarking on the second post mortem examination. That morning, he had arrived at his department knowing what would be awaiting him: another small mound under a white sheet in the dissection room, but this one even smaller than the last.

He steeled himself for the task and proceeded with all the professional detachment he had honed over the years, but it was still far from easy. He tried to lose himself in the puzzle before him rather than think about the dead child lying on his slab.

He began as always with careful and slow observation, taking in everything that his eyes could tell him before he so much as laid a finger on the corpse. The tight cloth in which the body was wrapped was heavily stained both from the soil and from the body itself, which was already undergoing decomposition.

As Morgenthal had noted at the site, there were a number of rather withered stalks protruding from the wrapping and adhering to the underside of the body. There was also a brown mass of matted material beneath the head that Cuthbert took to be some decomposing ferns that had been placed like a pillow as in the first grave.

He noted everything and removed the loose plants from the body before cutting the strings binding the cloth. The unwrapping was more difficult than before because in places the body fluids had seeped into the cloth and dried, causing it to adhere to the corpse. With gentle movements he was able to loosen it and cut away any that remained stubbornly attached.

The child was wearing a floral dress, a yellow knitted pullover, socks that had been white and small brown leather shoes. Unlike the ones the small boy had been wearing, these were laced and neatly tied in bows. When he removed the clothes and the undergarments, he confirmed that this was a small girl who appeared to be about 2 years old. Underneath her clothes, he again checked for any identifying marks or deformities and for anything that might indicate any violence, sexual or otherwise. He drew a blank with both, and he thought that at least that was one small mercy.

Although the body was in a much poorer condition than that of the boy, it was still possible to discern her features and the soft, almost straw-like colour of her hair. He checked her mouth but found no trauma and confirmed that she was probably aged between approximately 20 and 30 months old, based on her number of teeth. Her second molars were not yet fully erupted, but all sixteen of her other milk teeth were present and healthy.

Before he embarked on the internal examination, he had a series of X-rays performed, again to check for any old fractures that might aid identification and for hand and wrist films to confirm the child's bone age.

The remainder of the post mortem examination revealed

nothing except the same distinctive smell in the stomach lining, and Cuthbert thought the child had likely met her death in the same way as the boy, by poisoning with some form of ingested tansy. Despite this, he did not allow this early conclusion to sway him from a thorough investigation of other potential causes of death. Nevertheless, he found everything else to be normal for a child of this age.

When Morgenthal arrived back from St Gregory's, he saw Cuthbert at his desk writing up the examination report. He knew how his mentor felt about performing post mortem examinations on young children, and he hesitated before telling him that there would be another arriving in the morning for their attention. Instead, he went straight to his bench and began writing up his own field notes from the third grave. However, Cuthbert noticed him through his open office door and called to him. 'Anything to report, Simon?'

'I'm afraid so, sir. There was a third grave, and from the preliminary examination it looks as if we are dealing with another of the same – a child wound in a cotton shroud along with various plants and buried in a shallow grave in the St Gregory's wood.'

Cuthbert's face clouded with disappointment, but Morgenthal knew that it was the dreadful loss of young lives that was affecting him, rather than anything he had done.

'Are you sure there's only one more?'

'As certain as I can be, sir. I surveyed the site very closely and there was no further evidence of recent excavation, save for that done by animals, and there were no signs in the pattern of plant growth to suggest the presence of older graves. It's only this one.'

'So that's three. I suppose we should be thankful that it stops there, but it's still three too many, Simon. I've just completed the post mortem examination of the second victim, and I think we're dealing with the same cause of death. I suspect all three met their ends in the same way. Anyway, we'll know tomorrow.'

Morgenthal could see that Cuthbert was far from relishing the prospect of another child to unwrap and examine, so he offered to help.

'Would you like me to perform the examination of the third child in the morning, sir? It would be useful experience for me as we see so few young children.'

Morgenthal was only trying to be considerate in sharing the least palatable aspects of the work, but Cuthbert could not allow his junior staff to carry him. Therefore he decided on a compromise.

'Yes, I think you should, Simon, but I will be at your side throughout to supervise. I'm afraid you will have to examine the corpses of far too many children in your career, and you are quite right: it is important that you gather as much experience as possible. I expect the remains will be ready for us here at nine o'clock. After you've finished writing up your notes from St Gregory's, get yourself home. That family of yours must be forgetting what you look like.'

Morgenthal was indeed weary from the day's work, and he took a taxi back to his home in Mayfair. Sarah was in the nursery playing with little Jack when her husband's key turned in the lock.

'Is that Papa? Is it? Is it? Shall we go and see? Yes, let's go and see, my little soldier.'

She appeared in the hallway, smiling and holding their son in her arms. Morgenthal came to her and embraced them both and kissed her warmly on the lips. She could tell immediately it had been a difficult day. However, if he wished to talk about it, he would, and if he wished to protect her from the details of his daily dealings with death, he would do that too.

She loved her husband and she stroked his cheek and smiled just to let him know that she was there and always would be. Morgenthal turned his attentions to the healthy baby in her arms.

He was now just over a year old and was growing fast. He was no longer the helpless babe in arms he once was, and he was already tottering around the nursery, holding on to the furniture as he went. Any day, they expected him to break out on his own across the floor, unaided.

And best of all, he had uttered his first word, which to Morgenthal's surprise had not been the conventional 'Mama' or 'Dada' but the altogether more sophisticated 'book'. He now said this whenever he pointed at the picture books in the nursery, but in truth he also said it when pointing at anything he wished brought to him. Despite this, Morgenthal was now quite sure the boy would be nothing short of a prodigy. He reached for little Jack and raised him high at arm's length before bringing him close to his chest.

'How has our little soldier been today, darling? Any new milestones to report?'

'Well, he ate up all his lunch, isn't that right, Mrs Hastings?'

The white-aproned nanny had come from the nursery and was now standing impatiently beside Morgenthal with her arms out to take the child. She did not hold with such involvement of the father. In her experience, it just led to unruliness in the child. 'Do let me take him, sir. He's teething and will be drooling on you before you know it. There, that's better, isn't it? Come to Nanny.'

Morgenthal, who was just a little afraid of Mrs Hastings, handed over his son, but not without regret. He would see him again, washed and polished and ready for bed just before he and his wife dined. But wouldn't it be better if he just got down on the nursery floor, there and then, to play with him? Such a thing, of course, was beyond the nanny's comprehension. Jack was whisked away to the nursery and Sarah embraced her husband and kissed him again.

'Drink, darling?'

'Why not? It's been a long day. But why don't you tell me what interesting things you've both been up to?'

This was clearly one of those times when she was being protected, so Sarah simply took him by the hand into the drawing room and poured his drink.

*

As Morgenthal was sipping the chilled cocktail, Cuthbert had not yet left his office at the hospital. He had both files open on his desk – the 4-year-old boy and the 2-year-old girl.

He scanned the notes and compared the findings, trying to glean any other clues as to their deaths or identities. The Yard had been searching now for several days for any leads on the missing boy. How could a child like that disappear and be unreported, unless of course there was no one to report it? Even if he was an orphan, surely somebody would have cared.

The thought that the boy might have been all alone filled him with a new sadness that he had not expected, and he closed both files and decided he needed to go home himself. He was consoled that he had Madame Smith waiting for him at Gordon Square, and that in only a couple of days he would see Erich again when he returned from his business trip to Manchester.

He had known solitude in his life, and at times loneliness, but not now, not any more. He took his hat and coat and left, buoyed by that thought, and walked home briskly through the bustling rush-hour streets.

*

The following morning, Morgenthal was in the department before Cuthbert, as he wanted to make sure everything was in order for the examination of the third child. The remains had been transported the previous evening and were now waiting for them in the dissection room, covered in a clean white sheet.

He spent the time going over his notebooks on the proper procedures for the autopsy of young children, as Cuthbert would be observing him closely. His mentor's standards were high and, rather than bemoaning that fact, Morgenthal had learned to appreciate it. With very high expectations come high achievements.

When he discussed forensic matters with any of his peers working in other London hospital departments, he had yet to find anyone who followed such detailed and meticulous procedures as Cuthbert had taught him to do. The work of their department was also held in the highest regard, and he was able to share in that acclaim, even if it was largely reflected glory.

Cuthbert arrived shortly before nine o'clock and went straight to his office. When he emerged, he was wearing a fresh white coat ready to supervise the examination.

'Now, Dr Morgenthal, shall we proceed?'

His voice was formal and his face stern, not so much to show his assistant that he was in teaching mode, but to remind himself of the professional detachment he needed to be able to deal with another dead child. Morgenthal took the lead and, as he had been taught, narrated his findings as he made the initial observations.

'We have the tightly wrapped body of a child, length three foot, three inches. The cloth is stained with the grave soil, and adhering to the cloth are a number of stalks and stems of different plants. Protruding from the windings, there are also other plants, which appear to have been placed deliberately when the body was wrapped. The cloth is held in place by thick twine knotted about the neck, waist and ankles.' He bent over the corpse to look closely and also squatted down to view it at eye-level from the side of the slab. 'There are no additional grave goods evident other than further plant material which the body appears to be resting on. Once the shroud is removed, we will be able to determine more.'

'Very good, Dr Morgenthal, please carry on.'

Carefully, he slit the strings binding the cloth and began to unwrap the body. Most of the cloth came away easily, and he recovered the plant specimens that were wrapped in it, labelled them and put them to one side for further inspection.

'These plants look different from the previous ones recovered from the other graves. If anything, they are more wilted and discoloured than the others, which is odd given that the body does not appear to be the most decomposed.'

'There will be time for comparisons later, Dr Morgenthal. Please focus your attentions solely on the case before you. Such tangential thinking may force you to miss something.'

'Of course, sir. My apologies.'

With the body unwrapped, Morgenthal now proceeded to inspect the child's clothing. 'We have a child, approximately five years old, dressed in a pink cotton dress. There is a pink ribbon in her hair, and she is wearing socks and shoes. Her arms are crossed over her chest and the legs are straight. The dress is stained with soil that has likely seeped through the wrappings. Next, I need to remove the clothes to perform a surface inspection of the body.'

He looked to Cuthbert, who nodded. Morgenthal then used scissors and a scalpel to cut away the clothes while moving the body as little as possible. This was a time-consuming process, and once he had the clothes and shoes in a separate pile, he turned his attention to them.

'The clothes are unstained with urine or faeces and especially the undergarments appear to be clean. There are no identifying labels on any of the garments, suggesting they may not be commercially made. I doubt they can tell us much more, sir.'

His last statement was almost a question, and he watched Cuthbert's face as he said it, only to be told to proceed, so he turned his attention to the small naked corpse on the slab.

'This is the body of a young girl. She is well-nourished and there are no obvious physical deformities. The skin colouration and condition is consistent with death some months before. However, the body has not undergone any insect invasion, and there is no evidence of larval infestation. This may be due to the alkalinity and dryness of the grave soil and perhaps the deterrent effects of the plants placed in the grave, although these have yet to be identified. On surface inspection of the skin, there are no signs of physical violence in the form of contusions, abrasions or lacerations. There is also no blood staining. However, there is what appears to be a distinctive strawberry birthmark on her lower back. That may well help in identifying her.'

'And?'

Morgenthal looked at Cuthbert, unsure of what he had missed. However, from his mentor's grim expression he saw what was required. He parted the small girl's legs and examined her genitals and then inspected her anus for any tears. Morgenthal was pleased to report that there was no evidence of sexual violence.

'Good. What's next?'

'I would like to inspect the eyes, ears, nose and mouth before arranging for some X-ray studies to be performed.'

'Why?'

'The state of her dentition will aid in the ageing of the child and close inspection of the other orifices may reveal clues as to cause of death. The X-rays will help assess the child's bone age and may also reveal healed fractures which could again help with her identification.'

'All right, Simon, get all that done as well as some photographs of her face and body before you perform the internal examination. And write up your findings so far. I'll be in my office – let me know when you're ready for the next steps.'

Cuthbert left Morgenthal with the corpse and, unusually, closed his office door behind him. While awaiting the photographer, Morgenthal covered the small girl lying naked on the slab with a sheet. He did not need to be reminded to treat any corpse with respect for that had been the very first lesson he had learnt at Cuthbert's side.

In his office, Cuthbert sat at his desk but turned his chair to look out of his window. His view was limited, but it did include a large lime tree in one of the internal quadrangles of the old hospital. It was losing its leaves and many of the branches were already bare.

Death, he thought, was everywhere he looked. He turned back to his desk and opened his bottom drawer. He removed a wooden box and took out the cloth and polish. His boots had already been polished that day, and to anyone else they would have appeared perfect, but to Cuthbert's eyes, they were imperfect and the only way to correct them was to start again.

Slowly, in small swirling motions, he rubbed the oily black polish on the cloth into the leather of his boot. As it dried and became gritty under his fingers, he added some spit to the cloth and continued the buffing. He devoted a full half-hour to each boot, and as he polished them to the highest shine, he felt his anxiety subside. He was able to start thinking through the details of the cases, ordering them in his mind and looking for connections.

What did these children have in common? Why were

they all buried in a wood at the orphanage? What was the significance of the way they had been interred? No answers came, but at least he could now deal with the questions.

When Morgenthal knocked on his closed office door, he chose not to enter right away as he usually did but to wait. Rather than invite him in, Cuthbert opened the door and came out, already with his sleeves rolled up and wearing his rubber dissection apron.

'Are we ready to proceed, Dr Morgenthal?'

'We are, sir.'

The internal examination of the child proceeded with textbook efficiency, and throughout Morgenthal narrated all of his observations and his largely negative findings. Like the other children, this small girl had no obvious anatomical cause of death, and the only clue was again the distinctive smell in her stomach. This time, Morgenthal was careful not to describe the finding in comparative terms.

'The stomach is largely empty, but the lining smells strongly of camphor and rosemary. This may indicate ingestion of some poisonous agent derived from plants.'

'Tansy?'

'Yes, sir, that would certainly be a possibility, but unfortunately there is no specific test for the alkaloid toxin or toxins derived from that species, so we must rely on the secondary evidence of the odour.'

Cuthbert nodded in agreement, but nevertheless instructed Morgenthal to take the necessary fluid and tissue samples that could be tested for other common poisons. 'And the date of death? What are you thinking?'

'It's very difficult, sir, and dependent on so many variables. I think we are certainly dealing with months rather than weeks and I would estimate less than a year. I'm not sure how else we might pinpoint it.'

Cuthbert looked over the child's clothes piled neatly on the side table and the withered plants. 'I wonder if the plants might give us more information, Simon. These are certainly different plants from the other graves, so perhaps they may have been collected at different times. If they can be identified, that might pinpoint at least the season when these children were put in their graves.'

Morgenthal agreed with Cuthbert's thinking and suggested that he might invite his contact at the Botany Department to identify the plants recovered from the second and third graves.

'Yes, Simon, that would make sense. Do ask Dr Davenport if she might shed some light on this.'

He was pleased that he could see the lecturer from U.C.L. again for he was still troubled by the poor first impression he had made. He hated causing offence, especially when it had been done so needlessly.

When the phone rang in Janet Davenport's office it was a welcome interruption from the papers she was marking.

'Dr Davenport, Simon Morgenthal here from St Thomas's. I wonder if we might prevail upon your expertise once more.'

'Do you have another grave?'

'Another two, I'm sorry to say. They are in the same geographical area, and again there are flowers and plants associated with the burials. This time, however, the plants are much more withered, and I would imagine much harder to identify, but any information you could give us would be so helpful.'

'Of course. It goes without saying I'll do anything I can to help.'

She looked at the unpromising pile of exam scripts on her desk awaiting her attention and said, 'Would it be more convenient if I came to you? If the plants are more fragile, it might be best to limit how much they are moved about.'

Morgenthal was more than happy that she was willing to come to St Thomas's and was surprised that she quickly agreed to come that very afternoon. He popped his head around Cuthbert's now-open office door to tell him of the arrangements.

'Dr Davenport is able to come over to look at the plant specimens here, sir.'

'Excellent, do make sure she has everything she needs, Simon.'

Morgenthal paused to consider what Cuthbert had said and could not help himself from asking, 'I'm curious, sir. How did you know she was a woman?'

'Our paths have crossed, Simon. Janet Davenport is a first-rate scientist and an excellent botanist. We're very lucky to have her. Make sure you treat her with the respect that she deserves, young man.'

Had Cuthbert somehow found out about his clumsiness with the lecturer? He was still embarrassed by it and was determined not to make the same mistake again. In the meantime, he made a start on the next set of toxicological analyses to be performed on the samples from the other two victims. Neither he nor Cuthbert expected anything else to show up, but completeness was essential in this as in every case that passed through their department.

*

At three o'clock, one of the departmental secretaries came to find Morgenthal to inform him he had a visitor. He jumped up immediately, not wishing to keep Dr Davenport waiting, and went straight to reception. He welcomed her and took her straight through to the side room he had prepared. There, he had laid out the plant specimens from the second and third graves.

The plants were arranged on clean sheets of blotting paper this time as he had seen Dr Davenport do in her own laboratory, and she smiled her approval.

'Give me an hour, Dr Morgenthal, and then we can discuss anything I've been able to find.'

Before he left, he took her hat and coat and offered to lift the Gladstone bag, heavy with reference books, she had brought with her on to the bench.

'It's quite all right, Dr Morgenthal. I think I can get it from the floor to the bench without the help of a man.'

He looked at her, pained, feeling he had committed another blunder, but she smiled and told him she was only joking, which, of course, she wasn't. He left her to it and exactly an hour later appeared at the door, on which he knocked gently.

'Do come in. It's your department, after all. Now, let's go through things. I've looked at the plants you recovered from the second grave. Again, they're all probably local species, but the common factor is that they would all have been gathered in the winter. I would suggest December or January. We have traveller's joy or *Clematis vitalba*. It flowers in the late summer, but it has these feathery seed heads in the winter.'

Using her forceps, she pointed out and traced the spider-like fronds attached to the dry, stick-like stems.

'They were already naturally dried out before they were put in the grave, so they have survived almost unchanged. Its other common name is old man's beard, and you can see why. I suspect it will be growing somewhere in the estate, for it likes chalky, lime-rich soils.'

She moved along the bench to the next specimen, which Morgenthal thought was a faded green mess of stems and smudged material.

'And here, quite obviously, we have mistletoe, *Viscum*

album. This specimen has evidence of berries, which means it must have been cut at some time from winter to early spring. If there's an orchard nearby, it will likely be on the apple trees. Lastly, this rather prickly specimen is butcher's broom, *Ruscus aculeatus*, and again the presence of berries, this time red ones rather like those on holly, means it must have been harvested in the winter.'

Morgenthal was taking notes and wondering how she was able to identify the plants so readily given their state. But he expected she might be just as bemused if she were to attend one of his post mortem examinations. Each to their own, he supposed.

'Are any of these plants used by herbalists, Dr Davenport?'

'All of them. The old man's beard is used to reduce inflammation, the mistletoe is used for arthritis, and the butcher's broom is a diuretic. Of the three though, it's the mistletoe that's poisonous. The leaves and the berries, if eaten or made into some form of concoction, can kill.'

'And the third grave?'

She moved the blotting paper sheets with the plants that she had just identified to the back of the bench and brought the next set to the fore.

'Well, this is where it gets interesting because here we have a quite different set of species. These are spring flowers in the main. They are very withered and partly decomposed, but they are still identifiable. Such plants are not nearly as robust or woody as those gathered in winter and that explains their very different condition. This one I suspect even you could identify, Dr Morgenthal.'

She held up a very unpromising withered brown stalk with a lump of equally brown faded bloom at its tip. He regretfully shook his head.

'It's a daffodil, one of the *Narcissus* species, but in this state impossible to classify further without a lot more work. There are several in the grave. And this is common nettle, *Urtica dioica*; judging by the size of the leaves, I would say a young specimen, again suggesting a spring harvesting. This one, I'm reasonably certain, is yarrow, *Achillea millefolium*, but it isn't flowering yet. The blossom comes in late spring or early summer, which means it was probably collected in March to April. So, collectively, given the species, their state of maturity and the weather conditions earlier this year, I would estimate that these were all placed in the grave sometime during the second half of March or the first half of April. Does that fit with your other findings?'

He was still writing in his notebook when she asked the question, but he nodded vigorously. 'Yes. The first grave had been very recently dug, within a week of its discovery at most. The post mortem examination of the child in the second grave suggested a time of death and therefore interment around nine months previously, around the turn of the year. The third grave looked to be somewhere intermediate between the other two, so, yes, it very much fits, and it certainly narrows the range of possibilities considerably. Tell me, Dr Davenport, I note you've not identified any tansy in the other two graves. Tansy doesn't grow all year, does it?'

'It flowers in mid to late summer, but it certainly doesn't need to be fresh to be used by herbalists. It could have been collected at any time and dried to be made into a concoction. Fresh flowering tansy was only found in the first grave, I suspect, because it would have been unavailable in the winter and early spring. Whoever laid these plants in the graves likely took what was readily available at the time. Probably it was just what was growing nearby, and they also probably had a good knowledge of medicinal plants because they've certainly gone for ones with pharmacological properties.'

Janet Davenport packed away the reference books and instruments she had brought with her from the university and again carefully repackaged all the plants into their original envelopes. Everything was left exactly as she had found it, but of course all the plants now had names and again she had written these neatly on all the envelopes.

'It's so good of you to come, Dr Davenport. I would offer to show you around before you go, but I expect you're busy.'

'Not too busy to learn something new, Dr Morgenthal. Please, do give me the tour. It's not every day one gets to see what goes on behind the curtain of forensic medicine.'

Morgenthal smiled and led her through from the side room where she had been working, first to the main laboratory, then to the various other side rooms where specialised investigations were carried out. She was especially interested in the toxicological assays he was setting up to screen for common poisons in the body fluids. She also paused to take a closer look at the comparator microscope they had to examine bullet markings.

Finally, he stopped outside the main dissection room. 'I'm afraid I'm not permitted to show you this room. If it was vacant, there would be no problem, but two of the victims are still with us.'

'The children, you mean? How terrible. It's so easy to get lost in the science of it all and forget that the whole reason for all this is in there. Little lives so cruelly cut short. I'm glad I only have to work with dead plants. I'm not sure I could do your job, Dr Morgenthal.'

'It's like everything else – you get used to it.'

But as he said it, he knew he was unlikely ever to get used to dealing with such small corpses.

'May I offer you some refreshment, Dr Davenport? I feel it's the very least I can do after all your work.'

'No need. I was only too happy to help. And if anything else turns up, do call. I confess it has all been rather interesting. Perhaps I need to become more involved in this sort of work. Is there such a thing as forensic botany? If not, perhaps there should be. Now, I'll see myself out.' She nodded her head at the dissection-room door as she shook Morgenthal's hand. 'You have others who need your attention more than me.'

*

Cuthbert arranged for Morgenthal to attend the next case conference with him at the Yard. Not only did he think it would be good experience, but he also thought there was a lot of new information to report. And the more heads on this case the better.

When they arrived at the duty room, Sergeant Baker acknowledged Cuthbert and specifically welcomed Morgenthal and showed him where to sit. The young man was too taken by the pinboard to sit down, and he studied the photographs, the notes and the red string that had been pinned between items to highlight their connection.

'Did you bring photographs of the other victims, sir?'

'Yes, sergeant. Dr Morgenthal has them in his folder.'

Baker took them and rearranged the board to accommodate all three victims. And he prepared further blank cards ready to record their summary details.

'So two for the price of one today, Dr Cuthbert. Good to have you with us, Dr Morgenthal. Perhaps you'll be more use than the old man.'

Mowbray winked at Cuthbert as he said it and invited them both to sit down before starting proceedings. 'Right, where are we with this? I understand we have three bodies now. Is that correct, gentlemen?'

Cuthbert took the group through the post mortem findings

of all three victims, emphasising the similarities as he went. He also discussed the latest findings from Dr Davenport regarding the timings of the interments, based on the plants in the graves.

'Grave One: the four-year-old boy was buried on the fourteenth of September, and we believe died around two to seven days before. Grave Two: the two-year-old girl was buried, and we believe died, in December/January. Grave Three: the five-year-old girl was probably buried in March/April of this year and was most likely killed shortly before she was put in the ground. There are different plants in each grave, but all have interest to herbalists, and all are likely to be local. Given the similarities of how the bodies were arranged, I think we must be dealing with the same killer in all three cases.'

'And you're sure these children couldn't have died of natural causes? You're as sure as you can be, doctor, that all these children were poisoned?'

'Poisons mainly affect us in one of two ways: by acting locally or remotely. That's to say they either kill or menace life by destroying the tissues they come into contact with, or they produce the effects by being absorbed into the bloodstream and thus act on organs more or less remote from the point of their absorption, such as the brain or the heart. Of course, there are also common corrosive poisons that do both, such as arsenic.

'In the case of these children, however, there was no local anatomical damage in the gut, so we must be dealing with remote effects. Now, the main post mortem feature in common is the distinctive smell of tansy in the stomachs of all three victims. They had all drunk or eaten something containing large quantities of tansy oil not long before their deaths. We know that such concoctions are used by herbalists, but large enough doses can kill, especially in small children. There is no other explanation for their deaths that we can find.'

Mowbray was pacing in front of the board and scratching the back of his head. He looked at the photographs of the three dead children and asked, 'And is there no way to be absolutely sure that they were poisoned with this tansy you've got on the board?'

Cuthbert turned to Morgenthal and asked him to take this question.

'I'm afraid there's no specific test we can perform to identify the poison in their bodies, chief inspector, mainly because the poisonous element of the plant is still unknown. There is of course the possibility of performing what we call bio-assays, or animal studies, in such a case. In these tests, a suitable animal – a frog or a mouse say – is exposed to a concentrated preparation of the victim's body fluids. If the fluids contain the poison, whatever it is, it could have a similar effect on the animal. However, such an approach is prone to many variables and in the opinion of many pathologists the results are usually inconclusive – if for no other reason than that humans and animals are very different when it comes to their susceptibility to poisons. For example, chief inspector, did you know you cannot kill a rabbit with belladonna, or a hedgehog with opium, even though both are often fatal to humans?'

'I'll bear that in mind, Dr Morgenthal, next time I'm planning a hedgehog cull. So we're left with the distinctive smell. Well, that will have to do to be going along with. Baker, has any of this tansy been identified growing on the St Gregory estate?'

'We've looked and I'm afraid we can't find it growing wild. There are two gardens where it might also have been cultivated – the one at the main house and Briar Cottage, but we've drawn a blank there too.'

'So where the hell did it come from? I think we need to take another look. Get that organised, Baker, will you? Right, three dead children in shallow graves buried over a nine-month period, probably all killed by poisoning and laid to rest somewhat elaborately. Motives?'

Baker stood up and went to the board. 'Initially, we thought the children may have been inmates of the orphanage, but their records are pretty good and none of the sisters have admitted to any missing children. They still have exactly the same number now as they started the year with. So, apart from the fact that they were all found in the orphanage grounds, it's possible they had nothing to do with the place.'

'No, I would disagree, sergeant.' Now Cuthbert was on his feet. 'This is an environment with children at the very heart of it. Three dead children on their grounds means there must be a connection. But there is very little else apparently to link the children. We have one boy and two girls, all of different ages. The similarities that we see seem to be related to their deaths and burials. All may have been killed by the same hand in the same way, all were dressed in fresh clothes, and all were put to rest wrapped in cotton shrouds and with various plants adorning their corpses and the graves.'

Mowbray nodded. 'Yes, I'm with you, Cuthbert. Those fucking nuns have something to do with this or I'm a monkey's uncle.'

Morgenthal, who was unused to Mowbray's directness, was startled by the way he spoke, and Cuthbert was mildly amused to watch the young man shift uneasily in his seat.

'Do we have their real names yet, sergeant?'

Baker consulted his notebook. 'Yes, sir. After I'd spoken with Mrs Barnaby, I went back up to the main house and got a look at the files. Sister Margery, who found the second grave, was Edna Granton, originally from Ealing. Novice Sister Mary Frances was Claire Arnott from Wimbledon, Sister Hilda was Grace Frensham from Bristol, and the reverend mother was

Edith Burnett from Northumberland. I've run the names and details through records, sir, and none of them are on our files.'

'And do we know much about their pasts, sergeant?' Cuthbert asked the question before Mowbray did. 'I'm thinking perhaps if any of them have a background in herbalism, it might give us a connection.'

'They do have a herb garden, and it's Novice Sister Mary Frances that looks after it. I'm not sure how much of an expert she is, or if any of the other sisters have experience, but I can check, sir.'

Mowbray tapped two other names on the board with his index finger.

'What about these two, Mr and Mrs Barnaby, old Dickson and his wife Eliza. What do we know about them?'

'Not much, sir, other than that Dickson Barnaby has been the groundsman at St Gregory's for twenty years and his wife used to be the cook. She gave up this last year because the couple lost their daughter, Tilly.'

'She must have been relatively young, sergeant. Do we know what the cause of death was?'

'No, Dr Cuthbert, but she's buried in the churchyard. And so is her older brother. He died in the war and he has a Royal Berkshire headstone.'

Mowbray shook his head. 'Christ, some don't get it easy, do they? See what you can find out about the daughter, Baker. It might have some bearing on the case. What about the old dear – any herbalist link there?'

'She's certainly a keen gardener, sir, and there were all sorts growing when I looked in. Again, I can check that out when I go back.'

Mowbray took stock of the board and summarised where he thought they were. 'Nowhere, that's where we're at, gents. No-fucking-where! Right, what do we do next?'

Morgenthal shifted in his seat again, but this time he raised his hand to speak. Mowbray smiled and told him it wasn't a classroom and if he had something to say, he should say it.

'I know it might not be my place, chief inspector, but I think this case has so much to do with plants that we might usefully involve the specialist we've been working with. Her name is Dr Janet Davenport from U.C.L. and Dr Cuthbert knows her. If she could be allowed to survey the site, especially checking for the presence of the tansy plants, that might allow Sergeant Baker to concentrate on his interviews. It might speed things up . . .'

Mowbray stood up, leant over the young pathologist and said, 'Good idea.' Morgenthal, who had been expecting a mouthful, was relieved to get out of the case conference in one piece, and as soon as they got back to the hospital, he called Dr Davenport and asked her if she would like to go on a field trip.

Chapter 8

London: 25 September 1931

Walter Baker was finishing the last of his buttered toast and draining his teacup at the breakfast table.

'Off in the car again this morning?'

'Yes, love. Back down Lewisham way.'

'You're not enjoying this one, Walter. I can see it in your eyes. Want to talk about it?'

'No, you know me. Work stops at the coat stand in the hall. No need for you to hear about it all. But you can come here and see me off proper, old girl.'

Sergeant Baker smiled and kissed his wife, and it was only when he was outside sitting in the car that he could afford to let his guard down. She was right: he was certainly not enjoying this one, if indeed he could be said to enjoy any of the murders he had investigated. But with children, there was so much more to think about, and all that could so easily get in the way of the work.

*

When he arrived at St Gregory's, he made straight for the main house and his appointment with the mother superior.

'Back again so soon, sergeant. We are getting a lot of your attention.'

'There are three children buried in shallow graves in your grounds. I hardly think that's something we should take lightly. Now, if you could answer some of my questions, I can leave you in peace.'

The nun detected a very different tone in the sergeant's voice from his last visit. What might have changed? She showed him into the reception room where they had last spoken and invited him to take a seat.

'I won't, if you don't mind. I need to know a little more about the sisters here, including yourself. Who here has any background in herbalism – the culture of medicinal herbs, or their preparation?'

'Our Novice Sister Mary Frances, whom I believe you have already interviewed, looks after our herb garden.'

'Yes, but I'm talking about the past. Who has any experience of that sort of thing?'

'All convents have gardens, and many have herb gardens for culinary and medicinal purposes, so I imagine the other sisters will have had some exposure during their vocation.'

'And what about you?'

'I did have a little to do with the herb garden in the Mother House.'

'How little?'

'I worked with one of the older sisters during my novitiate and learned how to prepare simple remedies for minor scratches, bee stings and the like.'

'Did you work with tansy?'

'The name is familiar, but I can't say I have an intimate knowledge of its uses.'

All the time she was speaking, Baker was studying her, and he felt she was not telling the whole truth. She gave just enough of an answer to move the question on but not enough to be complete. He had seen the tactic many times, and he was in no mood for it today.

'Sounds to me like you had a pretty extensive knowledge of the herbs, reverend mother. We will of course be checking your account with the Mother House. I expect there are still those there who remember you.'

She just lowered her eyes.

'One more thing. The last time we spoke, I asked you about the girl, Tilly Barnaby, and you said . . . let me see, yes, here it is: "She had no right to a burial in that ground, none of them did." What did you mean by that?'

'Only what I said, and I also said you would need to take it up with Reverend Henshall.'

'Well, I'm taking it up with you, reverend mother, and I would remind you this is a murder inquiry.'

'Tilly Barnaby committed suicide. And so did some other girls that the reverend has seen fit to bury in hallowed ground. More than that I do not know. Now, if we are finished here, I have a very great deal to do.'

Without waiting for an answer, she rushed from the room before remembering herself and slowing to her usual stately pace, her shoes squeaking on the polished linoleum as she went. Baker smiled; he had finally ruffled her feathers. His next port of call had to be the vicar, but he first made a note to phone the Mother House in Northumberland as soon as he got back to the Yard.

While Baker had been speaking to the mother superior, Morgenthal and Dr Davenport had arrived by taxi and were now crossing the lawns towards the woods. Morgenthal explained the details of the case that he was permitted to share now that Dr Davenport was officially a consultant.

'The three graves were found in here. If you look through

the trees, you'll still see the rope cordons in place. The first we found, but probably the most recent, was just beyond the tree line. The second to be found, and the one that you found the winter plants in, was further over near the wall, and the last, containing the spring flowers, was much further over this way.'

As he was pointing out the graves, he noticed the botanist growing pale. 'I'm sorry, are you feeling quite well, Dr Davenport?'

'Forgive me. It's just it's all so theoretical in the laboratory, and then you come here ... and it's dreadfully real. Those poor, poor children. What can I do to help?'

'Well, the police officers have not been able to locate any tansy, and the chief inspector is keen to know if there is any in the vicinity. We thought you might have a better eye than some of the coppers.'

'I would hope so. There wouldn't be any in the wood itself – too dark – but around the edges maybe. I'll start there.'

'There are also two gardens we might check. The groundsman and his wife have a cottage in the grounds and Sergeant Baker tells us that they have quite a kitchen garden. And there's a herb garden at the main house.'

'Right, we'll check them all. Let's get started.'

Morgenthal watched her steel herself before she entered the wood. She had to get to the far side nearest the wall and it meant passing the first grave site and walking towards the second. When she reached the stone wall, she followed the edge of the tree line around the woods and occasionally bent to examine a plant but at no time did she ever pick anything. He followed a few paces behind, thinking he should be on hand if she needed anything, without having any idea what that might be. He did feel a little superfluous, but having roped her in to help on the case, he felt responsible.

She was meticulous, and he watched her take notes in a small black book as she went. After almost an hour walking the boundary of the woods, she shook her head.

'There's no tansy growing here that I can find, but it is late in the season for it. I've also been checking for any companion plants – ones that we might find growing in association with it, but again that's drawing a blank. I don't think the tansy that killed these children was gathered in or near these woods. Now, what about those gardens?'

*

While they were in the woods, Baker had made his way across the St Gregory's estate to Reverend Henshall's rectory. There was no answer, so he went over to the church in the hope of finding the vicar there.

He tried the heavy metal latch and the door opened. Inside, the air of the church was damp, and the place smelled of stone and dust and old hymnals. There was all the usual paraphernalia of the Anglican churches he had been used to as a child, but these days he was inclined to give any form of religion a wide berth. He knew many who had served in the trenches who felt the same.

Baker walked up the centre aisle towards the altar. Glancing from side to side, he saw various memorial plaques, some in marble and some in highly polished brass. Someone was taking care of that, he thought. The flowers were also fresh in the altar vases, even if the air was musty. A side door to the vestry opened and the reverend appeared, carrying a pile of song sheets. When he saw Baker, he was startled but then smiled.

'I didn't expect to see you again. I'm sorry if you've been kept waiting. How can I be of help?'

'I just came on the off chance of catching you, sir. Do you have a moment to answer some more questions?'

'Of course, why don't we go into the vestry? It's a little less churchy in there. If I have to start talking in here, I do have a habit of delivering a sermon.'

He led Baker through the side door and along a short passageway to the small room with its large window. There were wooden chairs around a table, and the reverend gestured for Baker to take a seat.

'So what can I tell you, sergeant?'

'I'm pursuing several lines of inquiry regarding the findings in the woods at St Gregory's and we're trying to find any connections between the children—'

'Children? I thought it was one child you had discovered.'

'No, sir, I'm sorry to have to tell you that three graves all containing young children have been uncovered.'

'Dear God. How did they die? I mean, were they killed?'

'That's what we're trying to find out, sir. Now, if I might ask you a few questions.'

'I'm sorry, of course, anything. It's just such a shock, such a terrible state of affairs.'

'I wanted to ask you about the Barnabys' daughter, Tilly. I understand there was some controversy about her burial here.'

'I suppose the reverend mother told you about that. What a spiteful, poisonous woman that one is. I'm sorry, I really shouldn't have said that, but sometimes she makes my blood boil. Tilly Barnaby was one of my parishioners and I'd known her since I came here. When she died suddenly, I buried her in my churchyard.'

'But wasn't there some suggestion that she should not have been placed there because of the way she died? Because she had taken her own life?'

'Do you know how this Church of mine treats those who are driven to take their own lives? They proclaim them as damned. No priest can bury a suicide; no churchyard will allow their interment. They have committed a serious crime in the eyes of the law and a mortal sin in the eyes of God.'

He got up from his chair, walked across to the window and leaned one arm on the frame. He looked out at the clouds that were running from the wind.

'We have the audacity to call it a sin, and we don't know the first thing about it. Suicide isn't a sin: it's a failure of hope, a last desperate act. Surely an act can only be a sin if we have a choice and we knowingly take the wrong path. This isn't a choice. A young mother only commits suicide when she has no choices left. Tilly Barnaby took her own life because she was pregnant and unwed. She got rid of the child, I don't know how, but probably some filthy back-street abortionist. Afterwards, she couldn't live with the guilt or the grief. The poor girl saw it as the only way out. Dickson came to me and begged me to give her a Christian burial. You know they lost their son in the war and he's buried here too. All her father wanted was for them to be together.

'It wasn't a difficult decision for me. Not at all. In my book, all suicides are really tragic accidents. Like fatal accidents there are no perpetrators, no sinners, only victims. And victims always deserve our compassion. I know dear Sister Eglantyne would not agree with me on that. In fact, we tend to disagree on most things – certainly on matters of theology. But I go to my maker with a clear conscience.'

All the time he had been speaking, he had been looking up at the sky as if he was giving his statement to a higher power.

'And I understand Miss Barnaby was not the only suicide that you consented to bury in the churchyard, sir. Is that true?'

'So I am the sinner now because of showing the most basic human decency to these poor young women. Is that what she told you? Everything seems upside down in this world now, sergeant. Yes, there were some others. I don't know how, but word does have a habit of getting about. Perhaps you think they saw me as a soft touch, but you didn't speak with those poor people. Parents old before their time, desperately trying to make sense of all that had happened, clinging to whatever hope I could give them. I didn't talk of sin, but of pain. Their daughters were victims. Can you even imagine what it must be like to live inside the mind of someone who is willing to take her own life, to leave her family behind? How dark and terrible must that place be that the only solution is to end it all?'

'I didn't see recent headstones in the churchyard. Where are the women buried?'

'By the east wall. Their graves are, I regret to say, as yet unmarked. The families had no money for headstones, and we have been unable to provide. What is it they call us – the Tory Party at Prayer? The Church of England has always been the bidding servant of the middle class and has had little to say to the poor. I was at least able to lay them to rest in sacred ground, so God knows they are there, and perhaps more importantly so do their families.'

'But you have records of their names?'

'Yes, of course. In the Parish Register. All baptisms, marriages and funerals are recorded there. Let me get it for you.'

He returned with a heavy ledger, laid it on the table and opened it at the page for January 1931.

'The first of the funerals was in the winter, soon after New Year, if I remember correctly. Yes, here it is, the twelfth of January. Her name was Mary Nightingale. She was just nineteen, the poor girl.'

'Do you have an address for her or her family?'

'Yes, I should have. Let me see. Yes, here it is. Her next of kin was a Mr George Grayson and he lives in Lambeth. I think he was her uncle if memory serves. A rather diffident man, I recall, but then we weren't meeting under the best of circumstances. And, of course, there was the child.'

'She had a child?'

'Yes, a young daughter. Not much more than a baby, but I don't have a note of her name. Sorry. In fact, I think they were all mothers.'

'What became of the children, sir?'

'I don't know. I never saw them. I only dealt with the family members who came to see me. The funeral services were conducted very privately and quietly, and I don't remember any children being present. I only know all three each had a young child. More than that, I can't say. The next one was a little later in the year. Now, let me check.' He ran down the column with his index finger and turned the page. 'No, no, no, yes, here she is: Margaret Webb. My word, she was young too, only twenty-two when she took her life and as I said, another young mother. From Clapham, I believe. Yes, here is her parents' address. Good people, but just broken by it all. Such a sad burial. And there was one more. It was the most recent, just earlier this month in fact, and only attended by one mourner, the poor girl's sister. Yes, here she is, Rose Smith, and the funeral was on the seventh of September. She was just twenty-one when she died.'

'And she also had a child?'

'Yes, I think so. As I said, certainly no one other than the sister attended the funeral, but then often small children are kept away from such things. Her sister was very angry about everything, as family members often are. Some of them blame themselves for what's happened, some of them blame the victim, and most of them are bewildered by it all. She said very little – only enough to arrange the funeral. Sometimes people just need to find the right shoulder to cry on and for some that's not me.'

Baker thanked Henshall for his help and took notes of all the names and addresses. Already he could see it was going to be vital to track down these relatives. They had three young children buried in the grounds and now three young mothers who had died apparently by their own hand buried nearby in the churchyard. Could it just be coincidence? Years in C.I.D. had taught him that rarely, if ever, could coincidence be used as an excuse for such a set of findings.

On his way back to the police car, he met Dr Morgenthal and the young woman. Morgenthal introduced Dr Davenport to the sergeant, who raised his hat to the lady.

'It's a pleasure to meet you, doctor. Have you had any luck yet with this tansy?'

'No, sergeant, but I'm just taking our expert to take a look at the herb garden in the main house and there's also Briar Cottage. If it's here, we'll find it.'

'I'll leave you both to it, then. Thank you for your assistance, Dr Davenport. One way or another, this case seems to be revolving around that plant.'

As Baker drove off, Dr Davenport said, 'He looks worried.'

'Yes, they all look like that during a case, especially one like this. The detectives get a lot of stick, but in my experience they all work very hard, and they all care very much about getting it right. It's a privilege to work with them. Shall we go around and find this garden?'

The herb garden of the main house was part of the walled kitchen garden on the original estate. Dr Davenport studied the beds one by one and found all the usual culinary herbs she would expect to see in a mild English autumn. Again, she took notes as she went, and occasionally bent to study or smell a specimen, but ultimately she shook her head again.

'Let's try the cottage. Perhaps third time lucky.'

Briar Cottage was as pretty as it sounded, and Dr Davenport

could not help but be charmed by it. In the front garden was Mrs Barnaby, bent over tugging at some plants, clearing a bed of its summer growth. Dr Morgenthal introduced himself and Dr Davenport and they were invited in.

'What is it I can help you with?'

'We're just looking to see the kind of plants that are growing in the area. It's just a routine part of the investigation – nothing to worry about, Mrs Barnaby. You don't mind if my colleague here takes a look around your garden?'

'Gracious, if I'd known I was going to have an inspection, I'd have had it a lot tidier than it is. You'll have to excuse my mess. Just that time of year. Trying to get the old out so we can start again for next spring.'

Dr Davenport smiled and realised they weren't being specific.

'You have a lovely garden. I rarely get to see one so full of fascinating plants. I can see you have an interest in the medicinal. Am I right?'

'Oh yes, plants have always been the best medicines. I'll go and put the kettle on. Gardening is such thirsty work, and I'm sure you'll both join me, won't you?'

'Too kind, Mrs Barnaby, but we'll not trouble you. We'll just take a quick look and be out of your hair in a trice.'

'Well, as you like it. I'll be inside if you need anything.'

Mrs Barnaby disappeared inside the cottage and Morgenthal turned to Dr Davenport, who this time was nodding her head.

'This garden is one big pharmacy. Every plant in it is on the formulary for any self-respecting herbalist.'

'Tansy?'

'Look over here at this bed. It's been cleared recently, but do you see these small yellow flower heads between the broken stems. Take one and crush it.'

He did and immediately recognised the distinctive smell. 'So she's growing it?'

'Looks like it. The whole bed, if I'm not mistaken. She's likely to have harvested it, so it might well be drying somewhere. Usually, the stems are hung upside down in an airing room, an outbuilding, that sort of thing. Maybe in there.'

Dr Davenport pointed to a large potting shed and when they went over and peered through the window, they could see it was indeed being used as a drying room. Rows and rows of tied bunches of plants hung from poles spanning the shed.

'She has all sorts in there, and, yes, over there near the back, that's unmistakably tansy. It looks like this is your source, Dr Morgenthal. Should we say something?'

'Well, I suppose we could ask about it and see whether she lies. She won't know we've found it, and if she denies it, she could well implicate herself.'

Morgenthal knocked on the open cottage door and was told to come right in.

'Mrs Barnaby, thank you for allowing us to look around. We were just wondering if you knew of any tansy growing nearby.'

'Tansy is it you're looking for? We call it "bitter buttons" hereabouts. Tansy tea is good for worms. We always gave it to our girl.'

'And they use it for other things too, do they not?'

There was a sudden change in Mrs Barnaby's expression at Dr Davenport's question. 'That they do, but I never held with any of that. That's an unspeakable evil, that is, to kill the unborn. Only God has the right to take those lives. He did with two of mine but . . .' As she spoke, she turned away to look up at the sky and the rest of her thought seemed to be lost on the breeze. The old woman just stood in silence, apparently oblivious of her visitors.

Concerned, Morgenthal looked at Dr Davenport and frowned. She nodded and spoke up again.

'Mrs Barnaby. Mrs Barnaby, you were telling us about the tansy.'

The woman was stirred from the moment and looked back at the botanist and the smart young man by her side. There was a moment before she seemed to recognise them.

'So where might you gather the tansy, Mrs Barnaby?'

She forced a smile and indicated the cleared bed with a sweep of her hand.

'Here in the garden. I grow it for one of the sisters. It's over just now and I've already been clearing out the beds. It needs a firm hand else it takes over, but no matter how severely you thin it out, it always comes back every year.'

'Which sister would that be, Mrs Barnaby?'

'The young one, Mary Frances.'

'That's really very helpful, Mrs Barnaby. Thank you for everything. We'll just see ourselves out.'

On the way back across the lawns to the main house, Morgenthal was quiet. Dr Davenport could contain herself no longer and asked what he was thinking.

'Just that this is important, possibly very important. And I'll make sure the chief inspector knows it was you who found the tansy in that shed. But Sister Mary Frances, whoever she is, sounds as if she's going to have some explaining to do. Surely one of the nuns couldn't be involved in all this? I mean, I'm a little out of my depth here, religion-wise, but I can't imagine a group of women in holy orders to be murderers.'

'That's rather your department, Dr Morgenthal, but for what it's worth, I think people often aren't what they seem. I think I'll get back to my laboratory now. Plants are so much simpler than people.'

*

At the Yard, Baker spoke with the former Sister Eglantyne's colleagues at the Mother House in Northumberland. They confirmed that not only had she worked in the herb garden there, but she had for some five years been in sole charge of it, along with the preparation of all their herbal remedies.

Things were moving fast, and he needed to take stock, so he took time to write up his interview reports from St Gregory's to make sure he had it all straight in his head. What was clear to him now was that the young mothers who had committed suicide must be connected to the dead children, and he had to find their families.

In the afternoon, he drove over to Lambeth to the address the Reverend Henshall had given him for Mary Nightingale's uncle, George Grayson. It was familiar ground for Baker, and he knew the run-down streets well. The homes were packed tight in dirty narrow rows, and the air was foul from the nearby gasworks.

He rapped on the door of number 46 and when there was no answer, peered through the letterbox and shouted in that he was looking for a Mr Grayson.

'You won't find him there, dearie.'

The woman popped her head out of the adjacent door and looked him up and down, trying to decide if he was the rent man or the law. She was wearing a wrap-around apron and had her stockings rolled down to her ankles and her hair up in a scarf. She saw him similarly look her over and barked back, 'Getting an eyeful, are you? I usually look better than this, but I'm doing my windows, see.'

'Do you know Mr Grayson, miss?'

'Mrs. Mrs Franks. Yeah, he's been there as long as we have – nigh on four years come February. But I haven't seen him for a while, to tell you the truth. Always did come and go a bit. Think he might have been a travelling salesman or such like.'

'Was there a child?'

'You mean his Mary's kiddie? That was a bleedin' shame that was. She just disappears, so he says, and leaves him right in the lurch, with a baby to look after. I mean to say, how's a man going to make a go of that? It didn't half squeal the place down, no mistaking. Don't think he even knew how to feed the little thing.'

'What happened?'

'Don't rightly know. One minute the baby was here, the next neither of them were. That might have been the last time he was here, but that was months ago. I just lose track of it, dearie. Time flies when you've got windows to do. But as I said, you'll not get an answer there.'

She closed her door on Baker, who took a look through the window of number 46. The room was bare and there was no sign that anyone had been living there for some time.

He knocked on some other doors and got much the same story from Grayson's other neighbours. He had obviously told everyone the story that his niece had gone off and left him to look after her child. All were scathing of her behaviour and sympathetic to his plight, but none of them had any idea where he or the child had gone.

Baker checked the next address on his list and hoped he might fare better with the parents of Margaret Webb, who lived in his old stomping grounds of Clapham, only a few miles from Lambeth.

He took a small detour along his old street and past his school. Little had changed, but then again everything had changed. Before the war he had lived above the cornershop with his parents and brother. His dad was a butcher and that's what his brother George was supposed to be too. He used to have him and his brother in the shop on Saturdays to help out and never tired of his joke for the customers. 'I'm the butcher,' he would say, and then pointing at him and his brother he would add, 'and this is the baker, George Baker that is, so this little one must be the candlestick maker.'

The shop was now a tobacconist's, and the sign was gone. His parents had never got over his elder brother's death in the war, and when he came home, they looked at him as if he had no right to be there when his brother was still lying in a cold grave in France.

Nothing was the same after that, and when he joined the force, that was the final straw as far as his father was concerned. He had been expected to take over the shop when George had died, but he had seen enough blood and dead meat in the war to last him a lifetime. His parents were still there on the street, having moved to the small end terrace house, but he had not seen them for some time.

Perhaps if he had been able to bring them a grandchild, things would have been different, but then again maybe not. He turned the car around and drove back into the present and found the house he was looking for on Ilminster Gardens near the station. A young woman answered the door and immediately said, 'We don't want any, thank you!'

'No, miss. My name is Detective Sergeant Baker, and I'm looking to speak with Mr and Mrs Webb. This is their home – is that correct?'

The woman had all but closed the front door in his face but was pulled up by the question. He held out his identification card and she peered at it before opening the door again.

'I'm sorry, it's just that we're plagued about here with salesmen. I'm afraid Mr Webb passed away last month. I'm his niece. Auntie is still here but she's not been that well.'

'Would it be possible to speak with Mrs Webb? It's very important.'

'You can try, but you'll see what I mean. I do my best, but by rights she should really be somewhere else. You'd better come in.'

'Your name, miss?'

'Oh, Mrs Davidson. I live three streets away and pop in whenever I can, just to check on her. But she's getting worse every day, poor soul.'

She led him into a narrow hallway and then into a small front room where an elderly woman was sitting at a table in the bay window. She looked up at Baker and smiled.

'Frank, is that you, love? Where you been to this time? I can't keep your dinner hot when you're out gallivanting.'

The young woman leaned towards Baker and whispered that Frank was her uncle and that her aunt spent her time waiting for him to come home.

'Mrs Webb, my name's Sergeant Baker. I'm from the police, and I just wanted to ask you some questions.'

'The police! What's my Frank been up to now? He's a good man, and a fine father to our Maggie. What d'you want with me?'

'I wanted to ask about your daughter.'

'She's sleeping. She been having a time of it with her teeth, poor little soul, but Frank can always get her off. Where is that husband of mine?'

Sergeant Baker looked up at the young woman, who shook her head.

Mrs Webb looked anxiously out of the window and turned back. 'Are you Frank? Where you been, love?'

'I'll leave you just now, Mrs Webb, it was kind of you to talk to me.'

Outside in the hallway, Mrs Davidson apologised for her aunt.

'Please, no need. I'm sorry to have troubled you.'
'Why did you want to ask about Maggie?'
'It's part of an investigation, Mrs Davidson.'
'You do know what happened, I suppose?'

Baker was hesitant in case he knew more than the girl's cousin, so he said that he only had very sketchy details, and it would be most helpful if she could fill in the picture.

'She was in a sorry state after that good-for-nothing left her. She was married, you know, with a kiddie and another on the way, when he upped and left. It was all just too much for her and, well, you know the rest, I'm sure.'

'What happened to your cousin's child?'

'Taken into care, I expect. I wasn't here at the time, you see. We only moved back this summer, and by that time Aunt Jean was getting worse. I expect it was Maggie's death that tipped her over even before Uncle Frank passed away. Now all she does is wait at that window, living in the past. She thinks Maggie's upstairs in her cot. I don't say anything. Best not to tell her the truth.'

The young woman clearly had her hands full, and Baker took his leave after thanking her. Outside in the street he looked around. Did this place still feel like home? He shook the past from his thoughts and decided to stop torturing himself before driving back to the Yard.

Chapter 9

Edinburgh: 16 February 1908

For the last year, Cuthbert had been the tallest boy not just in his dormitory set but in the whole of his year group. Abercrombie, who had had that honour when they all arrived six years before, was now no more than average, and while he said nothing he felt it sorely. As they had grown together, the group of four had found friendship.

One reason may have been the discovery that each of them was an only child. Devoid of siblings, they found brotherhood in each other. After lights out they would huddle around to talk of the school, its teachers and of everything they hoped one day to be. Now, as they were beginning to feel the first stirrings of manhood, their late-night conversations were becoming less open and more self-conscious, unsure of themselves and what they were becoming.

The schoolwork was also intensifying, and of the four only Cuthbert found it effortless. Cruikshank had always struggled with Latin although he found he had a facility for mathematics and science. Jenner was the history buff but battled with anything involving numbers, and poor Abercrombie was a duffer across the board. They helped each other, viewing their little group as nothing less than family.

Some of the older boys also knew Cuthbert by reputation and occasionally would come by their dormitory room to get help with their algebra or their Latin prose, but Cruikshank, Jenner and Abercrombie all had him to themselves, and for that they secretly gave thanks. They used him freely as a resource, and he was happy to help, finding that he was a natural teacher, but it was Abercrombie who always had the greatest need.

'*Amare* was the very first verb we learned in Latin, Abercrombie. How is it after six years you still haven't managed to remember the endings?'

'You're starting to sound just like Jampot, you know. Just show me where I've gone wrong, won't you?'

'All right. The word you need to translate here is *amabunt* and you've written "they were loving". That would be *amabant*. You should have translated *amabunt* as "they will love" because it's the third person plural future active indicative, not the imperfect.'

'The what?'

'I know it's a bit of a mouthful, but you just have to sit down and really learn the endings. It's a grind, Abercrombie, but it pays off. As for the translation, it's only one letter different, but in Latin just as in English one letter can make a world of difference. Think of the words "has" and "had". To say "he has five shillings" is very different from saying "he had five shillings". Do you see?'

'Not really, Cuthbert, but I'll take your word for it. You're always right. Jampot has it in for me, I think. Or should that be "had" it in for me because I think he might have given up on me altogether.'

'You know, you're much cleverer than you let on, Abercrombie. It's all right to know things. It's not showing off, you know. Look, have another go at the translation, now you know what tense it's in, and let me see it. We can go over it together.'

Abercrombie smiled his thanks as he always did when Cuthbert tried to make him feel better about himself. None of the masters were as considerate, and he knew they had him down for the wooden spoon in every test that was going. Maybe one day he would find something he was good at, but he was already pretty sure it wasn't going to be Latin.

Although Jenner could have turned to Cruikshank for help with his mathematics prep, it was always Cuthbert that he reached out to. Cruikshank certainly knew his trigonometry, but he was not nearly as patient as Cuthbert in sharing it. Like many people who find a topic easy, he had difficulty in understanding why others found it hard. And he had a tendency to raise his voice and occasionally his hands when he thought others, like Jenner, were being particularly stupid. Cuthbert, on the other hand, could be relied upon to be sympathetic, at least most of the time. He was only ever sharp when he was called upon to answer questions in the middle of the night.

'Cuthbert.' The whisper came from Abercrombie's bed, but no one stirred. 'Cuthbert!'

'What is it? We're all trying to sleep.'

'Cuthbert, I need to talk to you. Look, wake up, it's important.'

'Right, you great oaf, I'm awake. What is it?'

'I think I'm ill, and you know all about things like that.'

'What in heaven's name makes you think you're ill other than that you don't seem to be able to sleep or let anyone else sleep for that matter?'

Cuthbert was expecting some sort of obscene retort but all he heard in the dark was the sound of Abercrombie sniffing and choking back some tears. He sat up and got out of bed and went over to his roommate's bed by the window, sat on the counterpane and switched on his bedside lamp.

'What is it? Come on, tell me. What's got you so upset?'

'It's my body. I think I'm dying. Horrible things have started happening.'

'What do you mean, horrible things? You look healthy enough to me.'

'There's hair growing on my legs.'

'Don't be silly! Everybody gets that. Look at mine.' And he pulled up his pyjama trouser leg to show the dark hair growing on his shins.

'But it's not just there. It's other places too.'

'Where?'

'I can't say, it's too awful.'

'Do you mean your armpits and down there as well?'

Abercrombie nodded in alarm, concerned that Cuthbert recognised the signs and was about to make a devastating diagnosis.

'Please tell me. Do you know what's wrong with me, Cuthbert?'

'Yes, stupidity. I mean, have you never read a book about growing up? Do you not realise that everything that's happening to you is supposed to happen? It's how you change into a man, silly. It's all completely normal and you're definitely not ill. By the way, anything else to report while you're at it? Because there are a few other things in that book you've never read that you're going to have to get used to as well.'

'Like what?'

'Oh, you'll know when it happens. So now that you're not dying, only getting hairy, can we please get back to sleep?'

'Cuthbert, is it all happening to you too?'

'The hair on the legs, yes, but not much else yet. Everybody goes at a different speed, but I don't think it's a race. We all end up in the same place in the end, don't we?'

'You know everything, Cuthbert. Thanks. I don't suppose I'll ever be able to tell you anything.'

'Well, you could tell me what it feels like to be a gorilla! Now, get some sleep. It's Jampot's test tomorrow and you need all the rest you can get so you can dream about Latin endings.'

*

Over the year, the four boys would all gain six inches in height and would be troubled by voices that for a while could not decide whether to be boys' or men's. Cuthbert's theoretical knowledge of puberty was itself duly put into practice along with all the others and before long the changes in their bodies were starting to become more and more noticeable. Nowhere more so than in games.

In the changing rooms, Cuthbert would catch glimpses of the other boys as they self-consciously slipped from their shirts and trousers into their vests and shorts. He never saw anyone naked, but there were moments when he did see the flex of a new back muscle, a tuft of dark hair in an armpit or the growing bulge of a bicep. And each time it happened, he would feel distinctly odd.

But it wasn't until the summer term when things came to a head. Because of his height he had found himself on the third XV rugby team. The first XV were all senior boys, almost all in their final year at Lauriston. The second XV were those of the same age group who were not quite as skilled, and the third XV was a proving ground for the younger boys, mostly those who had shown some talent for the game or, in Cuthbert's case, those whose physical prowess marked them out.

Morton was also on the team, and of all the boys Cuthbert knew at the school, it was him who had grown and changed the most since that first day, six years before. He'd had to endure the nicknames – Moaning Morton, cry-baby and blubbery – for the first couple of years but when he started to develop physically ahead of almost everyone else, the ribbing soon stopped. Now, he was still only fourteen but stood almost as tall as Cuthbert, but with a much more developed physique.

The thick mop of blond hair that had made him such an attractive-looking child now framed a much more angular face, and his voice had acquired a depth that none of the others could yet aspire to. He had always been friends with Cuthbert, never forgetting the kindness he had been shown that first day of term. And Cuthbert always enjoyed being with him, talking to him and watching him race after the ball, toss it and kick it into touch.

Morton was a natural rugby player, and everyone, including the games master, expected great things of him. Captaincy of the first XV was a prize not beyond his reach. Now, though, he had to content himself with dominating the junior team and, as it turned out, Cuthbert's affections.

Cuthbert had only attended Lauriston as a weekly boarder for the first four years. Since his twelfth birthday, he had become a full-time resident of the college, along with the other three in his dormitory room.

Spending the weekends at school had a number of consequences, one being that he would participate more actively in sports and school-based recreational activities. And it was the Saturday morning rugby practice that was to prove so affecting. The games master, Mr Thomson, would take the third XV through their paces and try to get them working together rather than against each other. Some, like Morton, had considerably more talent than others, but Thomson was surprised to find that Cuthbert was not only a big lad for his age, but he also took to the game.

In his experience, the academically gifted ones were often the least likely to excel on the pitch, but here was Cuthbert racing up the wings and mowing his way through the opposition with a force that was at times unstoppable. He did note that wherever his teammate Morton was, Cuthbert was sure to be close by, and he did for a moment wonder, but just as quickly put it out of his mind to concentrate on the shocking indiscipline of the scrum.

Cuthbert enjoyed the practice sessions for the very reason that they allowed him to be close to Morton. For his part, his friend was oblivious to the attention and only saw in Cuthbert a fellow player whose speed and strength would likely prove useful against their opponents the following week.

In the changing room, Cuthbert stayed close, always trying to catch the scent of the boy, if not his sight. Morton worked hard on the pitch and was invariably sweating when he came in and Cuthbert found him all but intoxicating. Unknowing, Morton would smile at Cuthbert and even rib him about his thin arms, showing off his own much more developed muscles.

'Go on, feel that, Cuthbert. That's what your arms are supposed to be like.'

Cuthbert never took up the offer, for he knew if he did, he would have been unable to hide his true feelings. When Morton saw Cuthbert look away shyly, he mistakenly thought he had caused offence and would even put his arm about his shoulders and tell him he was only joshing.

Cuthbert could barely breathe when Morton spoke to him like this, and he found that he was starting to live just for these Saturday mornings. Every week was like the one before, and Cuthbert was becoming more and more infatuated with the tall blond boy.

He tried to rationalise his thoughts, calling what he felt admiration for the boy's sporting prowess. But he knew that if

Morton never touched the ball, he would still feel exactly the same way about him. He wrestled with his thoughts, but he was well aware what they were called. He had already read and understood enough Latin to know that such feelings between two males was far from uncommon in the ancient world.

However, he knew just as well that in his own time, his thoughts would be labelled as nothing short of an abomination, an affront to God and a sin.

He waited for the infatuation to pass, for that was surely what it was – something meaningless, however dangerous it felt at the time. But, if anything, it intensified. One Saturday, he had to stop himself from reaching out and stroking Morton's hair while they were actually on the pitch, and at that point he resolved to seek help.

As well as being his Latin master, Mr Robertson was also Cuthbert's house master. In theory, he was there almost as a surrogate parent to offer support and counselling to the boys in his charge. In practice, it rarely came to that, for most would not dream of troubling the old man with their adolescent woes. However, Cuthbert could not carry on the way he was going, and he wanted to be told to stop by someone whom he respected.

He knocked on Robertson's office door at the appointed time and was hailed with a hearty, '*Intra!*'

'Ah, Mr Cuthbert, reliably punctual as always. Do take a seat and unburden yourself. Now, how may I be of assistance?'

Cuthbert was sheepish and unable to look his master in the eye. He was now regretting asking to see him, unsure of what possible good could come of it. It was cut and dried. He was just as wicked in his thoughts as anyone who ate knowingly of the fruit of the tree of knowledge, just as tainted as anyone selfish enough to think they were above the law of God, which in this instance was hardly open to debate.

'Come now, Mr Cuthbert, no need to be shy. I think we know each other well enough by now to speak openly. Or do you perhaps think that whatever you have to say may shock an old man like me? Believe me, there is nothing you can say in that chair which has not been said before in the forty-five years I have been sitting on the other side of this desk. So tell me what is worrying you, my boy.'

Cuthbert could still not look at the kindly old eyes that were studying him. He began falteringly, incoherently. 'It's the rugby, sir. It's Morton.'

'As I understand it, Mr Cuthbert, your performance on the pitch has been somewhat of a revelation to Mr Thomson. Is it that you don't like rugby, or are you telling me you don't like Mr Morton, who I believe is your captain?'

Cuthbert looked up, his eyes watery from it all, and shook his head. 'Just the opposite, sir. That's the problem.'

'Ah.' Robertson sat back in his seat, now realising that this was not going to be as difficult as he thought. He had seen countless boys with the same 'problem', but he had to admit that few sought his counsel on the matter. Of course, Cuthbert had always been different, and he could see the boy was more than a little distressed, doubtless because he was trying to intellectualise his feelings.

'Tell me about it, Mr Cuthbert.'

'I can't, sir. It's too terrible to speak of. I just want to be normal, to be good, but then there's this. The way he looks, the way he runs, the way he smells.'

'Smells? Well, that can happen, Mr Cuthbert. Now, what do I need to tell you to make you feel better?'

'I know it's wrong, but I don't know how to stop. I'm frightened I might do something that embarrasses him. That I might be thrown out of the school.'

'Why might that happen, do you think?'

'Because these thoughts are sinful, sir. Because I have angered God.'

'Stuff and nonsense, my boy. You are a child. How can a child commit a sin? And as for angering the Almighty, I rather think He must be quite pleased with you as His creation. It was a fine day's work when He put your mind together. Really, Mr Cuthbert, there's nothing to worry yourself about. Many boys your age have feelings exactly like this and they are harmless – we call it having a crush. Everyone has a crush on someone at some point in their youth.'

The old man's voice was slow and soothing. He knew exactly how to deal with what he saw as such an everyday problem, but which Cuthbert thought of as the very end of his world.

'Here at a boys' school, the only people you meet are other boys, so it's only natural that they should become the objects of these new feelings. It's rather as if our bodies and our minds are practising for falling in love properly one day. But it's something we grow out of. Some day in the future when you are a fine gentleman, you will meet a lovely lady and fall truly in love. You will marry and through your love for each other you will have children of your own. I don't expect I have to tell you the details of how that part works, do I, Mr Cuthbert?'

Cuthbert blushed and shook his head.

'No, I thought not. All that time in the library has certainly not been solely devoted to the lyric poets. Anyway, I assure you that ladies are certain to smell so much more fragrant than Mr Morton. Now, run along with you. There is nothing wrong with you, my boy, that a good long Latin prose translation won't mend.'

Cuthbert looked up again at the master, and he was relieved. He felt he had been offered a sort of absolution, at least in the form of acknowledgement and understanding. Just being able to articulate his concerns, however clumsily, to someone he trusted had helped. As he was leaving, he realised he had been offered no real solution because Mr Robertson had not seen it as a problem to be solved, just one to be lived through. That, Cuthbert realised, would have to be enough for now.

*

There were only two weeks of the summer term left before the long holiday and then he would return to his grandfather's house. There, he would be relieved of any distraction that Morton might present, safely ensconced behind the high stone walls around the estate. And he would be able to spend time with Nanna.

She always welcomed him with such excitement, eager to learn of everything that had happened to him during the term. However, he thought he might need to be a little less forthcoming with his news from now on. He loved her dearly, but he could not imagine sharing some of his innermost thoughts with her.

She, of course, already knew what those thoughts were. She had brought him up from a newborn babe and had watched him grow, and she understood everything about him. She now saw him maturing in both body and mind and had little doubt about what he was becoming – a wonderful young man, but one not without his troubles.

In the last year, his nanny had become frailer with each visit. She would refer euphemistically to 'a little turn' she had had, and which had prompted Mr Dalrymple to effectively retire her within the house.

Now, she had been allocated a small suite of south-facing rooms where he arranged for her to be cared for. He was not about to forget everything she had done for his only grandson. Those rooms were the first ones Cuthbert would make for when he returned from the college, and he would invariably find her seated by the window, quietly reading or looking out onto the gardens. He would sit at her feet and, despite his age, he still needed a warm lap on which to rest his head.

She stroked his hair as he told her of his roommates, his studies, the wonders he was still discovering in the college library and of his dreams for the future. However, she listened to those dreams with some sadness because she was unsure just how much of that future she would be spared to see.

But for the time being, there were still two weeks to go before he might escape, and Cuthbert threw himself into his studies with even greater vigour than before. There were only two more Saturdays to test him on the rugby field and in the locker room, and he resolved to keep as much distance between himself and Morton as he could. Perhaps, he reasoned, that might help.

However, as a result, Morton made an even greater effort to find Cuthbert. He would look for him to pass the ball to, to mark and always ran alongside him when they were instructed to run around the perimeter of the pitch as part of their training. Because they were the closest in height, Mr Thomson, the games master, would also pair Cuthbert and Morton up whenever he wanted the boys to do training exercises that involved physical contact. When that happened, Cuthbert swallowed hard and tried to conceal what he was feeling.

In the locker room, Cuthbert would use his studies as an excuse not to linger, and Morton was beginning to think he had done something wrong. He was physically the most mature of the boys, but he still had a long way to go with his emotional development, as he had no idea what was going on in Cuthbert's heart.

After the last Latin class of the term, Mr Robertson, who

had been watching Cuthbert rather more closely since he had come to see him, asked the boy to wait behind. Cuthbert was alarmed that he might wish to speak about his 'problem' and he was far from ready to have another such conversation. However, the old teacher only wanted to ask him about his Latin.

'You have now been in my classes for six years, Mr Cuthbert. I remember you telling me not long after you started here at Lauriston just how much you enjoyed Latin. Would that still be the case?'

'Certainly, sir. Latin is by far my favourite subject here at the college.'

'And why would that be, Mr Cuthbert?'

'Latin is the language of the gladiators, sir, of the centurions, of the mighty Julius Caesar himself. The stories of great battles, and empires, and heroes were all written in Latin. Being able to read those words brings it all to life.'

'Indeed, Mr Cuthbert, so much cut and thrust to contend with. There are so many exciting tales of great heroism as well as great barbarity to stimulate the mind, but next year I hope I might also stimulate your soul with some of the greatest poets who ever lived. Not to mention that next term you will be starting a new language with me: Greek. And that brings with it a whole new world for you to explore.'

Cuthbert nodded eagerly and explained that he had already been reading ahead and had acquired, in his own time, the beginnings of elementary Ancient Greek.

'Homer awaits us, and I guarantee he will not disappoint. But so do Horace and Ovid and Juvenal. Voices from the past that I think will speak to you anew.'

Just as he was about to go, Mr Robertson asked him to wait a moment. He went to his desk drawer and removed a slim leather-bound volume. 'I would like you to have this,

Mr Cuthbert. His poetry is so often misunderstood, even proscribed, but I think he may have been writing just for you. So please take this and make a new friend.'

Cuthbert thanked his master and accepted the book. On the cover inscribed in gold were the words *Gaius Valerius Catullus, Carmina*.

'You may have already heard the name Catullus, but until you read his poems of love and longing you do not know the man. He does not form part of our syllabus and he is beyond most of my students, but I think you may be ready for this, Mr Cuthbert. Take him and keep him safe. Now, run along and do whatever it is you do now.'

*

On the last day of teaching before the summer recess, Cuthbert and his class had only one final lesson, with the Reverend Fleming. He was a difficult man to age. His face was unlined, but his hair, while thick, was as white as the chalk dust on his gown. He always wore his ecclesiastical dog collar, and all his classes were prefaced by short, somewhat menacing prayers.

He taught history at the college, but, once a week, he also took Cuthbert's class for religious instruction. His history classes tended to be heavily geared towards religious topics – the history of the Scottish Reformation being his pet subject – and his religious instruction classes took on a distinctly historical bent.

Today, in his final lesson of the year, however, he had decided to embark on a more theological topic. He stood at the front of the class of twenty boys and his eyes widened at the prospect of discussing his favourite subject.

'Let me ask you an important question, gentlemen. What is a sin?'

Jenner's hand shot up and with a nod from Fleming he offered a fairly stock answer: 'It is an offence against Almighty God, sir.'

'And how do we know what God wishes us to do?'

Another boy reached for this one with a straining arm: 'Because of His laws, sir. There are the ten commandments.'

'So,' Fleming mused, 'if there is no law, is there no sin?'

The boy who had answered looked at Reverend Fleming, unsure if it was a trick question, and chose to leave his mouth open and empty rather than risk saying the wrong thing.

'Anyone?'

Cuthbert raised his hand only after he saw that no one else was willing to take up the gauntlet. 'As long as there has been a God, sir, there has always been law. And God is eternal, so the law is eternal too. Long before the ten commandments, Adam and Eve broke the law of God in the Garden of Eden. And even before man was created, Lucifer transgressed the law of God and was cast out of heaven. So, with a belief in an eternal God, we must believe in His eternal law and we must acknowledge the eternal existence of sin.'

The other boys were used to these kinds of logical arguments from Cuthbert, but they didn't necessarily follow them or find them anything but annoying.

'Indeed, Mr Cuthbert, our first parents in the Garden of Eden were seduced by the subtlety and temptation of Satan and sinned in the eating of the forbidden fruit. And the rest of your argument is certainly worthy of discussion, but perhaps we should take a more practical approach.'

The master knew he needed to keep the class's interest and decided to bring the lesson back into the realms of their own experience. 'Gentlemen, can you name a sin?'

A forest of hands went up and the master called on them in quick succession.

'Killing someone, sir.'

'Not going to church, sir.'

'Stealing, sir.'

'Being proud, sir.'

'Having impure thoughts, sir.'

The last one caused those at the back to stifle their giggles, but they were quickly brought to heel by a stern glance from the Reverend Fleming.

'Indeed, Mr Cruikshank, thank you for that sterling example. No doubt one of the most relevant for a class such as this. Now, gentlemen, I want you to think again. This time, in your jotters I wish you to write a single word to complete this phrase.' He chalked on the board in large letters, *To sin is to be* . . .

Pens were chewed as the class thought what to write and some found their word of choice rather faster than others. Fleming gave them some time and enjoyed watching the almost visible machinations of their minds as they wrestled with their answer.

When he thought most had written something, he handed his chalk to Abercrombie and asked him to go to the board and write up his word. Never wanting to be first, he nervously rose from his seat and, in comparison to the master's fine script, the boy scrawled the word 'wrong'. The chalk was passed to Morton, who wrote 'evil', and Jenner, who carefully and very neatly wrote 'disobedient'.

'All very good, and what about you, Mr Cruikshank. What can you offer us?'

He wrote the word 'mistaken', which drew a slight frown from the master, who nonetheless decided to let it pass and turned his attention to Cuthbert. He took the chalk and wrote on the board in his usual small and precise script the word 'selfish'.

'Ah, now that is an interesting contribution. Would you care to elaborate, Mr Cuthbert?'

Of course, this was not a question but an instruction, and he remained at the board.

'We all have duties and responsibilities, sir. And some of those we owe to God. I think we commit a sin when we place ourselves before or even ahead of God. The commission of any sin is thus a selfish act.'

The Reverend Fleming looked the boy over as he stood expounding his theology with the wit and assurance of someone twice his age. Cuthbert was different, and the masters at the college had already been vying to take credit for his intellect. In truth, however, everything Cuthbert was, was his own. Now, he waited to be allowed to take his seat or to be invited to offer further explanation. Fleming would have dearly loved to engage in a debate about the very nature of sin with this boy, but he was well aware there were nineteen other pairs of eyes on him, waiting for another question.

'Quite so, Cuthbert. Be seated. Now, let us turn our attentions to what the Old Testament tells us. Let us read some of that fine and uplifting book, Leviticus.'

Like many boys his age, Cuthbert had an unwavering belief in God. He had known nothing else, and his entire education had been set against a Presbyterian backdrop. There was no possibility of any other way of thinking. Any outlets for dissent or for questioning could only be channelled into the subtle interpretation of scripture rather than any wholesale refutation of it.

He was still living in an age of innocence, and he was only just beginning to see, a little ahead of his contemporaries, that the world might be a more complicated maze to navigate than he had been led to believe. He had started to read books about other religions. In them, he would see just how devoutly opinions were held which were the antithesis of what he had been taught to believe. And, of course, he spent many hours in the company of the ancients who had very different views on what might be right and wrong, what might be considered virtuous and what might be called a sin.

The copy of Catullus' poems given to him by Mr Robertson only a couple of days before was already having its effect, for suddenly a new view of the world was opening up – a world of passion. However, Cuthbert firmly believed what he had said at the Reverend Fleming's blackboard. He did think sin was something eternal, and he did think it arose from selfishness.

Nevertheless, he was far from sure that what he was feeling for Morton was anything but generous, giving and, ultimately, a form of love. How could love, any kind of love, ever be selfish?

Chapter 10

London: 27 September 1931

Through a crack in the bedroom curtains, the thin morning light lit his head as he lay beside Cuthbert. He was still sleeping, lying on his side and Cuthbert could study him closely. His blond hair was short at the sides but longer on top, and the long strands that he normally had well under control with hair oil were loose and had tumbled across his eyes. His eyebrows were much darker, as were his lashes, but the blond morning stubble on his chin and cheeks almost sparkled in the sunlight.

He shifted in the bed without waking, and Cuthbert tried ever so gently to stroke the stray locks from his eyes, but not gently enough. Jaeger opened his eyes and looked up at Cuthbert, who was leaning on one elbow at his side looking down at him.

'Good morning. Did you sleep well?'

'You know I always sleep well in your bed, Jack. Don't misunderstand me, old man. It has nothing to do with you. It's just that you have such a damned fine mattress.'

Cuthbert mock-punched him on the shoulder, and they laughed and kissed.

'It's Sunday, isn't it? Does that mean we can just stay in bed?'

'No, it doesn't. Madame Smith will be making us breakfast and the least we can do is get up to eat it.'

'I suppose so. Just one more kiss, though?'

Jaeger rose naked from the bed, and Cuthbert took in the beauty of the man. The tall Austrian had been a competitive swimmer in his youth, and he still had the physique of a lean athlete. The blond down on his body formed an aura around the outline of his long limbs in this light. Cuthbert drank him in as he flexed and bent to stretch his muscles as he did every morning before bathing.

After ten minutes of his morning exercise routine, he turned to Cuthbert and asked him to come and wash his back for him. Just as his eager bathing attendant was getting up himself, there was a knock on the bedroom door. Jaeger, in a reflex move, reached for a robe to cover himself. Cuthbert called out from the bedroom, 'Yes, madame, what is it?'

She replied without coming in, 'Good morning, monsieur. I am sorry to disturb you, but I have brought you and Herr Jaeger some coffee. I thought, being Sunday, you may wish to breakfast in your room. I'll leave the tray outside on the hall table.'

Jaeger was smiling at Cuthbert's slightly embarrassed expression, and he threw down the robe he had been holding over his groin.

'Discreet, isn't she, Jack?'

'Always.'

Jaeger listened at the door. When the housekeeper's footsteps disappeared back down the stairs, he opened the door and went naked into the hall to collect the tray.

'Erich, please!'

'What? I'm sure even if she saw me, I have nothing that would shock such a woman of the world as that one.'

'Erich, you are the limit sometimes.'

'Am I? You see, I don't think we're anywhere near the limit of all this yet.'

Cuthbert got out of bed and put on the discarded robe. 'Here, let me take that tray, Erich. We can have it over here by the window.'

'Don't change the subject, Jack.'

'I'm not. I just don't want to let the coffee go cold.'

'So?'

'So what are you saying, Erich?'

'You great oaf. I'm trying to tell you that I love you, Jack Cuthbert. That I've never met anyone like you and that I want to spend a thousand, ten thousand, mornings like this one. I want to wake up and find you looking at me with those eyes, with that hunger. You might be a little late to this party, Jack, but you've been making up for lost time, and I'm glad you've let me into your life.

'Of course, there's so much I still don't know about you or you about me. All those years when we were alive in this world together but apart. There are so many stories still to tell each other. There are so many more days and nights that we need to spend together before we get anywhere near that limit.'

Cuthbert reached out to him across the breakfast tray and put his hand around the back of his neck and pulled him towards his lips. The kiss was long and deep and was everything Cuthbert had to say by way of reply, and Jaeger understood him perfectly.

He got up, took Cuthbert by the hand and told him that sometimes coffee was best drunk cold.

*

Later, when they were both washed and dressed, they relaxed in the morning room. There, Madame Smith served them more coffee with warm croissants and small rolls that Cuthbert did not recognise. When Jaeger saw them though, he smiled broadly at the housekeeper.

'*Kaisersemmel!* How did you know they were my favourite? Look here, Cuthbert, they are a Viennese specialty. I used to have them all the time at my Oma's house. *Merci, vous êtes bien gentille, madame.*'

'*De rien, monsieur. C'est mon plaisir de vous servir.*'

Madame Smith left them to their morning newspapers, but she had enjoyed the smile on Cuthbert's face. She had made the little effort as much for him as for his guest.

'She really is a find, Jack. Whatever you do, don't ever let her go.'

'Don't worry, I know exactly what I've got with that fine woman, and I am not about to do anything to lose her. The truth is, if she asked me to double her wages tomorrow, I would, but I also know she would never ask.'

'Well, I hope you do pay her well. I would be really quite cross with you if you didn't.'

'Don't worry, I'm quite sure she has everything she needs. Or almost everything. No one has it all.'

They settled into the comfort of a Sunday morning at home, sipping the hot, strong coffee and nibbling absentmindedly on the fresh pastries. Cuthbert was losing himself in a lengthy article in *The Sunday Times* on the record unemployment figures, while Jaeger was reading *The Sunday Graphic* and absorbed in an item about a double murder in Hammersmith.

'I say, is this one of yours, Jack?'

Cuthbert shook his head, not to deny it but to indicate he could not talk about such things. He put down his paper and felt the need to explain. 'You have to understand, Erich, there will always be things I can't talk about with you. I work in a world with rules that are unbreakable. You mustn't think less of me because of it. It's not a matter of trust but one of honour. I owe a great deal to those in my care – the living and the dead – and I must never give them anything less than total respect.'

Jaeger could see how earnest he was and how pained he was in the explanation.

'Jack, please don't worry about it. Of course, I understand. I just think sometimes you might need to talk. You carry a terrible burden in that big heart of yours. I want you to know that I'm here, that I'll listen, if you ever need me.'

'That means more to me than I can say. Just know that if I've been a little distracted of late, it is only because the case I'm working on at present is especially troubling. I cannot tell you any details other than to say it involves children, young children.'

'I see. I can't imagine what that must be like for you. I'm so sorry, Jack.'

'It's part of the job – and one I was only too aware of when I signed on. But I do confess it has always been the most difficult part of it all for me.'

'For everyone in your profession, I would think.'

Cuthbert threw his paper aside and got up to walk to the window. He looked out across the square through the trees to the terrace opposite and seemed to Jaeger to be lost in his thoughts. 'Erich, might I ask you something? Do you ever think what it might be like to be a father?'

'All men wonder that, I suspect, at least at some point in their lives. I know that when my own father died it did make me think about what it all meant. He was a good man, but a distant one for most of my life. He was ill for some time, you know, and towards the end we had some of the longest conversations together that we ever had.'

'Did he know?'

'About me? I think all parents know, don't they? He said

nothing, but I'm not sure he would have known how to, if he would even have had the words. But he did talk about what it had meant to him when I was born. He said his life changed for ever in that instant, and that it was the moment he felt he truly became a man.'

'So do you think you and I will always be incomplete?'

'Not if we have each other. I feel that you complete me, Jack. And I hope I might do the same for you.'

Cuthbert turned from the window and went back to the table. 'I know what you mean. Even when you went away a few weeks ago, I felt a part of me went missing. But when you're here in this room, it feels right, and I feel whole again.'

Jaeger threw his newspaper aside and got up. 'Is it something about a Sunday, Jack? All I want to do is lie down.'

'I doubt very much that's all you want to do, but Madame Smith will be leaving in an hour. It's her afternoon off and she is unlikely to be home before nightfall. Why don't we finish our coffee and when she's gone, we can perhaps take the papers upstairs?'

*

When they lay spent again in each other's arms, Cuthbert felt he had to ask Jaeger something he had never asked him before. 'Erich, did you ever think this was wrong?'

'How could this possibly be wrong?'

'I mean, when you were growing up, when it first dawned on you what kind of man you were.'

'Well, for one thing, it was a long time before I was a man. And it was the same way for you too, even if you've never admitted it to yourself. And to answer your question, no, I've never felt it was wrong. If it's wrong, then I'm wrong; I'm a mistake, something to be fixed. And I'm not. I'm Erich Jaeger and I'm proud of what I am. I don't hurt anyone, and I never have. This isn't a sin, Jack, if that's what you're getting at. It is, isn't it? You think God's watching you right now, lying here with me, and He's shaking his head in some sort of celestial disapproval. Well, as far as I'm concerned, God lost the right to pass judgement at the Somme, at Mons and at Ypres.' Jaeger struggled free of Cuthbert's embrace and sat on the side of the bed.

'I'm sorry, Erich. I didn't mean what we have is wrong. It's still so new to me and I've still got so much work to do to understand it. What I said was clumsy, nothing more. Forgive me.'

'You fool, you don't need me to forgive you. You just need to forgive yourself. Now, get ready because I'm taking us both out to dinner at the Savoy Grill, but I'm afraid you're paying. Sins always have to be paid for, you know. Didn't they teach you at Sunday School, old man?'

*

It was almost ten o'clock when Madame Smith slipped quietly home. She turned her latchkey in the lock, trying not to make too much noise, but when she opened the door, she could hear the two men joking loudly in the drawing room.

Normally, she would have gone straight to bed, but the joy in their laughter was infectious and she thought she might bid them goodnight. She knocked on the door and waited for Cuthbert to invite her in, which he did with great enthusiasm. Both men had been drinking but were far from drunk, although Cuthbert's mood was as light as she'd ever seen it.

'We've just had such a wonderful evening, madame. I hope you've enjoyed your time off just as much.'

'Indeed, monsieur. I have been to my club in Chelsea, and it was as enjoyable as ever.'

'What club is this, madame? Would we have been?'

Cuthbert parried Jaeger's question, knowing that Madame Smith probably did not wish to share that much with his house guest. 'You've probably been to every club in London, Erich. But tell madame about that wine you ordered at the Savoy. I had never heard of it, but it was sublime. French, of course. We really must get some for the cellar. What was the name of it?'

Madame Smith found Cuthbert's protectiveness endearing but could not help feeling that if anyone would understand the kind of ladies' club she chose to frequent, it might be Herr Jaeger. Nonetheless, she did not wait for his answer and, with a smile, left them to their brandies.

*

The next morning, Jaeger had to go home, but this time, rather than slipping away to catch the earliest of trains, he was able first to have breakfast. Cuthbert, who rarely drank as much as he had the day before, woke to find his constitution in a state of rebellion. His head ached almost as much as his limbs, and he struggled to get up.

He bathed and shaved and drank several glasses of water to rehydrate himself, and by the time he sat at the breakfast table he at least appeared unscathed by the night's revelries. Jaeger, for his part, was considerably more practised and was unaffected by it all. He did, however, find Cuthbert's delicate demeanour amusing and said so, much to his host's annoyance.

'Why don't you just sit quietly, perhaps on your hands, and drink your coffee? And before you say anything, I know that is a physical impossibility, but I think you get the gist.'

'You really are a magnificent specimen of male grumpiness, Jack Cuthbert, but don't worry, you're going to get much better at drinking red wine. Trust me.'

Even feeling the way that he did, Cuthbert still managed

to smile, and Jaeger brushed the back of his hand with his. When they said goodbye, once again to resume their separate lives, they agreed to spend the whole of the coming weekend together and that made their parting just about tolerable for them both.

*

By the time Cuthbert had walked to St Thomas's, the air had cleared away most of whatever was clogging his brain. Nevertheless, he knew he needed to take the morning a little more slowly than usual in case he should make a mistake.

Morgenthal, who saw him arrive, immediately greeted him a little too loudly and launched into a rhapsody on the colours of autumn. Cuthbert indulged him, for he did not have the energy to do otherwise. 'We have the case conference at the Yard this afternoon, sir. I can't tell you how interesting it is to attend. Thank you for making that possible.'

Cuthbert was aware that the working relationship he had built with C.I.D. was unusual and to some perhaps even inappropriate. However, he had firmly come to believe that he could make his greatest contribution to a case if he was regarded as part of the investigative team. He was keen to share that belief with his assistant in the hope that he might do likewise.

'You do know, Simon, that what we have there is a little unconventional. I'm sure you speak with your peers in the other centres, and you've no doubt learned that few forensic specialists, such as ourselves, ever see the inside of a place like the duty room of Scotland Yard's murder squad. Some would even say we have no right to be there.'

'But you're there at the chief inspector's invitation. He values your input greatly.'

'I hope that is the case, but I just want you to be aware that such teamwork is not always a given in our field. In fact, it has to be worked for. And I believe it is worth it, not just for the added satisfaction it can give to the job, but also, even in a small way, to help solve some of these terrible crimes.'

Morgenthal felt Cuthbert was very much underestimating what he gave to his colleagues at the Yard – his expertise, his insight, his experience and above all his formidable intellect. No one, he thought, would be foolish enough to pass up on that kind of help. As for himself, he was far from sure he could match that kind of contribution, but it was still early days and he reassured himself that he still had much to learn.

*

By the afternoon, Cuthbert was feeling human again and he was happy to walk together with Morgenthal over to Scotland Yard. Lately, when he had been coming to see the team with his assistant, he had allowed the young Englishman to deal with the constable on reception. For unfathomable reasons, after more than five years, Cuthbert's Scottish accent still posed a problem for the succession of young London bobbies who occupied the chair. Morgenthal's clipped vowels, however, always got them in first time.

At the case conference, Baker reported on his latest findings. He stood by the board and pointed at the name of each of the three women buried in the churchyard at St Gregory's.

'The only known relative we have for Mary Nightingale is a Mr George Grayson. Unfortunately, he's not at the address in Lambeth the vicar gave us, and by the looks of it hasn't been there for some time. A neighbour did say he had a young child in his care but only briefly. She wasn't able to tell me anything more.

'Margaret Webb's parents were not much more helpful, I'm afraid. The father has died since the daughter's suicide and the mother is not at all *compos mentis*. I spoke with a niece who was unable to give me much. I've still to visit Rose Smith's sister out by Battersea, which I'll be doing after this.'

'Do we have anything else on the background to these nuns?'

'I've spoken again with the mother superior, sir, and I've also been in touch with the Mother House of their order up in Northumberland. Seems that our head nun has quite a knowledge of herbs. Apparently, she was in charge of the medical herb garden up there in her younger days and was responsible for making all kinds of medicines.'

Mowbray stood up and went to the pinboard to peer at her picture. 'Was she really? Good work, Baker. What else do we have?'

'I've been looking into the Tilly Barnaby case, sir. I thought that might be a useful line of inquiry. According to the files, she was found dead just over a year ago on the eighth of September 1930. The post mortem examination showed that she had died as a result of drowning which was considered to be self-induced — a witness had seen her throw herself from Waterloo Bridge into the Thames. The report also states that she had recently been pregnant but had not carried the child to full term. There was no evidence of "mechanical trauma", and the pathologist concluded she had most likely undergone some form of chemical abortion around three weeks prior to her suicide.

'Well, well, and who do we know that is good at concocting the means to induce an abortion like that?'

'Are you suggesting this might be connected to the orphanage, sir?'

'Why not? You said this tansy was used for that, didn't you, doctor?'

Cuthbert looked at Morgenthal and urged him to speak.

'Yes, chief inspector, tansy tea has certainly been used for that for years, but it would be remiss of me not to point out that there are many other drugs Miss Barnaby might have used to rid herself of the child.'

'Nevertheless, do some digging, Baker. Find out if there is any connection between this Barnaby girl and the nuns. She lived in the grounds, so it stands to reason she would have come into contact with them. There's at least two of them who would have had the know-how to make this tansy tea. And let's not forget her own mother has been growing the stuff.'

A W.P.C. came over to the group working at the board and tried to catch Mowbray's eye. 'Begging your pardon, sir, but there's a telephone call for Dr Simon Morgenthal.'

Mowbray just pointed at the young man and the W.P.C. said, 'I believe it's your wife, sir, and she says it's urgent. She sounds quite distressed.'

Morgenthal looked up in alarm at the others, and it was Mowbray who said, 'Well, man, get going!' He leapt from the chair and followed the W.P.C. to the phone.

'Sarah, darling, what is it? Are you all right?'

'Simon, it's little Jack. He's burning up. He was irritable all morning but now his temperature is over a hundred. What should I do?'

'Stay calm and tell me some more. First, is he breathing normally?'

'Yes, yes, I think so.'

'And his colour? Can you describe the colour of his skin to me?'

'He's very flushed. His cheeks are bright red.'

'Does he have any sort of rash on his body? Check his chest and his back, Sarah.'

'No, it looks fine, I think.'

'That's all good. You're doing very well. Is the little fellow drowsy at all?'

'No, quite the opposite.'

'That's a good sign. Will he take anything to drink? Can he swallow?'

'Yes, I gave him a little water earlier and he took that.'

'That's good. Is he moving his head all right or do you think his neck might be stiff?'

'No, he's very agitated, and I can hardly keep him still.'

'All right. Here's what you have to do. Get two facecloths and soak them in cool but not cold water and place one on his forehead and another on the back of his neck. Also, give the little chap a sponge bath with tepid water. That will all help bring his temperature down. I'll come home right away but start doing all that just now. I'm at Scotland Yard, darling. I'll be home as soon as I can.'

Morgenthal was agitated himself at the thought of what he might be dealing with and with having to ask to leave the meeting. He went back to the group around the case board.

Mowbray looked him over and said, 'Well, should you still be here?'

'I'm terribly sorry, but I was hoping I may be excused, sir. Dr Cuthbert, it's little Jack. He's running a high fever, and I think I should take a look at him, with your permission of course.'

'Go, laddie. You can't take chances when they're that young. These little ones will still be here when you get back.'

Morgenthal thanked everyone and left quickly.

'You're training that lad up well, Jack.'

'Chief inspector, let's not forget ourselves. This is the duty room and Detective Sergeant Baker is still here.'

Mowbray took the rebuke on the nose.

'My apologies, *Doctor* Cuthbert. I was just saying that *Doctor* Morgenthal is developing into a fine *police surgeon*. Perhaps you should just send him over in your stead when you start to find the stairs a bit of a challenge. I mean, you are the oldest one here, after all.'

Sergeant Baker had to stifle his laughter as Cuthbert's left eyebrow arched high in response to Mowbray's apology, but the chief inspector saw him, and the chuckle promptly turned into an embarrassed cough.

'Let's call it a day there. Baker, get me a connection between Tilly and any of the nuns, and we'll overlook your insubordination.'

'Right away, sir.'

Baker thought it might be best to speak with Dickson Barnaby again rather than the nuns. He reasoned that the girl's father might be more willing to shed light on her friendships and her state of mind than the sisters, especially since he would have to get past the mother superior in order to speak with any of them. He drove out to St Gregory's and by good fortune met Mr Barnaby pushing a wheelbarrow up towards the main house.

'I'm sorry to disturb you again, sir, but I wonder if you could answer a few more questions.'

'Not a problem. Just let me get rid of this and we can sit over by the old oak.'

He parked the barrow and took off his gloves and tossed them in. He took Baker towards a circular bench that had been built around a mature oak tree halfway down the lawn.

'Still not too bad for the time of year, but I can see it changing by the end of the week. Lots to be done before then. Nature does a lot herself, but there's always a helping hand needed from the gardener if you want it looking like this.'

The grounds were indeed beautiful, and the views from the bench up across the grass and along the herbaceous borders towards the house were a credit to him.

'What is it I can help you with?'

'I wanted to ask you a little about your daughter, Tilly.'

'What for, lad? She's paid her price surely for what she done.'

'I know, Mr Barnaby. It's just that there are some loose ends we're trying to tie up. Did Tilly have much to do with the nuns?'

'Well, I don't rightly know. She were brought up here. She and her brother used to play with the children. So they would have come into contact with the nuns. I did see her a few times chatting in more recent years with the young one. What is it they call her, Mary Frances? They were about the same age, I expect, so maybe they had something in common. Not sure what, though.'

'And we know your daughter was pregnant not long before she died and that she lost the baby.'

'You mean got rid of the baby, don't you? Don't be frightened of saying it like it is, not to me.'

'Do you know how she went about it?'

'I didn't even know she was pregnant, poor lass. I don't think she told anyone. She must have been so alone in that, so frightened. She were never away anywhere, though, so I don't think she went off to have it done. All I remember is her being really ill for a couple of days. Something she ate or drank, she said. But it looked worse than that. She were right pale and being sick all the time. I wanted to call a doctor, but she wouldn't have it. I should have done. I know that now.'

'Did she have much to do with the mother superior?'

'Oh, no. Nobody has much to do with her. She wouldn't have had time for my Tilly. She barely has time for me.'

'Thank you, Mr Barnaby. That's been very helpful.'

'You don't think what happened with Tilly has anything to do with all this other business, do you?'

'We're trying to keep an open mind, Mr Barnaby.'

*

When Simon Morgenthal got home, he was breathless from racing up the stairs. Sarah met him at the door and told him that their son's temperature had already come down a little.

'He's still hot, but the sponge bath and the cool flannels seem to be helping. He's a bit more settled.'

'Where is he? I need to see him.'

In the nursery, the boy was in his cot. As his mother had said, he was still hot to the touch and his cheeks were flushed. Morgenthal went through a quick physical examination and contented himself that there appeared to be no serious cause for the fever.

'What do you think it is, Simon?'

'Honestly, Sarah, it could be a hundred and one different things, and most of them just run their course. He's hot, but he's not gravely unwell, and I think we should continue doing what you've been doing, just keeping his temperature down and keeping him comfortable. If he stops drinking, if he stops responding, if he stops wetting his nappy, then we can start to worry, but as long as he's doing all those things, he'll get better. Little ones get sick so quickly, almost before your eyes, but they also get better just as fast. So you're not to worry, my darling.'

'I just thought we might lose him. I couldn't imagine anything more awful, could you?'

Morgenthal could not possibly share with his wife just what he had to imagine when it came to young children. But looking down at his own son, unwell now but soon to be thriving again, he could not help but think of those terrible photographs pinned to the board in the duty room. They were three small children, not that unlike his own son, who were let down so badly by the adults around them. The thought of anyone deliberately harming his boy filled Morgenthal with an almost primordial anger.

He stayed with Sarah and the child, sponging him and cooling him, helping him drink and watching him slowly return to normal. By late evening his temperature was back to normal, and he was looking for his dinner. The boy was also confused to find his parents too worn out to play with him.

'It won't be the last fright that little soldier gives us, but it gets easier as they get older, and at least they can tell you where it hurts.'

'It hurts here, Simon.' Sarah took her husband's hand and pressed it to her heart.

'I know, my darling, but now it's your turn to get some sleep. Come on, let's get you to bed.'

Chapter 11

London: 28 September 1931

Finding Rose Smith's sister was Baker's last hope of tracking down any of the relatives of the suicides. According to the Reverend Henshall, she lived in Wandsworth, near the vast building site that was soon to be the new Battersea Power Station. Already two huge chimneys were thrusting their way up from the great red-brick cathedral of a structure on the bank of the Thames, and it was rumoured that two more were planned to follow.

Her street was like all the others he was used to in the poorer parts of London, south of the river – lines of squat brick buildings, cramped and overcrowded, facing off against each other across cobbled streets smeared with horse manure. His police car was the only one in the street and was already drawing a crowd of scruffy young boys eager to peer through its windows and admire the dashboard. Gruffly, he waved them away and made it clear that if he found so much as a fingerprint on the paint work, he'd run them all in.

The door was answered by a woman who was probably in her late twenties but looked ten years older. She was carrying a toddler on her hip, and another slightly older child sucking at his thumb was clinging to her skirts. She was heavily pregnant and when she saw him on her doorstep, she sighed and rolled her eyes.

'Look, when I've got it, you'll get it. I can't give you what I haven't got. It's payday today, so he'll be back at six. Can you not wait three more hours?'

'I'm sorry, madam, I'm not here collecting.' He took his warrant card from his jacket pocket and held it out for her to read. 'Detective Sergeant Baker, Scotland Yard. I'm trying to locate a Mrs Price, a Mrs Evelyn Price.'

'I'm Mrs Price. What's this about? Has something happened to my George?'

'No, no, nothing like that, Mrs Price, please don't upset yourself. I'm conducting inquiries in connection with a Miss Rose Smith, who I believe was your late sister.'

She sank back from the door, stiffened and pulled the children closer to her. 'What do you want to be asking about Rose for?'

'Perhaps I might come in, Mrs Price. It's a bit delicate.'

The house was cold, with little comfort. There were no rugs on the floors and the few pieces of furniture were old and scraped. A large damp patch on the wall of the front room was causing the paper to peel back and the curtains on the street window were little more than old sheets. She sat down awkwardly in the only chair in the room and Baker removed his hat. She looked the policeman over suspiciously. Nothing he was about to say could possibly be good.

'Am I right in thinking that Rose Smith was your sister, Mrs Price?'

The woman nodded and pulled the toddler in her lap closer and caressed his thin blond hair for comfort.

'I realise this is very difficult for you, but I need to ask you about your sister's death.'

'She had no right to do what she did. No right at all. She just left us. She put her head in the oven and didn't even give a tuppenny damn for any of us, not even her own little Charlie.'

'So she had a son. How old would he be?'

'Charlie's four, almost the same age as my little George here.' She put her arm about the small boy standing at her side, who, hearing his name, dropped his eyes to the floor.

'And where's Charlie now? What happened to him, Mrs Price?'

She looked at Baker with a frown that was as defensive as it was an admonishment. 'Why do you need to know about Charlie?'

'It's part of our inquiries, madam. Please, could you tell me what happened to the child?'

She shifted her weight in the chair, trying to find some support for her back, and winced in sharp discomfort. He thought she might be unable or unwilling to talk, but then she sighed heavily and told him.

'The day it happened, I was due to meet her. She lived just around the corner, see, and we would walk the kiddies together. She hadn't been right for weeks, and I should've seen it, but I suppose I was too wrapped up in my own worries.

'Anyway, when I got there, I could hear her Charlie crying blue murder in the house, but there was no answer at the door. When I pushed the letterbox, I could smell it, the gas. I panicked – I mean, what was I supposed to do? I got Mr Greene, the man next door, and he managed to force the lock.

'Charlie was in the front room, bawling his eyes out, and she were lying on the floor in the back in front of the oven. She'd shut the kitchen door and put towels down. I suppose to make it quicker for her and to save Charlie. But everybody said he was lucky to be alive. Mr Greene smashed the kitchen window to let in some air – the smell was something awful – and he pulled her out of the oven, but there was no life left in the poor cow. I got left with everything to sort out. It wasn't fair. It wasn't fair on little Charlie most of all.'

'So you looked after him?'

'Well, what was I supposed to do – just leave the poor soul? I brought him here, but you can see for yourself it's no palace, right enough. Honest truth is we can hardly feed ourselves, let alone another mouth. And he was so upset, always crying for his mum.

'When she came and said she could make it easier, I didn't know what to do. She was nice enough, but I didn't know who she was. She knew all about Rose though. She said the kiddies often had a hard time when they were left like that, that it was for the best if they were taken away from it all and allowed to grow up differently. She said she could take him somewhere in the country, where he'd be with other kiddies the same. I didn't know what to say, though. I mean, he was Rose's little one and I was his Auntie Evie.

'By rights, I should have been taking care of him. But look at us. Look at me. Two little ones of my own and another on the way. What could I give the poor little sod? Not somewhere nice, that's for sure. So I let her take him. Just like that.'

Baker was taking notes as she spoke, but he could see that she was conflicted about the choice she had made. He could not imagine giving a child away to a relative stranger, but then he was not her, living like this, with two young children and awaiting a third, fighting to keep the rent collector from the door.

'Who was this woman, Mrs Price?'

'She probably told me her name, but it was all so mixed up at the time. She seemed kind. And, of course, she was one of the nuns. I'd seen them at the church when we buried Rose.

They weren't at the service, but some of them were watching from over by the wall.'

'Can you describe her?'

'They all look the same in that get-up, don't they?'

'Have you seen the boy since he was taken away?'

'Oh no. She was very firm about that. It was for his own good, she said. It needed to be a clean break. He would have a better life if he was allowed to forget all about his mum and where he came from . . .' Mrs Price's voice cracked and she fought back tears.

Then she broke down completely, and the child in her lap started to wail along with her. Baker took a step towards her, but the older child who was leaning into his mother's side recoiled. Baker kept his distance in case he made the situation even worse and allowed the woman to compose herself again.

'I'm sorry. If truth be told, I'm sorry I ever let him go. But why are you asking about all this? I know Rose broke the law, but you can hardly blame the little one for it.'

Baker could see she was already distressed and wasn't sure whether he should tell her the truth, but she had to know.

'I'm afraid I might have some more bad news for you, Mrs Price. You see, we've found the body of a small boy, and we think it could be your nephew.'

She looked at him in disbelief and shook her head. 'No, you've got that wrong. Charlie's in an orphanage. He's safe. He's with other children. There must be a mistake.'

'That's possible, Mrs Price, but we need to be sure. Tell me, did Mr Price know Charlie well? Might he be able to identify him?'

She sat in silence.

'Mrs Price, are you all right? Is there someone I can get for you?'

She was staring into space. Her imagination was trying to

hold on to everything that should have been, but all she could find was darkness.

'It's all my fault. I let her take the boy. She said he would be safe, and I believed her. I'll go to hell for this, won't I?'

'Mrs Price, I know this must be a terrible shock, but we need to find out if this little lad really is Charlie, and if he is, we need to find out what happened. We're going to need your help. Do you think your husband might be able to identify the body?'

'I'll do it. He was mine to look after. It should be me that does it.'

'No, Mrs Price, we can't ask that of you.'

'I said I'll do it. Just tell me where.'

*

When a relative had to view a body in the mortuary at St Thomas's, Cuthbert was meticulous in the preparations. He had gone through the procedure countless times, but for every grieving parent, sibling or child, it was likely the first time for them and very probably the worst day of their lives.

Some departments allowed the viewing of bodies in the main dissection room, but Cuthbert had never considered this appropriate. Why did people have to see where their loved ones had been examined, surrounded by all the medical implements and apparatus? No, he preferred an altogether more respectful solution and had dedicated a side room for such purposes.

There, the body could be laid out on a table rather than a slab, where there could be flowers instead of forceps and saws, and where there could be some dignity for both the living and the dead.

When Mrs Price arrived with Sergeant Baker the next morning, Cuthbert was at once concerned. She was by his reckoning almost at full term in her pregnancy and looked worn out by everything. The very last thing she needed in her life was to identify a dead child.

He took her hand. 'My name is Dr Cuthbert. Thank you for coming here today, Mrs Price. Would you like to have a seat and perhaps we can get you some tea?'

She looked up at the tall, handsome gentleman who was speaking to her so kindly in such a soft Scottish accent, and she could not help but feel comforted. However, she wanted to get this all over with, and she declined.

'I understand perfectly, Mrs Price. Let me tell you what will happen. In this room here, we have prepared what we need you to look at. When you go in, the boy will be covered in a white sheet. I will raise the sheet to allow you to see the boy's face, and all you have to say is yes or no – is it your nephew Charlie or not. I know this is very hard, but is that all right, Mrs Price?'

She took a breath and asked him to open the door.

Cuthbert went in first and stood on the far side of the table. She hesitated on the threshold, unsure of what she was about to see. All there was in the plain room was a long rectangle covered in white, with an odd mound at the top end.

'Are you ready for me to show you, Mrs Price?'

She swallowed hard as she nodded, and Cuthbert deftly lifted the top of the sheet and held it up, revealing only the boy's small face. He had been washed after his post mortem examination and any incisions were well hidden. His hair had been carefully smoothed back and parted and the only real clue that he wasn't sleeping was the pallor of his skin.

The woman recoiled slightly when she saw the body and took a step back into the sergeant, who was standing behind her waiting to catch her in case she fainted. All the time she was nodding and crying, she did not take her eyes off the boy, and only when Cuthbert covered him again did she lunge forward to try and embrace the dead child. But Baker took her by the arms and firmly steered her from the room and out into the corridor.

There, a seat had been placed by Morgenthal, and he helped the woman to sit down. Cuthbert came out and squatted down to meet her eyes, then took her hands in both of his.

'Mrs Price, I can't tell you how brave that was, and I am so sorry for your loss.'

'How? How did it happen? How did he die, doctor? Was it quick? Did he suffer? Tell me he didn't suffer.'

'He would have died instantly, Mrs Price. There would have been no pain. And he's at rest now. You can be sure of that.'

She squeezed Cuthbert's hands and thanked him. Baker took her back to the reception area where she was given tea and allowed to rest before he drove her back to Wandsworth. Before Baker left, he told Cuthbert and Morgenthal that he would return prior to the case conference with the chief inspector.

'I would value your thoughts on it all, doctors. The boss is going to want answers, and to be honest I'm not sure what this is all about. Maybe if we could talk it through, it might clarify things.'

Cuthbert assured the sergeant that his door was always open to him, and they arranged to meet at the department an hour before going across to the Yard together.

While he was gone, Morgenthal arranged with the technician to move the body of the child who had now been identified as little Charlie Smith from the viewing room back into the mortuary refrigerator. As he was passing back through the department, he saw Cuthbert at his office desk and knocked on the door.

'May I ask you something, sir?'
'Anything. You should know that by now, Simon.'

'Do we really know, sir? I mean what you said to Mrs Price about the way the boy died. Surely, the boy suffered a seizure, possibly cardiac arrhythmia. It probably wasn't instantaneous, and it might well have been painful, or at least unpleasant.'

Cuthbert looked at Morgenthal and shook his head. 'Do you not think I know all that, Simon? But that woman was not asking a question, she was not seeking an answer. It was a plea for absolution. There is no sin in giving people comfort and the ability to go on living with themselves. The truth is sometimes what people need it to be rather than an account of the hard facts.'

'I meant no criticism, sir.'

'I know, but there is so much more to this job than the search for scientific truth. There is also the much more complex task of dealing with what that truth leaves behind it in its wake.'

Morgenthal was well aware of the conflicting demands of the job. He needed to be an objective scientist sifting the facts to get at the truth, but he had to do so against a human backdrop of emotion and pain. He understood exactly what Cuthbert had said, but it worried him. Might he be found wanting when called upon by a similar plea not for the truth but for some form of mercy?

When Baker returned, both Cuthbert and Morgenthal were waiting for him.

'Let me update you, gentlemen. As you know, Mrs Price, who is the sister of Rose Smith, one of the young women buried in the St Gregory's graveyard, has now positively identified the four-year-old boy as Charlie Smith, her nephew. When questioned, she states that shortly after her sister's suicide, she was visited in her home by a nun who offered to take Charlie into care at an orphanage. This woman was insistent that neither Mrs Price nor the family should visit or have any further contact with the boy, in her words, "for his own good".'

'Was she able to describe this nun, sergeant?'

'Not initially but I asked her again on the drive back to Wandsworth. All she could really remember was the habit she wore, which from her description sounds very like that of the sisters at St Gregory's.'

'Well, given where the child was found, that's hardly surprising.'

'But what I don't understand, sir, is why a nun would take the child to live in an orphanage and then kill him. And from the dates that Mrs Price gave me and your own estimated time of death, I think we are looking at both events happening about the same time, maybe even on the same day.'

Cuthbert pondered Baker's question and asked, 'And the other two children – do you think we might be dealing with a similar story?'

'There's no evidence for that yet, sir, but there's no evidence to the contrary either. I haven't been able to speak with anyone who can tell me how the two little girls disappeared. One relative of the older girl just said she thought she'd been taken into care.'

'So we have three dead children and three young mothers who have all committed suicide lying in graves only a stone's throw away from where the children were buried. The approximate dates of all three children's deaths tie in closely with the dates of their mothers' suicides. And we have evidence that the last of these children, Charlie Smith, was taken from his home by a nun, ostensibly to be brought up in the care of the orphanage.'

Morgenthal looked puzzled. 'Would it really be normal practice, sir, to forbid any contact with the child's family? I realise they might not be able to look after the child, but surely family is still family and would be important for the child.'

'I suspect if your plan is to dispose of the child, the last thing you want is relatives coming to visit. But it is important because it does rather suggest that this was premeditated. I don't think these poisonings were any kind of accident. Whoever took these children planned to kill them.'

The sergeant was still shaking his head. 'But why kill them?'

'That, sergeant, is the mystery here, but the only connection the children have is that they were all the orphans of suicides and that their mothers all lie in St Gregory's churchyard, where we know some would say they have no right to be.'

Baker, who had been taking some notes, looked up and asked, 'Because they had committed a sin?'

'You may call it a sin; I say it was an act of desperation. I think it might be time to exert some more pressure on the nuns, especially the mother superior. When you tell the chief inspector all this, he'll want to rip that orphanage apart, and I'm not sure that would help anyone, especially the children who are living there.'

'But could they be in danger, Dr Cuthbert? Whoever has done this has already killed three children.'

'No, sergeant, I doubt this has anything to do with the orphans in their care and everything to do with the suicides. Remember, none of the victims were children in the orphanage. Let me speak with the chief inspector first before our meeting. Perhaps I can try to settle him down and urge him to bring the mother superior in for questioning in the first instance. That might well get us some answers.'

*

Mowbray's office on the second floor of Scotland Yard had a view out over the Thames towards the South Bank and

Waterloo Station. When Cuthbert knocked on the door and entered, he found the chief inspector standing with his hands in his trouser pockets staring out across the city.

The autumn sky was still blue in patches, but the clouds were massing dark and heavy in the west, and before the day would be out the rain would be washing the gutters of London clean. Cuthbert was unsure if Mowbray had heard him come in and cleared his throat to announce his presence. When Mowbray still did not move from the window, Cuthbert said, 'You seem to be deep in thought, Jim, or are you just ignoring me as a matter of course?'

'I know you're there. Take a seat, and I'll be with you as soon as I'm finished.'

Cuthbert sat down and only after another full minute did Mowbray take a deep breath and turn to face his visitor.

'What was that all about? Have you taken up meditation?'

'Do me a favour, Jack. I mean, do I look like the sort that meditates? I needed to get my thoughts straight, that's all. This case is annoying the hell out of me. I fucking hate nuns, and I fucking hate anyone who messes with children. And if I find out one of these nuns has been being doing that, they won't have to hang her 'cause I'll already have broken her bloody neck. So what was it you wanted?'

Cuthbert couldn't have wished for a worse opener to the discussion he needed to have with Mowbray, but there was nothing else for it but to tell him everything that had happened. As he related the story Mrs Evelyn Price had given to Sergeant Baker and told him of her positive identification of the first victim as her nephew, Cuthbert could see Jim Mowbray become more and more agitated.

'I fucking knew it! I'm going to go in there and rip their fucking throats out, the sanctimonious bitches.'

'Listen. Listen to me. We don't know anything yet that

would justify anything of the kind. All we have is a witness who says a woman dressed as a nun came to take the child away. That is not the same as saying it *was* a nun. Let's gather some more facts. Why not bring the mother superior in for questioning?'

'No! She's had her chance to explain. Baker's been to talk with her more than once and she's not been straight with him. She's hiding something. They're all hiding something or running away from something. They're damaged goods, women who want to live like that.'

As he spoke, Mowbray was shaking with rage and Cuthbert knew he had to intervene. 'Jim, sit down and stop. Stop what you're saying and stop what you're thinking. I'm not asking you to tell me what happened to you. I'm not sure I need to ask because I can see it. You've been hurt badly – I assume as a child, and I assume at the hands of a group of nuns not that unlike those we're dealing with here. But they're not all the same.

'All policemen aren't the same either; neither are all doctors. There are good and bad everywhere. You can't tar them all with the same brush. You're better than that. I admit there are unanswered questions here, but that's what you do: you get answers from people. Well, question her. Find out what's going on there.'

Mowbray was in his chair where Cuthbert had ordered him to sit, and his head was down. He said nothing in response to Cuthbert's pleas for reason but after a few moments he started to laugh. 'You know I was twelve when I first ended up in a children's home. My parents weren't exactly what you'd call love's sweet dream. One day my dad came home and found my mum packing a suitcase. She was going to leave him – and me as well by the way – so she could run off with the meter reader. Dad had had a skinful and he went for her. I watched him do it.

I was terrified of him, you know. I was small for my age, and by God he was big, and he'd always been quick with his fists and his belt buckle.

'I remember cowering in the corner and seeing him go for her throat. He throttled the life out of her, and I did nothing. And then he just let her drop to the floor as if she were nothing. And you know what he did then? He went and got another bottle of beer and sat at the kitchen table and drank it, all while she was lying at his feet.

'The neighbours had heard the commotion. It's surprising just how much noise a woman dying can make even when she's being choked to death. They came in and found us there, him at the table drinking, her on the floor in a heap and me in the corner where I'd pissed myself. They took him away, and I never saw him again after that day. A few months later they hanged him.

'The day they arrested him, I was placed in a home, a church-run place like your St Gregory's. It was a brutal place, though. Lots of bigger boys from even tougher backgrounds than mine, and they were all somehow broken. But the nuns who ran the place were even worse. They should have been there to care for us, to protect us, but they were the real enemy.

'One was called Sister Joan, and she was the one who would laugh as she was beating you. She was high on it all, a proper sadist. When you started bleeding, that was when she really got excited. I've still got the scars on my back. I had an aunt, my mum's sister, who kept in touch, but she would never hear a word said against the nuns. It was only after eighteen months of it when I showed her my back that she took me out to live with her. That didn't last long either, but that's another story.

'So, the long and the short of it, Jack, is no, I don't have a lot of time for the good Christian sisters.'

Cuthbert was not prepared for such a shocking confession.

He'd had no idea just how much Mowbray had been through and could see how he was still reliving the memories of those years through his anger and frustration.

'I'm sorry, Jim. No one deserves a start in life like that. To lose both your mother and father and then to suffer such abuse. I don't know what to say.'

'I didn't tell you because I wanted your sympathy, Jack. I just wanted to explain my position and to emphasise what I said before. I realise the terms I used may have been less than professional, but I meant what I said. I regard the mother superior and her nuns as prime suspects in the abduction and murder of three innocent children. I will question her, and if I find she has a case to answer, I will press for the harshest punishment possible. She will hang for what she has done.'

Mowbray was icily calm, and his words were clear.

Cuthbert nodded and suggested that it might be useful if he were present as a medical observer during the interview.

'I have no objection to that, but why? Do you think she's a madwoman, or is it that you think I might kill her?'

'In truth, I think anyone who lives in a religious order has to be a little mad, but more than that, anyone who could do what was done to those children has to be of unsound mind.'

'That or evil, Jack. Let's not forget that as a possibility. We've both seen enough of that in this game. They're not all mad. Some of them do it because they enjoy it.'

Cuthbert nodded in silence, although he had always had the hardest of times reconciling such thoughts. He had seen many sick minds in his career, and he could not help but wonder if the very definition of madness should include those warped notions that others labelled as evil.

Anyone who could kill a child, in his opinion, had to have a mind that was no longer working normally. Such extreme, aberrant behaviour was surely symptomatic of dysfunction.

But, of course, there was also the chance that he was merely rationalising it all to protect himself from the alternative. An alternative that Mowbray was quite sure about.

A detective spends his life studying human behaviour and sees the worst of it on a daily basis. There is perhaps no greater expert on the extremes of what we are capable of. That there were people like that – people who could understand the consequences of their actions but who did not care because they held the lives of others in such little regard – was almost unthinkable for Cuthbert. In contrast, Mowbray not only thought it, he knew it to be true.

Chapter 12

Edinburgh: 2 September 1910

In the assembly hall of Lauriston School, Cuthbert stood towering over the new intake of boys. They looked up at the young man before them and had it not been for the warmth of his smile, they would likely have remained clinging to the skirts of their mothers and nannies.

All Cuthbert's school friends had already celebrated their sixteenth birthdays months before, but he was the youngest of the group and would not be joining them for another two weeks. Although he was still destined to grow even taller and much stronger, he was already, despite his youth, the biggest boy these small children had ever seen.

At the other end of the hall, Cruikshank stood on the dais and read out the groups of names assigned to each dormitory room. He wore the enamelled badge of Head Boy, a role he, or more correctly his father, had been working towards since that first day in this hall some eight years earlier.

Cuthbert was now a prefect, and although many thought he would have been the natural choice for the top job, he was more than happy to see his first friend at the school in charge of the room. Cuthbert loved the college because of the education he received there, but Cruikshank loved the college as an institution, and a family one at that. His father had narrowly missed being appointed Head Boy in his own day at Lauriston, and he was determined not to let it slip through his fingers a second time.

Cuthbert corralled his group of four youngsters and led them like a trail of ducklings up the stairs towards the junior dormitories on the second floor.

'Room three, gentlemen. This was my room when I started here at the college, and now it will be yours. It's a good room – in fact, don't tell anyone else because they'll only be jealous, but it's actually the best room. You'll have a lot of fun in here, and you might even on occasion get some sleep. Now, find your beds as quick as you can. Your trunks have already been brought up, and you can get unpacked and settle in. The principal will be speaking to the whole school in a little over an hour, so you might even have time to do a little exploring. I recommend the library. But don't be late. Remember, you only have one chance to make a good first impression. Now, is everyone all right?'

He looked at the four bright faces staring up at him, all too frightened to speak yet too excited to stand still. 'Good, I'll leave you to it.'

He wandered along the corridor, looking in the other rooms and reliving that first day of his own. The faces were all different, but the little boys in their new, slightly ill-fitting blazers and caps were all busying themselves with bags and books, and he even spotted one pot of marmalade being unloaded. Perhaps a future head boy, he mused. You can never be too careful where food is concerned.

There was noise from every room, but in the corridor, one small boy was standing alone at the window. Cuthbert didn't want to startle him, so he coughed to let him know he was there, but the boy didn't move.

'I say, are you all right there?'

The boy turned and looked up at Cuthbert, who was now standing at his side, but who quickly squatted down to find his eye level.

'Tell me, what's the matter?'

'I want to go home,' the boy said before his eyes filled with tears and he stood sobbing, arms clamped to his sides.

Cuthbert stood, took a small hand in his and led him into the nearest empty room. 'Let's get ourselves sorted out in here. Now, what's your name?'

'Jack.'

'Well, what do you know? That's my name too. But, you know, to prevent any confusion they like to use your surname here. I mean, imagine if one of the masters shouted, "Jack, please come here!" and we both came running. That just wouldn't do, would it? So I get called Cuthbert because that's my surname. What's yours?'

'Harrison.'

'Harrison it is. Well, I know it's all very strange, but this really is a great place to go to school. I was very frightened on my first day too.'

The boy looked at Cuthbert in disbelief and between his tears, which had now slowed to a trickle, he said, 'You were?'

'Oh, yes. I didn't know anyone, and all I wanted to do was go home, just like you. But then I started to meet some of the other boys, and I made friends right away because, you see, today is the best day of all for making new friends. Everybody wants to be friends. So what we've got to do is get these eyes of yours all dried up, take a big brave breath and go and say hello to your new roommates. Shall we do that?'

The boy nodded and took a large handkerchief from his pocket that had doubtless been supplied by an anxious mother who suspected it might be needed. He wiped the tears from his face, and Cuthbert straightened the boy's blazer and adjusted his tie.

'There, perfect. Now, do you want me to take you back in?'

'No, sir, I mean, Cuthbert, I'll do it myself.'

'Good idea, and I'll probably see you later at the assembly.'

The boy ran from the room and threw himself into his new school life without a backward glance, and Cuthbert smiled at the thought of all that was still to come for the little ones.

*

As the autumn term was coming to a close, everyone's thoughts in the senior year were on what was to come next. The leaving certificate exams would be held the following spring but applications for university places were already at the forefront of many of the boys' minds. In Cuthbert's group, Jenner had announced his intention to read history at the University of Edinburgh.

'And what are you going to do with that – come back here and teach at Lauriston?'

Abercrombie asked the question with the same sneering tone he had been cultivating since the start of term for the discussion of all things university-related.

'No, I'm going to join the Foreign Office after that. There are amazing opportunities for chaps with a good degree. This empire of ours is just getting bigger and needs administration. But I don't suppose you've given too much thought to further education, have you?'

Abercrombie scoffed again, but inside he was angry that he could not be part of it all. His own academic performance at the school had been little short of dismal, and already the masters were trying to steer him towards taking a position in a bank rather than considering a university course.

'I suppose university isn't for everyone, Abercrombie. And there'll always be a need for insurance clerks.'

Abercrombie lunged at Jenner, and Cuthbert had to intervene by lifting him bodily off his prey and placing him firmly back on his bed.

'What about you, Cuthbert? University, I suppose, but what will you read?'

It was a question to which Cuthbert himself would have liked to have known the answer. He had been struggling with it for some weeks, and just when he had decided on a course of study, he would pick up a different book or attend another lesson and be back to square one.

He was a true all-rounder, excelling in everything he studied and equally at ease in the humanities as in the sciences. But he had to make a choice. He could only go to university once. Not surprisingly, several of the masters at the college were having quiet words with him, canvassing for their own subjects. He was largely unaffected by their arguments, all that is except Mr Robertson, his classics master.

'Tell me, Mr Cuthbert, what options are you considering for your university career?'

'I have rather too many options, sir, and that's the problem.'

'A fine problem to have, no doubt. I would be remiss, however, if I did not put my own tuppence worth in. Have you considered reading Greats at Oxford? It is, I confess, my own alma mater, and I am therefore justly accused of partiality, but I have never met any pupil more suited to that course.'

Cuthbert had indeed thought hard about that path. Of all his subjects at school, he felt most at home in the worlds of Latin and Ancient Greek. He could read both with fluency and had little difficulty understanding the deeper meanings of all that he read. However, he could not help wondering what would happen after such an education. He thought of Jenner's dream to be some sort of petty official in a far-flung corner of the empire. Was that as good as Cuthbert could hope for too?

'I realise education is an end in itself, sir, but this is the twentieth century and I wonder if I have the luxury of studying for its own sake. Things are moving so fast, and who knows what the next few years will bring?'

The old man was used to the impatience of young men, always in such a hurry to make their mark on the world. None of them, not even the one before him now, had any notion of just how long their working lives would be and how insignificant in some ways were three or four years at university. Insignificant in time, yet not on the impact they would have on everything that would follow.

'And what might prepare you for this new century of ours?'

'I am thinking of studying medicine, sir.'

'Ah, a noble profession, indeed. Might I ask why?'

Cuthbert's desire to study medicine was, he had to confess, somewhat visceral, and he found it difficult to articulate his reasons. However, many others would ask this question, and he needed a better answer both for them and for himself.

One of his first loves at school had been Latin, but that was because it gave him the opportunity to solve puzzles. That love had never left him although Latin itself had become something much more. Now, when thinking about the greatest puzzles of all in his own life, he always came back to people – their bodies and their minds. Perhaps the proper way to spend one's studies, he reasoned, was in trying to solve the problems at the heart of the human race. But there was more than that.

He had always felt for the underdog, whether it had been the small squirrel who could never reach the nuts in his palm, or the little boy crying in the corridor. He was drawn to weakness, perhaps because of his own strength, and often wondered if he had been given his size to protect others. Few were weaker and more vulnerable and in more need of protection than those who were ill. This he now tried to articulate for Mr Robertson, who listened with interest and humility and could offer little by way of contradiction; although he felt the need to add one final argument.

'Do remember, Mr Cuthbert, that to study the classics is not to study a subject. It is not like a skilled apprenticeship as in law or even medicine, but a training of the mind preparing you for anything you wish to tackle. Our greatest thinkers, our great statesmen, our leaders have their educational roots in the classics. This, I believe, could be your destiny, young man. However, as the great Horace said, *Caelum non animum mutant qui trans mare currunt*.'

'They change their sky, not their soul, who rush across the sea, sir.'

'Indeed, and whichever sea you choose to cross, young man, I know you take with you a good soul. It must be your choice, for only you must live with it. And remember there is no right or wrong decision, only one with which you are content within yourself.'

*

As the year wore on, the senior boys became lost to their studies. They were regularly reminded of the importance of the impending examinations and were left in no doubt as to the dire consequences of failure.

Abercrombie was taking it particularly hard, and his mood had darkened since the start of the year. Cuthbert was unsure how much he could help at this relatively late stage, but he resolved to try. And he enlisted the less than willing assistance of Jenner and Cruikshank, who at first felt they had enough on their own plates to concern them. Nevertheless, Cuthbert was persuasive and reminded them that they had started at the school together, had grown up together and that they needed to finish it together.

So, every evening, Abercrombie was schooled by one of them in the subject in which they excelled. Jenner naturally took history, Cruikshank mathematics, and everything else was left to Cuthbert, especially Latin.

'It's no use. I appreciate what you're all doing, but it just doesn't stick with me. I'll never get through these damned examinations.'

'No, you won't, Abercrombie, not with an attitude like that. Look, we're not trying to get you an A, you chump, we're trying to get you a pass, and that's more than possible. So buckle down and do what I tell you.'

Cruikshank had become very forthright since he had been made Head Boy and was not about to accept any such attitude. He, almost more than any of them, now viewed Abercrombie's success or otherwise in the examinations as a personal challenge. And when Cruikshank set out to get something, history so far suggested he would succeed.

*

By the New Year, Abercrombie had settled down to the extra workload and was spurred on. He now had three friends whom he would let down if he failed, whereas before he only had himself to disappoint.

As the daffodils in the school grounds were at their finest, the first of the examinations was held in the assembly hall. That first week would see the senior boys take papers in English, mathematics and Latin. The following week was the turn of history and then science.

Cuthbert and the others had prepared a careful study plan for Abercrombie in the preceding weeks. They had all come to realise that their roommate's main failing was one of organisation rather than lack of intellect. Cuthbert had also spent considerable time strategising for Abercrombie. He scoured the past papers that were available, looking for patterns and reasonable certainties for the questions that might come up.

'Never forget, Abercrombie, this is all just a game like any other. There are rules and you have to know what they are, and you also have to seek every advantage, no matter how small, to tip the balance in your favour. So here are my predictions for what might appear in the Latin and English papers. Jenner's done the same analysis for the history papers and Cruikshank, the mathematics. Science seems to be a lot less predictable, I'm afraid, so we might need to take a bit of a punt there, but if you focus on these topics, you've every chance of getting through.'

All of them took advantage of Cuthbert's analysis of past papers and almost hooted with joy when they opened the first of the English papers on their examination desks and found almost word for word his predictions. The same happened for Latin, with the very passage that Cuthbert predicted for the prose translation there before them.

Abercrombie was feeling a lot more confident by the end of the week, but Cuthbert knew it was far from over and forced everyone to redouble their efforts for the history and the much less predictable science papers in the week ahead. That weekend, when other pupils were lounging under the trees in the late spring sunshine, he had them going over dates in Scottish history and reciting Newton's Laws of Motion.

When the last paper was handed in to the invigilators the following Thursday, the collective weight lifted from the shoulders of the senior boys was palpable. They walked taller and found the frivolity of their youth again as they ran about the grounds. There was only a matter of weeks left of their school days and it was Jenner who asked what it was all for.

'I mean, why can't we all go home now? The exams are done, so what more do they have to teach us?'

'Says the man who is about to go off to university to read history. Don't you think when you get there, there might be a little more to learn? And that perhaps you should start that now? These last weeks are a preparation for the biggest change in your life since you started at this school. University is going to be a fish of a very different kind, Jenner. Best you realise that and get yourself ready.'

Cruikshank had started to sound more and more like his father. None of the boys had ever met Cruikshank senior, but they were reasonably sure that his son was doing a fair imitation of him. He had even started wagging his finger as he spoke. Jenner looked across at Cuthbert and mouthed the word, 'Fish?' Cuthbert just nodded seriously at Cruikshank, and the head boy was pleased that someone had the good sense to agree with him.

*

On their last day at the school, there was much ceremony to be attended to as well as the practicalities of packing up a childhood and an adolescence into a few bags and trunks. While Cuthbert was wondering how to fit all his books into a trunk that was already full, a small face appeared at his dormitory door.

It was Harrison bearing a folded note. 'Please, Cuthbert, Mr Robertson asked me to bring you this.'

'Thank you, and how are you faring? Has it been a good year?'

'The best, Cuthbert. I'm all right now.'

He nodded at the small boy, took the note and read Mr Robertson's invitation, written in Latin, of course, for Cuthbert to attend him in his office at his pleasure. Cuthbert smiled and knew he would miss the old man's ways.

'Ah, Mr Cuthbert, I was not at all sure you would be able to find the time in such a busy day to accept my invitation.'

'Sir, there will always be time for you.'

'How kind of you to say so. I simply wanted to speak with you one last time before you go off into this wide world. In truth, I wanted to ask you a question. I have asked you this question before, on more than one occasion, but I am intrigued by how your opinions may have changed as you have grown from the child that came to us almost ten years ago into the young man you are today. Tell me, why do you like Latin?'

'Some say studying the classics is to live in the past, sir, and that it's all about looking backwards. I only look back in the hope of finding those people who have spent their lives looking forward. I do so in the hope that our eyes may meet, that I may engage with them and look into their souls to learn some sort of truth about what it is to be human.'

The old man sighed with delight at the answer.

'You know, Mr Cuthbert, this will be my last term at Lauriston. In truth, I should have been put out to pasture years ago, but I wanted to stay, and I think it was so I could hear you say those words. I was there at the start of your classical studies, and I resolved to be here at the end.

'A teacher is always blessed by their pupils, but now and again something wonderful happens and you get to play a small part in creation. I have taught many remarkable young men in my career, but you, sir, will be the one I remember above all.'

Cuthbert was by now used to receiving praise, but to hear such words from his first and favourite teacher moved something within him. He reached out for the old man's hand, and he was given it freely.

'You know, Mr Cuthbert, I've watched you. I've seen the way you look at the other boys in that way altogether different from the way they look back at you. In spite of what I said all those years ago, you never did grow out of that, did you? For some, that is the way, but it will be a difficult path to tread. I would not wish it upon you.

'I myself have never found that fragrant lady we once talked about, and I suspect it is a little late for me now, don't you think? A word of advice from an old man: please do not be unkind to yourself on your path through life. Do not think that you are a sinner simply because of the way God has made you. He does not fashion sinners, Mr Cuthbert. It is man that does that. You please Christ in so many other ways.'

'If I am being honest, sir, I think I have stopped trying to please Christ. I realised a while ago that if I am God's creation then He must bear at least some of the blame if I am imperfect. I work hard and I try even harder not to hurt others. If what I think when I look at other boys displeases God so much, perhaps He should have given me different eyes.'

The old teacher smiled and could see that the young man before him had found enough strength, perhaps even enough defiance, to accept who he was, even if he had yet to find the confidence to do anything about it.

'Shall I let you into a little secret, Mr Cuthbert? Christ, in my view, has always been something of a political rebel. I believe if He were alive today, He would be standing shoulder to shoulder with the poor, the oppressed and the unemployed. I doubt very much if He would give two figs for who or what might turn our heads in matters of the heart. There are so many more important things to concern Him. Now, run along with you and see if you can't change the world for the better.'

Cuthbert closed his eyes, swallowed to hold back the tears and bowed his head. As he was walking away, the old man called after him, '*Sapere aude*, Jack Cuthbert, *sapere aude!*'

Abercrombie, who had heard the cry, ran to catch up with Cuthbert. 'What's that old duffer on about now?'

'Dare to be wise! And that's what I intend to do.'

*

In his grandfather's study, Cuthbert stood as he often did, taking in the walls of fine leather-bound books. He had come home from school the week before but had yet to see the old man, who was becoming increasingly frail and reclusive.

When he had arrived at the house, Cuthbert was met by Mrs Blackwell, the housekeeper, and he went straight to his room. It had been two years now since Nanna had died. After her death, coming back had been about returning to his grandfather's house rather than about coming home.

When she passed away, Cuthbert's links with his childhood died too, and he could no longer even bear to go into the nursery where they had spent so many hours together. Now, the house was empty of the love and warmth she had brought to it. His thoughts of happier times were interrupted by the hacking cough of the old man who came in behind him and went to his desk. He looked pale and tired and barely looked at the boy as he passed him. Cuthbert was not invited to sit and did not expect to be.

The only time he had sat in this room was when he was 4 years old, and then it was on his grandpapa's lap. Dalrymple shuffled some documents on his desk and then looked up at his grandson, who stood tall and erect, with the raven hair and piercing blue eyes of his mother, and the physique of his father.

'So, university. What are your plans?'

'I wish to study medicine at the university here in Edinburgh. It is one of the finest institutions in the world and second to none for medicine.'

'I see. And that is your final choice?'

'It is, Grandpapa.'

'Then I will not stand in your way. You will lodge in the city, I take it?'

'Yes, I imagine so, sir, but I have yet to be accepted.'

'Oh, I wouldn't worry about that. I have already received a letter from Sir William. It's here somewhere. He's the principal of the university, indeed an old friend. He's been asking what you plan to do. They're very keen to have you. And not just because you're a Dalrymple. Apparently, you've created quite a stir with your examination results. It appears the world is your oyster, sir. Now, the matter of your allowance. A thousand a year perhaps during your studies, and we will obviously review that on your twenty-first birthday.'

'That's very generous, Grandpapa. Thank you.'

'It's nothing of the sort, and I rather expected you to negotiate, but then your father never was a businessman. Ask me for two thousand a year, and I'll give you fifteen hundred. Ask me for three, and I'll grant you two. That's the way this works.'

'A thousand will more than meet my needs, Grandpapa.'

'So be it. I would like you to dine with me this evening at seven. Tomorrow, I shall be leaving for Italy and summer climes. This chest of mine, you know.'

With that, the old man bent to study the papers on his desk, and Cuthbert showed himself out. It was still warm outside in the late afternoon, and he took a stroll through the grounds. He looked across the lawns to the oak and horse-chestnut trees under which he had spent endless hours, and then he smiled, for scampering between them were some old friends. He approached them slowly, knowing how shy they were with strangers.

Gone was the sad little boy coaxing them to eat nuts from between the buttons of his jacket. Now, here was a confident young man, dressed in his summer linen suit, coming stealthily towards them. He got close enough to see their russet tails flick and swish and the staccato movements of their alarm before they disappeared, leaping up into the foliage above. He sat on the grass in the shade of one of the largest trees and waited in vain. They may have come back for the boy, but not for him.

*

The next day, his grandfather left on his travels. There was no sad parting or even a perfunctory goodbye. All Cuthbert heard from the breakfast room was his grandpapa coughing as he climbed into the carriage, with Osbourne in the driving seat as usual.

When he went to the window, the brougham was going down the driveway and onwards, he imagined, to Waverley to catch the train south. He went back to the table to finish his coffee and a maid appeared with the post on a silver tray. She bobbed a curtsy, and he took the letters. One was from the University of Edinburgh and indeed it was the acceptance letter that his grandfather had anticipated. The other was a handwritten envelope in an unfamiliar hand. He opened it eagerly and saw with some surprise that it was from Morton.

> *Dear Cuthbert*
>
> *Well, what do you know? Here we are, free men at last, having shaken off the shackles of old Lauriston. I expect you have your summer all planned out because you always were so much more organised than the rest of us, but I thought I would write on the off chance.*
>
> *The thing is, old sport, I find myself at a loose end. My*

parents are taking the steamer to New York to visit my sister and her ghastly new husband, and I've cried off. Would you fancy a little company? I'm up for just about anything, but it might be nice to get a little sun before we settle down to the books this autumn. What do you say? Are you up for a little trip with me?

In hope,

M

Cuthbert almost laughed to himself as he read the letter. What he wouldn't have given a few years ago to have been alone in the sun with Morton. As it was, he had spent the last three years of school training himself to hide everything he felt, sometimes even from himself. Now, here was Morton all but offering himself on a plate. He folded the letter and put it back in the envelope. He would reply after he had communed with the squirrels and told them his good news about medical school.

When Morton arrived with his bags that evening, he was shown by Mrs Blackwell to one of the guest suites in the south wing. At eight o'clock, he appeared in the drawing room dressed for dinner and Cuthbert met him warmly. He took the young man's hand and shook it.

Although they had last seen each other only the week before, then they had both still been schoolboys dressed in their Lauriston uniforms. Now they were elegant young men dressed in their evening wear, their hair oiled back and their smiles as sparkling as their eyes.

'I can't tell you how much I appreciate this, Cuthbert. It's so good of you to have me.'

'The pleasure really is all mine, Morton. So what's this I hear about you and Oxford?'

'Yes, indeed. I'm off to the dreaming spires. Reading economics and politics, would you believe? I'm really quite excited, to tell you the truth.'

'And so you should be. Very well done. You'll be a cabinet minister before we know it.'

'I thought you might have been joining me. There was a rumour you were going to take Greats. Is that off the cards?'

'Yes, I'm staying in Edinburgh. Medicine.'

'Really? My word. Dr Cuthbert, I presume, and all that. Well, good for you too.'

'Can I offer you a drink?'

'Oh, won't we be waiting for your grandfather to join us?'

'No, he's gone off to the sun himself. It'll just be us this evening. I hope that's not too much of a disappointment.'

'Not a bit of it. It'll give us a chance to have a real chinwag. You can tell me what you really thought of me at school.'

Cuthbert hesitated for a moment, unsure of what he meant. Had Morton known all along? But he said nothing, smiled and led his guest into dinner. They ate and drank well in his grandfather's dining room and Morton commented more than once on the opulence of the surroundings.

'I had no idea you were such a nob, Cuthbert. This place is practically a palace. You kept all that quiet.'

'I've never really thought of this as mine. This is my grandfather's house, and he just took me in when I was orphaned.'

'I don't think I knew that about you, either. How did your parents die? Or is that too personal a question, old sport?'

'Oh, there's no need for any secrets between us. But there's not much to tell. I never knew my mother for she died having me. And my papa died when I was four, so I barely remember him.'

'What rotten luck! How did he die?'

'An accident, I believe. It wasn't talked about. Too painful for everyone left behind, I expect.'

'But surely you know now.'

'No, not really. The only one who might enlighten me is my grandfather, and he doesn't say much to me about anything these days. Look, shall we retire to the drawing room? The one thing my grandfather does do is keep a very good brandy.'

Cuthbert led Morton up the stairs of the mansion. The drawing-room fire was lit as it always was, even in summer, and Morton felt the heat and the oppressive air in the room as soon as he entered.

'I say, this is a bit of a cavern, isn't it? But what wonderful paintings. Is that the Battle of Culloden?'

'Yes, one of a series. You can work your way through Scottish history just by studying the paintings in this room.'

Cuthbert poured them both generous brandies and invited Morton to sit, not quite sure what there might be to talk about. Apart from the fact that they had attended the same school, he wasn't at all sure they had anything in common. To Cuthbert's eyes, Morton was undoubtedly still beautiful, but he was not as attractive to him now as he had once been.

Morton reached for the glass and took it eagerly. 'Tell me, Cuthbert, what do you think you'll miss about school?'

'I'm very much hoping that everything I enjoyed I'll still be able to do. I was a bit bookish for your tastes, I expect, but going on to university will suit me just fine.'

'I'll miss rugby.'

'Really? I think that'll be the last thing I'll miss! And I expect it won't miss me.'

'Nonsense, you were a damn good rugby player, Cuthbert.'

'Not as good as you.'

'That's true.' Morton dissolved into a fit of childish giggles, which Cuthbert might have found charming when they were thirteen, but not now.

'Why don't we have a game now? You've got the space for it here. Look, we can use this for a ball.' He picked up a velvet cushion from an armchair in the corner of the room. 'Try and stop me getting past you.'

Cuthbert asked him to sit back down by the fire. While he was still one of the most attractive young men he had ever seen, Morton was really nothing more than a little boy. Already he was having second thoughts about inviting him to stay and the suggestion of some European odyssey together was filling him with dread. For now, he just had to get through the evening.

*

The telegram arrived early the next morning before anyone in the household was up, and it was brought to Cuthbert in his room by the housekeeper. He opened it in his dressing gown, while she waited to see if anything needed to be done. He had to read the words three times before their meaning sank in:

> REGRET TO INFORM DALRYMPLE DIED SUDDENLY ON
> LONDON TRAIN STOP RETURNING TONIGHT STOP PLEASE
> ADVISE OF ARRANGEMENTS STOP OSBOURNE

Cuthbert handed the housekeeper the telegram for her to read, and she immediately put her hand to her mouth and gasped.

'Mrs Blackwell, please gather the staff in the drawing room. I'll be down in a moment to speak with them.'

'What about Mr Morton, sir?'

'Oh. Why don't we let him sleep in and I'll inform him shortly? There's going to be a lot to do, Mrs Blackwell. I'm going to need your help and that of all the others. I hope—'

'Sir, we'll be right by your side. That's the way the old master would have wanted it.'

*

The following days were a storm of activity with Cuthbert at the eye of it all. As the heir of the Dalrymple Estate and fortune, everyone wanted to speak with him. Mrs Blackwell orchestrated everything in the house, including discreetly packing Morton off to his family home in Edinburgh.

Lawyers, business associates, funeral directors and bank managers all trooped their way through to the study where Cuthbert received them, although not at his grandfather's desk. He found from the lawyers that the funeral had already been planned in meticulous detail and all he was expected to do was attend. The business was in safe hands and the bank accounts were full to overflowing. His grandfather had clearly anticipated exactly this eventuality and had left only the smallest decisions for the young man to make, which he did more thoughtfully and efficiently than any of the functionaries had expected.

*

The last time Cuthbert had been in the graveyard, he had been 4 years old. Now, he found himself as the chief mourner at his grandfather's funeral. He was laid to rest with all the pomp his wealth and social standing demanded.

Over the coffin, the minister read lines from Psalm 103 at the graveside in front of the large ornate memorial to Dalrymple's wife, who had predeceased him by almost thirty years. He would be laid to rest beside her and together they could sleep through eternity.

The minister's words were slow and measured, and, as he read, a soft drizzle dampened the pages of his psalter.

As a father cares for his children,
so does the Lord care for those who fear him.
For he himself knows whereof we are made;
he remembers that we are but dust.
Our days are like the grass;
he flourishes like a flower of the field;
When the wind goes over it, it is gone,
and its place shall know it no more.
But the merciful goodness of the Lord
endures for ever on those who fear him,
and his righteousness on children's children.

Cuthbert recognised that the last line was meant for him. He was the child of Dalrymple's child, and he was being reminded of the transactional nature of grace. He could expect the enduring presence of God's mercy in his life, but only if he feared the Lord. His grandfather would soon be dust, a fragile flower of the field blown away by the wind, and Cuthbert was not entirely sure a life of fear was a price worth paying for anything.

Most of the mourners were strangers to Cuthbert, but he carried himself with decorum, determined to behave as impeccably as his grandfather would have expected. He greeted each and every one with a firm handshake and took upon himself all of their kind words.

When they had gone, he stood alone at the graveside, accompanied only by the sextons, resting on their shovels. He silently thanked his grandfather for giving him a home and an education. He would have liked to have told him how much he had loved him, but the truth was, at that moment, he realised he barely knew the old man.

Cuthbert nodded to the gravediggers and turned to walk away. After taking only a few steps, he decided there was another grave he had to visit. Quite some way from his grandparents' plot was the white marble memorial that was so overwhelming in his memory. Now, he saw that it was much smaller and more modest than he remembered, and the text was simple:

> *In loving memory of*
> *Alexandra Archibald Dalrymple*
> *1870–1894*
> *Beloved wife of William Cuthbert*
> *Taken too soon to be with the angels.*

And in smaller text beneath:

> *Also*
> *William Sutherland Cuthbert*
> *1862–1898*

He stood at their side in silence. What does one say to dead parents lying together in a grave? To Cuthbert they were just names. One had only ever been a painted portrait, and all that was left of the other was a tall shadow of a memory in his nursery. He searched for words, but none came, and he thought it best to leave them to whatever was left of the love that had bound them together in life.

*

The following week, he had been invited to attend a meeting at the offices of his grandfather's lawyers, Bissett, Brodie & Jenks. Osbourne drove him to the New Town, where their chambers occupied one of the sandstone Georgian terraces on Charlotte Square that faced on to a tree-lined garden.

Cuthbert was met at the door by one of the senior partners,

Mr Brodie himself, such was the magnitude of his grandfather's estate. He was led into a large, airless room and invited to take a seat in a heavy, studded leather armchair that had supported many heirs like him over the years. The far less comfortable wooden seats by the desk were doubtless reserved for those with more meagre means and prospects.

'Mr Cuthbert, you are John Archibald Dalrymple's sole surviving relative, but I must inform you that you are not the sole beneficiary of his will. Make no mistake, you are now a very wealthy young man, but he has chosen not to bequeath to you the entirety of his estate, but rather only a portion of it.'

Cuthbert, who had been so privileged that he had never once thought about money in his life, was unfazed by the revelation, and much less concerned by it than Brodie, who was sitting opposite him with knitted brows, expecting this to be the beginning of a lengthy dispute. As such, the senior partner had prepared a conciliatory speech which he now thought he should deliver even though it might be unnecessary.

'I expect you would like to know the reasons for this state of affairs, and your grandfather gave me leave to provide you with the following explanation. He wanted to leave you sufficient funds to ensure your comfort and to allow you to live as a gentleman, but, knowing that you wished to pursue a medical career, he did not wish to encumber you with the kind of fortune that would force you to administer it, and which thereby might serve as a distraction from your studies or from your future career.

'He has bequeathed the house to the Church for them to either sell or use as they see fit. He has settled more than generous sums on all his staff and retainers. His considerable business interests will be liquidated and shared between a number of charities.

'He has left you a large proportion of his capital, which will service your allowance, and he has arranged for a further sum to be held in trust for you until you are twenty-five. There are also two other bequests. These are items he wished you to have, but they are also to be held in trust for you until a later date. The terms of the will do not permit me to share the nature of these bequests at this time.'

Cuthbert politely listened to everything Brodie said with interest, but not enthusiasm. 'My understanding was that I might have an allowance of a thousand a year until my twenty-first birthday. Is that still possible under the terms of the will?'

The old lawyer sat back in his chair and shook his grey head, smiling at the young man. 'My dear Mr Cuthbert, your annual allowance will initially be ten thousand a year, and that will only increase on your maturity. As I said, you are a very wealthy young man, and I do hope we may continue to serve your interests as we have done your grandfather's these last forty years.'

On his way back to the house, Cuthbert's head was full of the future, but his most immediate task was to take care of those in his grandfather's employ. Brodie had already told him of the financial provisions made for them, but there was more that needed to be done. As soon as he got back to the study, he sat at the desk for the first time and started writing letters of thanks. He also took the time to speak personally with Mrs Blackwell and Osbourne to assure them that they would be taken care of.

With the second post came more letters of condolence, which were still arriving daily since his grandfather's death more than two weeks ago. Amongst them was one with a familiar scrawl, and he knew at once it was from Abercrombie.

Dear Cuthbert,

Just found out and wanted you to be the second to know. I passed the Certificate. It was your doing more than mine and I will never be able to thank you adequately. I am not sure what the future holds, but it is certainly looking much brighter today than it was.

If ever you need my help — although I can't imagine such a thing — I will be happy to do anything for you.

Your old friend,

Abercrombie

Cuthbert held the letter to his heart and immediately wrote off a reply, reminding his friend of just how much work he had put in, and that everything he had achieved he had done on his own. He concluded with a postscript: 'Remember the old school motto, *Omnia mea mecum porto*, which as you are so qualified now in Latin, I won't trouble to translate for you. Just to say that what you carry with you, Abercrombie, is yours and no one else's. Never forget that.'

Chapter 13

London: 30 September 1931

Cuthbert was watching the mother superior from the adjacent observation room as she sat alone at the table in the interview room. She was turning the plain gold band on the ring finger of her left hand. When Mowbray entered the room, she barely looked up, and if she was expecting more respect, she did not betray it in her expression. He studied her in silence and arranged his notes on the table. She said nothing and would not until she was spoken to.

'A wedding ring?'

'Yes.'

'Why?'

'It is symbolic of my spiritual marriage to our Lord. It is engraved with the words *Delectus meus mihi et ego illi* – My beloved is mine and I am His.'

'Is that so?'

Mowbray had taken a dislike to this woman as soon as he had laid eyes on her, and nothing she said or the way she said it was about to change that. However, as an experienced detective, he was aware that such prejudice was a weakness on his part, leaving him vulnerable to error. He tried to clear his mind of such thoughts, but it was a crowded mind.

'I understand that your Reverend Henshall feels strongly about the treatment of those who have committed suicide.'

'That, chief inspector, you must take up with the reverend father himself. But he is known for his unconventional views.'

'You mean his tolerance?'

'If that is what you wish to call it.'

'Does the Bible not teach us to be tolerant and to forgive?'

'There is a single example of a suicide in the New Testament. That of Judas Iscariot whose remorse at betraying our Lord drove him to hang himself. Are you seriously suggesting we should hold him up, the blackest of all sheep, as a role model for morality?'

For the mother superior, the question was not a rhetorical one and she waited for a response. When Mowbray said nothing, she invoked further examples to strengthen her argument.

'Our dear St Augustine pointed out that the commandment "Thou shalt not kill" applied to suicide as well as homicide. Unlike the commandment against bearing false witness, it does not say, "Thou shalt not kill *thy neighbour*", it simply says that all killing is forbidden and therefore that must include the killing of the self – namely suicide. St Thomas Aquinas in his turn taught us that suicide is always a mortal sin, as well as being contrary to the natural law and to charity. Put simply, chief inspector, throughout history, the Church has always viewed suicide as an abomination, as the outrage against God that it surely is.'

She said her words and quoted her theology without rancour. Her expression was calm, almost smiling, her words no more than whispers. Baker, who was observing, could not help feeling chilled by her, especially when he compared it to the passionate and deeply held views of Reverend Henshall. Mowbray, however, resented her lecture, finding her tone patronising. On the other hand, now that he had made her feel a little superior, it was time to pivot to a new, more important, subject.

'Tell me about Sister Mary Frances, your novice. Do you know much about her life before she joined your order?'

'I am reasonably confident I know everything about her. We choose very carefully, sir.'

'What do you mean by that?'

'No one motivated by grief or frustration would ever be considered. The life of a sister, even in the orphanage, is to deal on a daily basis with great pain and loss. We cannot afford to take anyone who carries with them even greater problems than those we are called to ease.'

'So you would vouch for her honesty?'

'Completely.'

The chief inspector knew that others of whom he would ask such questions would be demanding to know his reasons, but apparently not this woman.

'She arrived two years ago – is that correct?'

'That is correct.'

'And she is due to complete her training when?'

'Six months as a postulant and three years as a novice. Only then will she take her vows. She is currently in the second year of her novitiate.'

'And she has taken a special interest in the herb garden while at St Gregory's?'

'She has, and I have encouraged that. Many find God's true meaning in the works of His creation.'

'Is that a fact? She cultivates medicinal herbs, I understand.'

'I believe she grows many plants, but amongst them there will be those with medicinal properties, I'm sure.'

'Including some that are potentially poisonous?'

'Many plants are poisonous if taken in injudicious quantities.

An important part of any herbalist's knowledge is to know what can be administered safely.'

'And you would know all about that, wouldn't you? Didn't you develop a special interest in herbs and herbal remedies when you were serving your own novitiate in Northumberland? So, for example, you would know how to prepare a safe dose of tansy tea, and, if you so wanted, a fatal dose.'

She looked puzzled by the chief inspector's question and bowed her head to consider her answer, but when she spoke, she could not hide her annoyance. 'I cannot imagine anyone deliberately setting out to prepare a fatal dose of any herb, and I have certainly never done so. The plant you mentioned has many purported medicinal qualities, but it is also well known to be dangerous.'

'Well, someone in your community thought it was a good idea to feed a fatal dose to the little boy who's lying in our pathologist's refrigerator, so if you could just stem your self-righteousness for a moment, Miss Burnett, I'd like to get to the bottom of this.'

Gone now was any pretence from Mowbray about the special status of this suspect. To him, she was nothing more than a self-important old maid, who very possibly had a hand in the deaths of three children in the grounds of an orphanage she was supposed to run.

'So let's start again. Do you know how to make so-called tansy tea?'

'Yes.'

'Have you, while at St Gregory's, done so or instructed others how to do so?'

'Yes. I have shown Novice Sister Mary Frances how to prepare the concoction.'

'Why?'

'As a remedy for worms in the youngest of the children.'

'Did Mary Frances ever make it for any other reason?'

The flow of the mother superior's answers was abruptly stopped by this question. She dropped her head again and brought her hands together in prayer.

'I'm waiting, Miss Burnett, and I don't have all day.'

'I discovered by chance that on a separate occasion Novice Sister Mary Frances had indeed prepared a stronger concoction for the purposes of helping . . .' She stopped and almost held her breath, such was the enormity of what she was about to say. She looked as if she might be sick before saying the words, so Mowbray helped her.

'. . . of helping a young woman rid herself of an unwanted pregnancy? Is that it, Miss Burnett?'

The mother superior closed her eyes and brought her clasped hands to her lips before nodding. She was obviously now in some distress.

'With your full knowledge and approval?'

'No!' She almost screamed the word across the table, and her body began to heave with waves of nausea. She staggered to her feet and rushed to the corner of the room, where she retched violently. She wiped her mouth on her scapular and began to apologise between her sobs. Whether this was for her vomiting, or for her part, however peripheral, in all this, Mowbray was unclear, but he wasn't about to let it derail him.

'Please sit back down, Miss Burnett. This interview is not over.'

The woman who now sat opposite the chief inspector was no longer the composed leader of the religious house. She was trembling, trying to hide the stains on her habit, and her face was blotchy from crying.

'Why exactly should I believe a word you say, Miss Burnett? Or would you rather I call you Sister Eglantyne, or perhaps reverend mother?'

'You know none of that matters, sir. What matters is that I had nothing to do with Mary Frances's actions and I had nothing to do with the deaths of these children. I can see in your eyes you hate me. You hate everything about me. I've seen the same look in many people's eyes, and frankly I can do nothing about that, but I will answer any question you put to me with complete candour. I have nothing to hide.'

'So I should believe you because you tell the truth. A little circular as an argument, I'm sure you'd agree, quite apart from the fact that you don't always tell the truth, do you? You lied when Sergeant Baker first asked you about Eliza Barnaby's daughter. You knew very well that Tilly Barnaby had died by her own hand. Indeed, that's why you said she should never have been afforded a burial in the churchyard. But you told my sergeant that you had no idea how she died. That was a lie. So how many other lies have you been telling?'

'I did not think it my place to reveal such an intimate detail about the Barnaby family. That was the only reason I had for concealing the truth.'

'No, not concealing the truth, Miss Burnett, telling a lie and misleading a police officer, even potentially obstructing a murder investigation.'

'Yes, you're right. I did lie. And I will have to answer to God for that transgression.'

'Oh, I would be much more worried about having to answer to me for it. Now, let's discuss the other young women – Mary Nightingale, Margaret Webb and Rose Smith – who are also buried in the churchyard. I understand you objected to them being there as well as Tilly Barnaby. Is that correct?'

'I did.'

'And did you also object to their children?'

'I don't know what you mean.'

'We believe their children are the ones lying in shallow

graves in your grounds. Did you object to the children too? Did you decide to punish them? To poison them with your herbs?'

'That's an outrageous suggestion! I could never harm a child. Why would you even think such a thing?'

'It's my job to think such things, and it's my experience that many of the things I think turn out to be true. So maybe less outrage and more answers. Did you have any hand in the deaths of these three children?'

'No!'

'Do you know who may have been involved?'

'No! I don't know anything about their deaths.'

'But you're very keen to tell everyone that their mothers have no right to be buried in the churchyard, aren't you?'

'Only because they sinned, chief inspector.'

'Says who?'

'The Church.'

'So your Church not only takes it upon itself to be the arbiters of sin, to define what it is, but it also holds the monopoly on forgiveness? And from your pulpits you tell ordinary people that their lives, everlasting after death, will be lived out either in the paradise of heaven or the damnation of hell according to those sins. You really do think you hold all the cards, don't you?'

'Is it my faith that's on trial here, or your lack of it?'

Mowbray suddenly appeared to Cuthbert as if he might reach across the table and slap the woman then and there, but he held his anger in check. However, he decided to test himself no further, to leave the interview room and allow the nun to simmer in her own ire. When Cuthbert saw him get up, he left the observation room and met him in the corridor outside.

'What's your take on the nun, Jack?'

'I don't think she's any more insane than anyone who

believes unreservedly in scripture and who is willing to give up everything on earth for the promise of an eternal life.'

'You know you have a lot in common, you two. You both live in fantasies – you in the past and she in some fairytale future. Both of you seem happy to sacrifice living, really living, in the here and now, for your respective theologies.' Cuthbert was shocked by this comparison to the veiled woman seated in the interview room, but Mowbray barely noticed the effect his words were having. 'But do you believe her?'

'I do. I know she's not been completely truthful with you or Sergeant Baker, but I've been watching her closely. She looked genuinely horrified at what Sister Mary Frances seems to have done for Tilly Barnaby, but when it comes to the suicides and their children, I think she likes words probably more than she likes actions. She believes those young women were sinners. She firmly believes they should not be in that churchyard. But would she take children to St Gregory's to punish them for their mothers' sins? I don't think so. There is no evidence at all that any child in her orphanage is anything but well cared for. I don't think she could hurt a child.'

'I've had different experiences at the hands of her type, Jack, and I'm more than willing to believe she's capable of hurting them, but murdering them is another step, and I'm inclined to agree with you. I'm going back in, but I don't think we'll be keeping her unless I can charge her with aiding and abetting the novice. Much as I would like to, I doubt I have the evidence of malicious intent. I do wonder, though, whose mind she might have poisoned with all this talk of suicide and sin. Before she goes, I think I'll see what she has to say about that.'

The mother superior was sitting just as he had left her, slightly hunched over with her hands clasped in desperation as much as in prayer. Again, she barely acknowledged him as he entered.

'So who have you been talking to about these girls in the Reverend Henshall's churchyard? The ones you say have no right to be there.'

'I have spoken with the reverend father and with the bishop.'

'Running to tell on him to his boss. That's nice, I must say. Very Christian. Anyone else? Did you discuss it with the other sisters?'

'I'm sure they already knew. Everyone knew that the Barnaby girl was buried there, and I suspect they also knew about the others.'

'What about the Barnabys themselves – did they know about the other girls?'

'Mrs Barnaby was broken-hearted when her daughter took her own life. But she knew as well as I did how grave a sin it was. She came to me to discuss it. And, yes, we talked about it all. When the first young woman was buried there after Tilly, she was as shocked as I was, and we both agreed that it was wrong.'

'Or did you tell her it was wrong?'

'Scripture tells us it is wrong. All I did was clarify the sacred word of the Lord for her.'

'I see. And when the second girl was buried and the third, did you talk with Mrs Barnaby about them too?'

'She came regularly to see me. She was in great need of spiritual support. She could hardly go to Reverend Henshall, could she?'

'What exactly did you talk about? What did you tell Eliza Barnaby to do?'

'I told her to pray, to ask for God's forgiveness for her daughter's sins, and I asked her to pray for the others too. We even prayed together.'

Mowbray gathered his notes and sat for a few moments looking at the woman. 'I think you are very possibly the poison that killed those children. I am compelled to release you, but if

I find a shred of evidence that links you directly to their deaths, I give you my solemn vow that I will come for you, and I'll see you hang from a tree just like that blackest of sheep you enjoyed telling me so much about.'

As soon as he got out of the interview room he consulted again with Cuthbert.

'You could very well be right, Jim. There are loose ends, but Eliza Barnaby could have had her mind poisoned by all of this. She was already likely disturbed by her daughter's death. It might not have taken much to put some very odd ideas in her head.'

'Right, we need her and her husband in. And the helpful Mary Frances has some explaining to do. If she could assist in the killing of an unborn child, what else might she have been capable of?'

Mowbray summoned Baker and told him to bring in the Barnaby couple and Novice Sister Mary Frances for questioning immediately.

'If any of them refuse to come freely, arrest them. When they get here, you start with the old man and see what you come up with. And I'll take the wife. The nun can stew in a cell until I'm ready for her. Cuthbert, can you stay to give me a second opinion on them as well?'

'Of course, chief inspector.'

*

The Barnaby couple were brought in first by Detective Constable Marshall, who persuaded them to come without fuss. He placed them in separate interview rooms, and, as instructed, Sergeant Baker started with the husband. Just before he went in, he checked with Cuthbert.

'I'm not sure what we'll get out of him, sir. I've spoken to him several times now and I doubt he can tell us much.'

'Perhaps if you can get him talking about his daughter, sergeant, that might open the door a little.'

Dickson Barnaby was already seated when Sergeant Baker entered. He looked up and nodded in recognition. Baker took a seat opposite him and set about arranging his notes. He also took those first moments to study the man.

Barnaby looked older than Baker remembered him when they had talked by Tilly's grave at St Gregory's and later by the oak tree. Being a man who spent his life outdoors, his face was dark and weather-beaten, but his eyes were grey and sunken. There was now a bone-deep weariness about him that had not been there before. Baker knew he could not have been responsible for taking the children, but there was always the possibility that he had had a hand in their deaths and very possibly their burials. What motive he could have had for any of it, though, eluded the sergeant.

'Now, Mr Barnaby, I would like to—'

'I did it. I killed them. Those little children. I'm the one.'

Baker was stopped short. He looked at the man across the table with suspicion. What on earth was this one thinking?

'Mr Barnaby, I would remind you that you are being interviewed here under caution. This means that you do not have to say anything unless you wish to do so, but what you say may be given in evidence.'

Barnaby said nothing in response to this, and Baker noticed that he was twisting his cap in his hands and they were trembling.

'Mr Barnaby, why did you kill these children?'

'It were an accident. Eliza had brought it home. That were wrong, and she shouldn't have done it, but there it was in the house, and I took it upon myself to calm it down until I could take it back where it belonged, with its family. I must have picked the wrong tea. I just meant to keep it quiet, and help it sleep, like. But it didn't wake up.'

'How did the child die, Mr Barnaby?'

'I don't know. Just slipped away, I suppose.'

'And what then? What did you do?'

'I did it all. Eliza wasn't involved. She wasn't even there. I put it in the ground in the woods.'

'Is that all you did?'

Barnaby looked at the sergeant, searching his eyes for a clue as to what he was being asked and then said, 'Yes, that was about the extent of it.'

'And the other children?'

'When the next one came, I knew I had to get rid of it just like the first one. You see, I knew no one would believe the first one was an accident. And I knew the tea I'd used would sort it, so, God forgive me, I fed some to the second one and then the last one as well. Three all told. Three little children.'

'Why did you report the last one to the police not long after you had buried the body?'

'Guilty conscience, I suppose. I knew I couldn't leave them there in the woods. They had families, and I thought if I told you about one, you'd find the others, and you did.'

'What did you tell your wife had happened to the children she brought to the cottage?'

'I told her I'd taken them back.'

'And she believed that?'

'She wasn't thinking straight when she took them. She's not been right since our Tilly. She has good days and bad. Some days she just stares into space. It's almost as if she doesn't recognise me, or even know where she is. Then the next day she can seem as right as rain, but she's not. Not really. You need to go easy on her. She made a mistake bringing them to the orphanage, but she meant them no harm. That was all me. You have to believe me.'

Baker could see the desperation on the man's face. Dickson

Barnaby had spun a whole web of lies hoping that he would catch the guilt that he knew the police were trying to assign. However, the sergeant had spent too long interviewing suspects not to know when a husband was trying to protect a wife from the noose even when it meant taking her place on the scaffold.

He wasted no further time on the interview and retired, feeling sorry for the old man. In the corridor, Cuthbert, who had been watching the proceedings from the next room, shook his head.

'Well, I think we can be reasonably certain that Mr Barnaby had nothing to do with these murders. He has no idea how the children would have died, the seizures they would have undergone, the preparation of their corpses, the ritual of their burials. I don't think he was anywhere near them, sergeant.'

'I agree with you there, sir. It's all rather pathetic, really, isn't it? We could charge him with wasting police time, but I'm inclined just to tell him to go home. I doubt the chief inspector will see it like that, though. When is he interviewing the wife?'

'He's just about to start. We should both observe. Unfortunately, this might be an even more sorry affair.'

Eliza Barnaby was sitting up straight in the chair and twisting the corners of her shawl. She looked neither worried nor fearful, which Cuthbert immediately thought strange. Who wouldn't feel uncomfortable if they were about to be questioned at Scotland Yard as part of a murder investigation?

Mowbray was clearly thinking along the same lines and began rather unconventionally by asking her if she was feeling all right.

'Oh, as right as ninepence, sir.'

'Mrs Barnaby, can you tell me how long you've lived at St Gregory's?'

'Twenty-odd years. My Dickson is the groundsman, see. And I was the cook at the orphanage.'

'Why did you give up that job?'

'I'm not as young as I used to be. Old bones, you know. Dickson says I creak sometimes.'

'Wasn't it because of your daughter, Mrs Barnaby? Didn't you give up after she . . .'

The woman dropped her eyes and then looked up and about her as if she was suddenly awake to where she was.

'Your daughter, Mrs Barnaby. What about Tilly?'

'She died.'

The woman's eyes suddenly filled with tears, and she began to stroke the shawl she had bunched up in her hands. Just as suddenly, she let it go and swallowed back her grief, and with altogether harder eyes she carried on.

'She was seduced by the Devil himself and paid the price. She was driven mad by it, you see, but she had no right to do what she did. First, she killed the unborn child and then she killed herself. And she should never have been laid in that church. Not alongside decent folks. He wanted it. It was all him.'

'Mr Barnaby?'

'She was always her father's daughter, and he couldn't bear that she wouldn't lie in the church. I think he really did forgive her for what she had done. But she shouldn't have been there, not near my Robbie, not near my darling boy.'

'Did you feel the same way about the other young women the Reverend Henshall buried?'

'They shouldn't be in hallowed ground. None of them. That's not the old way. Their spirits are evil, and they are neither in Heaven nor in Hell. They walk the Earth searching for what they've lost. Their spirits are corrupt and need to be controlled. They need to be pinned into the very earth they lie in. They need to be staked through the heart. That's the only way. And they should be buried at night and at busy crossroads to confuse them. The wheels of the traffic help keep them down, you see, and if they should escape their pits, they won't know which road to take.'

'What about the children, Mrs Barnaby?'

'It was the only way to stop them, can't you see that? It needed to be done to keep those wicked, wicked girls in their graves. As long as their children were alive, they would be sure to come looking for them.'

'How did you know about the children, Mrs Barnaby?'

'I clean the church brasses and do the flowers for the reverend, and everybody thinks a skivvy can't hear or that they must be stupid. Well, there's nothing wrong with my ears. I could hear them all talking when the relatives came begging for his help, the same way my Dickson must have done. Sad folks, but they had no right to ask the reverend to do what he did. And he would always ask about any family the girls had. That's when I learnt about the little ones, and I knew I had to do something to help. Any decent Christian would have done the same. I got their addresses from his book in the vestry and went to see them.'

'Did you tell them you were one of the sisters? Did you go dressed as a nun, Mrs Barnaby?'

'Of course, because I am one of the sisters. I have more of a right to wear their habit than they have. I mean, what did they do to help? Nothing! No, I told them the truth. I told them I was from the church and just like that they'd let me in.

'They were all struggling just the same way me and Dickson were after our Tilly died, and I knew what to say. I told them about the orphanage attached to the church and that I could arrange for the little one to be cared for there.

'With the first little girl, she was being looked after by an uncle who was only too pleased to get her off his hands. He packed her bag there and then, and I took her away with me that afternoon.

'With the second one, it was the grandparents. I could see they were exhausted by it all, but they still didn't want to lose their little one. I had to work harder for her, but I convinced them it would be for the best. But I told them, like I told them all, that it would be unfair on the child if they tried to visit, in case they stirred up a lot of bad memories. In fact, it would be best for everyone if they just forgot about the child altogether.

'It was only with little Charlie that I had real problems. He was being looked after by his mother's sister, along with her own two. She wasn't for letting him go at all. I explained it would be for his own good. After all, it was obvious that she had more than enough work looking after her own children, and I could see she was in the family way herself.

'The church orphanage, I said, would be able to provide for the little boy better than she could. None of the families had anything to speak of. They couldn't even pay for headstones for the girls, so what chance did they have of feeding another mouth? In the end, they all came to me, and I looked after them until it was time.'

'What about your husband? He must have known what was going on.'

'My Dickson? He were away. Doreen, his sister up in Norfolk, has been right poorly this last year. First she was widowed and then she had a stroke. He's been visiting her, trying to help out and staying the week. He was away each time I went to get the little ones. By the time he got back it was all sorted. He never knew anything about any of it. Not until I told him last night. He were going on about it all. How sad it was. How he would never feel the same way about the place. Well, I couldn't have that, so I put him straight. I told him what I'd done and why I'd done it. I knew he would understand when I explained it. I mean anyone with sense would see that.'

Baker, who was observing alongside Cuthbert, was incredulous at what he was hearing. In particular, he was struggling to understand how families could just relinquish their children to a stranger and agree to sever all contact under the pretence of doing what was best for the child. As he was shaking his head at the thought of it, Mowbray picked up the question.

'And no one ever came looking for them?'

'No. You see, I offered them a solution to their problems. It was practical. They couldn't afford to look after the children, or they didn't have the time. But it was also a blessing of sorts – every time they looked at the child, they were reminded of what its mother had done, of the shame she had brought on the families. This way they were never going to have to explain away the child. It was all very straightforward, really.'

'Tell us, Mrs Barnaby, how did you put the children to sleep?'

'I gave them tansy tea and they sat in my lap and we sang hymns. They were a little sick, but only a little, and the little girls just slipped away. Only the little boy had trouble going off. He had a fit, but soon he was quiet. I held them all and I spoke to them. I told them why it had to be and that it was because of the wickedness of their mothers. I made sure, though, that they knew it wasn't their fault, the little loves. I washed them afterwards. I thought it was important they went clean. And I changed their clothes.'

'Where did you get the clothes, Mrs Barnaby?'

'When I took the children away from their families they would come with a little case of their things. And I could always get something from the store in the main house if I needed it. The sisters keep quite a lot of clothes that have been donated in there. All sorts. Little Charlie didn't have much at all with him when he came, and anything he did have was only fit for the ragman, so I got him a new outfit. I think I done him proud.'

'And you did this all by yourself? Are you sure you didn't get any help? From one of the nuns, say? From Sister Mary Frances? Mr Barnaby didn't help you at all?'

'Dickson? No, no, not a bit of it. He's useless when anything important needs done. All he can do is tidy that girl's grave. He thinks I don't know, but I see him. Talking to her like she's really there instead of in Hell. No, he couldn't even say anything when I told him. But he could see I'd done the right thing. And as for the nuns, what use are they to anyone?'

'It sounds like you thought of everything, Mrs Barnaby. Perfect, in fact.'

'Oh, there's no perfection on this side of Glory, sir.'

'Did you not think, though, Mrs Barnaby, that you might offend God by what you did? You do believe in God, don't you?'

'God? Of course I believe in God. But I don't think He's the same God that them sisters believe in. I know we have souls – spirits that live on after us. And I believe in evil, sir. I know about that because I've seen it. I've seen the way my Robbie was taken from me and then given back to us in pieces. And I've seen the wickedness of our Tilly. There was evil working in her. It took her over and made her do what she did.

'At least she's in the same place as the child of hers now, wherever that might be, but it certainly isn't paradise. None of the others would have rested, though, no matter where you buried them. Not as long as their children were in this world and they're in the next. These are wicked spirits, and they would walk the Earth searching for their little ones, like I said. I needed to reunite them or there would be no peace for any of us. I needed to give the children back, so their innocence could heal the damned spirits of their mothers.'

'And the children? Are they damned too?'

'Their mothers were seduced by the Devil into taking

their own lives and we have no dominion over what God has created.'

'Didn't God create the children too? What dominion do you have over them?'

She looked around the room again, almost as if she were seeing it for the first time. She smoothed the shawl in her lap, looked straight at the chief inspector who was still waiting for her to answer his question, and smiled. 'It had to be done. It was the only way, you see.'

Chapter 14

London: 7 October 1931

When Eliza Barnaby was charged with the abduction and murder of three children, she looked at Chief Inspector Mowbray with surprise. She couldn't remember where she was or who this odd man with the broken nose might be. Had she met him before? Perhaps he was one of Dickson's acquaintances. That must be it because he seemed to know her. Anyway, she was ready to go home to Briar Cottage just as soon as all this confusion was sorted out.

The policewoman who helped her along the corridor was sweet, she thought, and even reminded her a little of Tilly. She asked if she was one of her daughter's friends, but the W.P.C. shook her head. Not the talkative type, she thought.

The room they took her to was very plain, but it was peaceful, and although the window was high, she could barely hear the traffic outside. They closed the door to give her some privacy, which she was thought was considerate.

She sat down while she waited. Dickson must be coming soon to fetch her home, but he was such a forgetful man. Always getting distracted by something or other. Might as well make herself comfortable while she waited.

*

Cuthbert met Sergeant Baker in the stairwell at Scotland Yard a week later and asked how things were going since the interviews.

'All done now bar the paperwork, sir.'

'And the trial?'

'We don't think it will come to trial. The judge will likely rule her unfit to plead. The psychiatric evaluation was pretty cut and dried. You saw her yourself, sir.'

'Yes, she was seriously deluded at times. There were moments of lucidity, but I would say she has no real understanding of what she's done. It's also doubtful whether she would have any meaningful understanding of the judicial process. That said, she's a dangerous woman. What will happen to her? Will she be held in a secure facility?'

'Yes, and no doubt held for the rest of her days, sir. She'll never see another child again.'

'And the nuns, sergeant? What will happen to them?'

'Sister Eglantyne, as I believe she is again, has been recalled to the Mother House up in Northumberland. Whether it's a punishment, or a bit of re-education, I'm not sure, but she's certainly out of the picture.

'Mary Frances is being charged under the Infant Life (Preservation) Act for performing an illegal abortion on Tilly Barnaby. We have her on remand now. She'll certainly be looking at a custodial sentence if she's found guilty. As for how long, that'll depend on which beak's sitting on the bench. But it could well be life.

'The other sisters are all still at St Gregory's and are being joined by a couple of new ones to keep the orphanage going. They still have sixty-two children to look after, and to be honest, from what I saw they were doing not a bad job of that — however odd that sounds given the circumstances, sir.'

'I know. It's always sad to think of children being alone, but if they have somewhere decent to live and there is some love in their lives, perhaps they will be all right.'

'I was wondering, sir. It might not be my place to ask, but what will happen to the little ones we found? It seems to me that the families weren't that able to cope with them when they were alive, never mind now they're dead.'

'I've arranged for them to be returned to their closest families, sergeant. They will be buried properly in their mothers' graves. I've spoken with the Reverend Henshall, and it's all been agreed.'

Baker sighed and nodded his appreciation. 'That's a good thing, sir. It's fitting. A child should be with its mother after all.'

'Indeed, and a mother with her child.'

*

The next day at Gordon Square, the morning post brought the usual collection of official correspondence and bills as well as a few more personal items. Amongst them was one in a rich cream-coloured envelope bearing ornate lettering and a Royal Warrant. However, the message inside was simple and consisted of the arrangements from Constantine's for the delivery of the painting, which would take place the following week.

Cuthbert had been expecting to hear from them after he had been contacted by his grandfather's firm of solicitors in Edinburgh, informing him of the fulfilment of the old man's bequest. He had all but forgotten about the arrangements for him to receive a further legacy in his maturity. Now he learned he was to receive the painting of his mother, Alexandra Dalrymple, that had hung in his grandfather's study. He had not seen it for almost twenty years, and his heart warmed at the thought of being reunited with her again.

The delivery itself was dealt with by Madame Smith, who supervised the manhandling of the large wooden crate, its careful unpacking and the precise hanging of the painting in the upstairs drawing room where Cuthbert wished it to be displayed.

When his housekeeper first saw the size of the canvas, seven by four feet, she was taken aback. And then when she got her first glimpse of the work itself, she could do nothing but stare, transfixed by the gaze of the beautiful woman in the portrait. They were unmistakably Cuthbert's eyes, and yet they were dazzling and feminine in a way that was so different from his strong masculinity. The brushwork was delicate and exquisite, the colours rich and the fabric of her dress, the petals of the roses and the sweep of her hair were all present and real. Madame Smith stood in silence before it when the portrait was in position, and even the delivery men, who had seen more than one masterpiece, took a moment to appreciate it.

When Cuthbert arrived home that evening, all traces of the delivery had vanished from the hallway and Madame Smith welcomed him with a smile.

'Is she here?'

'Yes, monsieur. I had no idea she would be quite so beautiful. Everything has been placed as you requested.'

He looked up the stairwell and hesitated. 'Perhaps later,' he said, and after she had taken his hat and coat, he went into his study. She had not seen this expression of his before and wondered what it must be like never to have known your mother other than the way she was in a painting on her twenty-first birthday.

*

When he did brave the stairs to enter the drawing room, he was overwhelmed with memories. Her image had been such a dominating presence in his early childhood, and he had sat for long hours cross-legged on the floor looking up at her in his grandfather's study.

Now, although he stood tall before her, he felt the need to lower himself and he crouched and then sat on the floor almost in worship. The painting itself was more lovely than his memory of it, and to see it now in the light and airy surroundings of his London home rather than in the dark, oak-panelled room where it had originally hung made it appear fresher than ever.

With the passing years, she had not aged, and the roses on the table beside her had not withered. Mother and child were together again. The more he looked at her, however, the more he realised just how little he knew of her and of his father. There were so many questions that he had never asked about his family, and there were so few left who might answer them. There was one person, though, to whom he might reach out. And although he had not seen her for almost thirty years, he thought it might be now or never.

*

When his Aunt Helena answered his letter, he was surprised by her tone. He remembered her as a severe woman, angry at his grandfather and maybe even angry at him. Now, her words were softer, even generous, and, yes, she would love to meet her only nephew after so many years. She had married soon after he had last seen her as a child, but she had been widowed by the war. She was now living alone in her husband's family home, a grand pile in Berkshire. Lady Allerton, as she was now, agreed to visit Cuthbert in Gordon Square the following Saturday morning. As she wrote:

It is always a delight to find a reason to get out of the country and into town, and I'm sure you and I have much to talk about. You are all the family I have and as your letter did not mention anyone else, I suspect I may be your only blood relative too.

Quite why he had waited this long to find his aunt, he couldn't fathom. For so many years she had been part of a past he had left behind. But neither had she sought him out; perhaps because he would only remind her of the brother she had lost.

Whatever the complications of memory and emotion that had kept them apart, he now keenly anticipated their meeting and was eager to find out more about his parents. He knew, however, that some things are best left sleeping in the past, and that thought tempered his excitement with a niggling anxiety.

*

On Saturday at ten o'clock, Madame Smith met Lady Allerton at the door and welcomed her into the morning room. Helena Cuthbert had been a tall, imposing woman in her youth, and little had changed in the intervening years. She was dressed expensively, and Madame Smith recognised the work of fine couturiers as she took her coat. She was wearing dove grey with silver fox trim and her equally silver hair was fashionably bobbed. Cuthbert came in and bent low to kiss her on both cheeks. She smiled her approval.

'It's so good of you to come all this way, Aunt Helena. And it's wonderful to see you again after such a long time. How on earth did we let this happen?'

'I lost you a long time ago, young man, and I wasn't sure that you might wish to be found. Nevertheless, here we are.'

She looked about the room and raised a pencilled eyebrow high at the oriental minimalism of it all. 'This is all terribly modern, Jack. Your choice?'

'Yes, indeed. I live alone and I'm afraid I am to blame for it all.'

'Then you're not married. Why is that?'

'I'm rather married to my work, Aunt Helena. There's never been room for anyone else.'

'Really? And that work is medicine, I understand. I saw from your letter that you are Doctor Cuthbert now. The first one of those we've had in the family. Each to their own, I suppose.'

Cuthbert thought it best not to go into too much detail about the precise nature of his work unless she asked, which, mercifully, she didn't. As she sat in the morning room, he could see how uncomfortable she was, perhaps regretting that she'd come. Now that she'd seen him, what else was there to say? Perhaps they had left it too long after all and the gulf between them was too great to span with polite conversation.

He needed to get her talking about the past if he was ever to find out anything about the family, and what better way than to invite her to view the portrait upstairs. That proved to be the spark that would ignite not just her memories but a fire that would almost consume him.

'My, my, my. I haven't seen that for almost forty years. It was painted by John Singer Sargent, you know. She sat for him here in London at great expense to her father. The painting was rumoured to have cost him a thousand guineas – an unheard-of sum for such a thing. But when you see what that painter did with her, he almost held her beauty in aspic, and it's still there. I can almost smell those roses, can't you? And I can almost smell her perfume too. Exquisite! She was simply the most radiant creature I ever set eyes on, and she still is.'

The woman's eyes filled as she was transported back across a lifetime to the first time that she had seen the painting when it hung in the Dalrymple mansion in Edinburgh. She turned quickly to Cuthbert and summoned him to her side.

'Let me look at you in the light, boy. Yes, you have William's build but everything else is your mother. You've certainly inherited the Dalrymple features. A family too handsome for their own good, some said. But your father was only human after all, and who could fail to be bewitched by Alexandra?

'The first time I saw her, when he brought her to the New Year's party at the Braes, I thought she looked as if there was a light on inside her. We were almost the same age, and I felt like an awkward little girl in comparison. I don't mind telling you, I was terribly jealous. She attracted the moths to her flame and more than one of them singed their wings, I can tell you. But my brother won her, the greatest prize of Edinburgh society.

'Their wedding was quite the splash – everyone wanted to be there. I was a bridesmaid, and I must say the dresses were ravishing. They came from Paris, you know, which at the time was considered such an extravagance. I thought I was so beautiful – all the bridesmaids did – but then we had to stand beside her, and she made everyone else look so dreary. She simply sparkled with life.

'At the time, it all seemed so dreadfully unfair. Of course, none of us could possibly imagine that less than a year later we would be attending her funeral. She burned so brightly, but so briefly. But you, dear boy, are carrying her flame now. Alexandra's eyes in that portrait are still looking back at me when I look at you.'

He looked again at the portrait. It had been so familiar to him as a boy, hanging in his grandfather's study. But now he looked at it with fresh eyes. The resemblance was striking. Cuthbert had inherited the beauty of her face but, in him, it was transformed into a striking masculinity. There were the same intensely blue eyes, the same raven hair, but her long neck, graceful pose and stunning figure were all hers. This was how she looked when his father first set eyes on her, and it was easy to see how he fell in love with her at first glance.

'You must tell me about them. You see, I know so little of my own history. My grandfather was never unkind, but as I grew up, I think I reminded him more and more of my mother. By the time I could understand, he had become rather distant.'

She sat down in the armchair at the foot of the painting and arranged the silk of her skirts.

'William had a thousand a year, but it was whispered that she had ten – with more to come when she inherited. The Dalrymples were one of the richest families in Edinburgh; old money swelled by the enterprise of her father.

'John Dalrymple, your grandfather, had been the younger son, and not set to inherit, but fate, as it so often does, intervened. His elder brother died unmarried at thirty-five, and John got the lot. By the time he inherited the family money, he had already been building his own empire and was doing very well indeed.

'Alexandra was his only child and he doted on her. When he lost his own wife, the girl became his world. And when he lost her too . . . well, you know better than most what that did to him. He should never have kept you there in that mausoleum. It was nothing more than a glorified shrine to his beloved daughter. And he blamed you for her death.'

'No, Helena, that's not true. He showed me nothing but kindness in those years. I think if he blamed anyone for my mother's death, it was my father. And he blamed himself for his early death. He gave him the pistols, after all, as a present. The ones that caused the accident.'

'Accident? Is that what you've been telling yourself all these years?'

Cuthbert was perplexed and waited for her to explain. Instead, she turned to look back at the portrait.

'No, if it was anyone's fault, it was hers. If she hadn't been so damned beautiful, my brother would still be alive today. He simply couldn't go on living without her. William didn't die because of an accident. He shot himself in the head because of her.'

Cuthbert slumped in the chair beside his aunt. He was shocked by her words but not by the revelation, for somehow he had always known.

None of the adults around him when it happened could have found the words to explain a suicide to a 4-year-old child, but even if they had, there was a world of difference between being told and knowing, between being informed and understanding.

But as he grew older, it became so natural to talk about the 'shooting accident', that no further questions were invited. Questions such as: how does a professional soldier accidentally shoot himself with a pistol? How does a gun accidentally go off and discharge into your temple? How does the sudden, violent death of a deeply depressed, grieving man go uninvestigated?

Of course, he knew the answers to all these questions. He was the answer – a surviving child whose life everyone thought had been torn apart enough. Better for everyone to agree to disbelieve the truth, to bury his father in the hallowed ground of his mother's grave and to move on with a different life, unencumbered by the sins of the past.

His aunt now looked at him sitting there and could see something of the sadness of her brother in him. 'You didn't know, did you? Perhaps I should have kept up the pretence, even after all these years, but no matter how painful, I have always felt we should know the truth. Only when we know what really happened to those whom we love can we truly move on.

'It was that way with me, with my husband. I needed to know how he died in that silly war, to know exactly what happened. It took me a while, but I discovered the truth, and it was bloody but no bloodier than my imagination in the middle of the night, wondering what had become of him.

'I realise knowing that William took his own life when he had a young child to look after raises new spectres, but we cannot live with lies as our bedfellows, Jack. The truth of the matter is that he could think of nothing other than his own grief. He really loved her, you know, in an all-consuming, destructive way. When she died, he was broken.

'Every day, you were a reminder of how and why she had died. I don't imagine he was the first widowed father to resent the life of his child, but that was the fact of it. There was nothing you could do, nothing you could ever have done, to make it better. Had he lived, I doubt your relationship would have improved any. In fact, looking at you now, looking into your mother's eyes, I can only imagine how acutely he would have felt his loss.'

Cuthbert said nothing as she spoke, layering grief upon grief, all but blaming him for the death of her brother, as his father had blamed him for the death of his painted mother. She had waited decades to have this conversation, and he wondered whether she might be relishing the effect it was having.

'Now, on that note I must take my leave of you. I do hope we do not leave it for another thirty years before we speak, but then again perhaps there is little left to say.'

He remained in the armchair in silence, and it was only when she stood up that he leapt to his feet, remembering his manners, and opened the drawing-room door for her. In the hallway, Madame Smith was expecting to be called to serve coffee, but instead Cuthbert asked her to bring his aunt's coat.

'Thank you for coming here, Aunt Helena. I cannot thank you yet for what you have said, but perhaps you are right in that we need to know the truth. It's just such a pity that it has taken so long.'

He shook her gloved hand but did not kiss her goodbye, and he waited in the hallway while Madame Smith showed her out. She closed the door and turned to find Cuthbert standing in the hallway, looking almost lost in his own home.

'Monsieur, can I get you anything?'

He looked up and held out his hand which she took. He held her small hand to feel some warmth and to reassure himself that he was not as alone as he felt at that moment.

'I think I need to go to work.'

'On a Saturday, sir?'

'Yes, madame. I need to escape from the stale air of the past that that woman brought into this house. Please open all the windows, will you? I would like the place aired.'

*

When he walked home that evening, unusually for London, the stars were out overhead. There would be frost in the morning and he could already feel the nip of winter on his face. Going to the hospital had distracted him as he hoped it would, but, turning his key in the lock, he knew the past was still waiting for him on the other side of the door. But so was Madame Smith, whose smile was more welcome than ever.

'Monsieur, a package arrived for you while you were out. I have placed it on your desk.'

'Thank you, madame. I expect it will be the students' examination scripts. I have rather a lot of marking to do this evening. Let us hope that at least some of them have read a book or two before attempting to impress me with their knowledge.'

'No, I think it is from Edinburgh, monsieur. And it arrived by special delivery.'

Cuthbert was intrigued and went straight to his study. There on the desk was the package, wrapped in heavy brown paper. The postmark was indeed from Edinburgh, and he undid the string and inside found a box with a letter attached. It was from his grandfather's lawyers. The note was short and to the point:

> *Dear Sir,*
>
> *Please find enclosed the withheld bequest from John Dalrymple, Esq. (deceased) to be fulfilled on 14th September 1931, being the 37th birthday of John Archibald Cuthbert, Esq. The delivery of said bequest now completes the terms of the late Mr Dalrymple's last will and testament.*
>
> *I remain, dear sir, your most obedient servant,*
> *William H. Moffat*
> *Corresponding Secretary for*
> *Bissett, Brodie & Jenks*

Cuthbert had forgotten about the second part of the belated bequest, so taken had he been by the arrival of his mother's portrait. Now, however, he remembered that he was also to receive another item from his grandfather, although he had never been told what to expect. He lifted the lid of the box; inside was something wrapped in tissue paper which he now unfolded.

Within the tissue paper was the slim blue book his grandfather had once shown him on his lap all those years ago. He took a deep breath, for these were his mother's poems, and all he could remember was the swirling copperplate of her delicate hand. He hardly dared open the book, knowing that within would be words he could now read, and he was far from sure he was ready after all these years to hear her speak. For so long, she had lived inside his imagination as the mute figure in the long blue velvet gown standing with the roses at her side, but here before him was her voice. He could feel the panic rise in his chest as he opened the soft leather.

On the first of the cream-coloured pages was written her name, Alexandra Dalrymple Cuthbert, and the date, June 1894. She had written these words when she had carried him in her womb, some three months before he would be born, and she would die.

This, in itself, was almost too much for Cuthbert to contend with, and he thought about closing the book and putting it away for another, stronger day. But her name drew him to the page, and he traced the ink that wove the curving letters of her handwriting, and he felt the need to turn the page.

There on the next page was the title of her work, and now he was sure she had written this book for him. The penmanship was beautifully ornate, and perhaps this had been the page his grandfather had shown him when he was 4 years old. All he remembered thinking at the time was that this was a book filled with wonderful drawings.

Now, he realised that these were her words written by an accomplished hand. He traced the lines and whispered the title: 'Sonnets for an Unborn Child'. He had been that child, and he still was despite the manly frame he now inhabited.

Unmothered by fate, a part of him had never grown up, and he longed now to hear his mother's sweet voice calling to him across the years. He longed to hear her soothe and comfort him in the way she had been so cruelly denied in life. But what could he expect? How could a few pages fill in for all the lost years? How could she have written anything to someone not yet formed? What if her words were bland or meaningless? There was no discussion now to be had, no possibility of redress or clarification. There was no way now to be grateful or to express his sorrow.

He closed the book and pushed it away from him, altogether unsure that he ever wanted to know. He couldn't bear to lose her again, and perhaps it was best if she lived on as the great beauty in the painting: ravishing yet silent.

He laid his hand on the book, as if trying to absorb its contents without having to engage with its reality. This was more than an object, and every moment he spent looking at it, touching it, made it seem ever more important and ever more daunting. He resolved to put it away until he was ready. When that might be, he did not know.

*

That evening he expected Jaeger to join him for dinner. Madame Smith was pleased he would be coming, for she knew how much Cuthbert needed a friend. While she could offer a hand, a smile, even a word of solace, Herr Jaeger could offer him love.

She had prepared a fine dinner for them both, and as she served it, Cuthbert relaxed and started to smile again. She caught moments of their conversation and began to realise how painful he had found Lady Allerton's visit and what that second parcel might contain.

'Will you read them for me?'

'Of course I will, but don't you want to know what she wrote?'

'I don't know. It's almost as if I couldn't bear to be disappointed. And then I feel so wretched at having such a thought. I'm only alive because of her – the very least I could do is give her a hearing, to read her words, the words she wrote for me. But I cannot bring myself to do so. Please, do it for me and then tell me what to do.'

The weight of the task seemed to Jaeger much heavier than that of the asking. However, he could see Cuthbert's distress and that pained him. He reached across the table and took his hand. Cuthbert interlaced their fingers, as if in joint prayer.

'Of course, if that's what you want.'

Jaeger took up the book that lay on the table and opened it, but Cuthbert winced and said, 'Not here, not yet. Do it when you're alone, and we need never talk about it, if you think that's best.'

*

After dinner, Jaeger found Cuthbert sitting in the upstairs drawing room sipping whisky and looking at the painting of his mother. Cuthbert turned to see him standing by his side, holding his mother's book. He was trying to see anything in Jaeger's expression that might indicate what he had read. Jaeger in turn could see how anxious Cuthbert was and immediately put him out of his misery.

'Jack, you need to read this, all of it. Your mother had so much to say to you, and she said it all with such honesty and urgency. This was her message in a bottle to you across the years. You must open it and let her speak to you.'

'I don't think I can. It's too much.'

Jaeger knelt beside Cuthbert in the armchair and put his hand on his shoulder.

'Would you like me to read the first of the poems to you? Perhaps if you could hear her words spoken aloud and not simply read them on the page, that would make it easier.'

Cuthbert wasn't sure it would make a difference, but Jaeger

was right: he had to hear what his mother wished to say to him. He nodded and took a large sip of the whisky from the crystal glass he was cradling in both hands.

'This is the title poem: "Sonnet for an Unborn Child".'

Jaeger's words were slow and smooth and deep. His recital caught the rhythm and the rhyme of Alexandra Dalrymple's thoughts perfectly, even though they had been formed before he was born. Cuthbert listened at first in pain and then with sorrow and finally with a sense of peace that he had not expected.

'Read it again, Erich. Please.'

He had listened the first time with his eyes tightly closed, frightened of what he might see. Now, he listened looking up at her portrait, at how she had been when she wrote these words:

Sonnet for an Unborn Child

> Within this frail and feeble frame of mine,
> Swells sweetest life; beats fresh a heart anew,
> Some magic thou hast work'd to make me thine,
> Entwined our souls until this life be through.
> In sunlit dreams thou comest to mine eyes,
> I see thee in these arms as clear as hope.
> I hold thee close to hear thy gentle sighs,
> But rough winds blow me down this sliding slope.
> Nine moons must mend themselves before we meet,
> And I ache sore with fear for what must come.
> There's peril in our parting, bittersweet;
> I must outrun the beat of death's dark drum.
> When life is done with us, what's left but dust?
> But e'en in death a shadow cast we must.

As Erich recited the poem, Cuthbert imagined he could see his mother's lips move, forming the words, and it was only when Jaeger finished that he closed his eyes and let the tears spill down his cheeks.

'She's still here, isn't she? She's always been here inside me, still calling to me, still telling me everything will be fine. She's nothing but dust now, but her long, beautiful shadow protects me. It always has. Thank you, Erich. Thank you for helping me find her again.'

Epilogue

London: 3 November 1931

Madame Smith, who took care of all the household accounts, was accustomed to opening bills addressed to Cuthbert, but amongst those from the various tradespeople who serviced their lives, she noted one rather unusual invoice that she brought up for his attention over breakfast.

'There is an invoice in this morning's post, monsieur, but I am not sure it can be correct. It is from a stonemason's in Lewisham.'

'That's correct, madame. Just some unfinished business. I would be obliged if you could see that it is paid promptly.'

'Right away, monsieur.'

*

The Reverend Henshall was unsure when they had been placed, but it was the morning of All Souls' Day when he first noticed. There was a sharp frost, and he was out early, walking across the churchyard, thinking about the sermon he would be delivering later that morning and still trying to order his thoughts. The text he had taken was from *Lamentations* 3:21–23.

This I call to mind, and therefore I have hope:
the steadfast love of the Lord never ceases,
his mercies never come to an end;
they are new every morning.

'New every morning' seemed such appropriate words as he looked about him. The world was falling asleep as winter crept on, but everywhere there were still such vibrant signs of life. On a bare bush there were the delicate frozen strands of silk woven by a spider overnight, and a sharp robin, unsure whether its territory was being encroached upon, twitched his head to look sidelong at the vicar. It took flight and alighted a few yards away on the old east wall, and, as the reverend followed its path with his eyes, that was when he saw them.

He went over the grass as if summoned by the bird and stood solemnly. By the wall of the churchyard, three white marble headstones had been placed side by side. The inscriptions were carved simply in the stone:

R.I.P.
Mary Nightingale
(1912–1931)
And her beloved daughter
Jeannie
Aged 2 years

R.I.P.
Margaret Webb
(1909–1931)
And her beloved daughter
Katie
Aged 5 years

R.I.P.
Rose Smith
(1910–1931)
And her beloved son
Charlie
Aged 4 years

The vicar removed his hat and stood by the graves, all of which bore fresh posies of wildflowers placed there by Sister Hilda. He bowed his head and said a silent prayer for the young women and their children who had now been laid to rest. Pain and despair and madness had taken them all to their graves. Whether sin had any hand in it all, he really could not say.

Author's Note

This is a work of fiction, and Jack Cuthbert did not exist, but I like to think he could have, so I have placed him in a world that is painted as plausibly as possible. In the past, people did not just dress differently and speak differently, they also had very different ways of thinking about the world. Ideas that we take for granted had yet to be articulated and notions that we see as outdated, even dangerously so, were still common currency. That must be remembered, especially when discussing subjects as delicate and emotive as suicide in an historical context.

The forensic detail, so important to the authenticity of my created world, is as faithful to the time period as I can make it. If Cuthbert and his team were investigating an unknown cause of poisoning today, they would have some very sophisticated artillery at their disposal, but not so in the early 1930s. However, despite the passing decades, the most important tool that any pathologist has is observation, and I hope I have made it clear that this was just as important for Cuthbert as it remains today.

As with the other Jack Cuthbert novels, I have relied heavily on historical accounts of the time period, always preferring to read the words of those who were there rather than those who have interpreted those words after the fact. That said, I am also indebted to the authors of a number of more modern accounts. A selection of the most important works of both kinds are listed below.

John Glaister's 1915 3rd edition of his *A Text-book of Medical Jurisprudence and Toxicology*.

The Royal College of Pathologists' 2005 *Guidelines on Autopsy Practice, Scenario 6: Deaths associated with epilepsy*.

June Callwood's 1953 article, 'A Day in an Anglican Convent'.

Albert C. Cain's 2002 paper in *Psychiatry*: 'Children of Suicide: the Telling and the Knowing'.

Russell Blacker's undated article, 'Suicide Down the Ages – A Judeo-Christian Perspective', on the Christian Medical Fellowship website.

James Stewart Watt Irvine's 1930 PhD thesis: 'The Doctrine of Sin in the Theology of John Bunyan'.

Catherine M. Carmichael's 2001 PhD thesis: 'A Post-Christian Perception of Sin and Forgiveness'.

John MacPherson's 1882 treatise: 'The Westminster Confession of Faith'.

THE DR JACK CUTHBERT MYSTERY SERIES

BOOK 1 *The Silent House of Sleep*

Death is a lonely business

No one who meets Dr Jack Cuthbert forgets him. Tall, urbane, brilliant but damaged, the Scottish pathologist is the best that D.C.I. Mowbray of Scotland Yard has seen. But Cuthbert is a man who lives with secrets, and he is still haunted by demons from the trenches in Ypres. When not one but two corpses are discovered in a London park in 1929, Cuthbert must use every tool at his disposal to solve the mystery of their deaths. In the end, the horrifying truth is more shocking than even he could have imagined.

BOOK 2 *The Moon's More Feeble Fire*

She was someone's daughter

In 1930, the killing of a Soho prostitute is hardly a priority for Scotland Yard. But when a second, similar murder comes to light, and then a third, everything changes. Cuthbert and his team find themselves in a nightmarish world of people-trafficking, prostitution and drug use amongst the upper classes. Using all his forensic skills, Cuthbert sets out to solve one of the most baffling cases of his career. One final question remains unanswered until a faded photograph reveals its tragic secret.

BOOK 3 *To the Shades Descend*

The dead all have stories to tell

A visit to Glasgow for a job interview in 1931 unexpectedly places Cuthbert at the centre of a devastating crime. Unwittingly, he finds himself working at the intersection between rising British fascism, antisemitism and the infamous Glasgow razor gangs. To solve the case, Cuthbert needs to rely on all the expertise he can gather from those around him. But who can he trust?

BOOK 4 *The Shadows and the Dust*

Sins never stay buried

Like all pathologists, Cuthbert finds dealing with dead children the hardest part of his job. However, when the body of a young boy is found in the grounds of a church orphanage, Cuthbert not only has to steel himself for the task ahead, he is also forced to revisit his own childhood grief. The boy in his shallow grave has been interred with some ritual, but just how did he die? And why was he killed? Working closely with his assistant and the team at Scotland Yard, Cuthbert slowly and painstakingly reveals the terrible truth.

Acknowledgements

Any novel owes its existence not just to its author but also to a diverse team of people who have helped make it possible. When that novel is the fourth in a series, it is also in large part a product of the readers of the previous three.

Without the encouraging comments from many readers and reviewers for the first three Dr Jack Cuthbert novels, I would not have had the confidence to publish a fourth. So a heartfelt thank you to everyone who has left a written review or who has pulled me quietly aside to tell me they enjoyed the books.

As for the team, I must first thank my early readers, especially Ellen, Alec, Anne, S.J. and Alex, whose feedback was invaluable in helping shape the final manuscript. Thanks also go to Sharon Mail, who once again took the story and assisted me in developing it.

My publisher Polygon has again made the whole process a thoroughly enjoyable and enriching one, and I am grateful for the time and expertise the team there has put into the project. Alison Rae, my editor, deserves special thanks for her consummate skill, tireless enthusiasm and endless tact. Without her input, this novel would not be what it is.

And, of course, nothing would be what it is without Moira.

Polygon

AN IMPRINT OF BIRLINN LIMITED

Head over to our website to find more
Birlinn books across fiction, non-fiction, sport,
poetry, children's books and academic history.

You can also sign up to our newsletter. Keep up
to date with all our new publications, launch events,
author interviews, special offers and much more.

http://birlinn.co.uk/birlinn-newsletter/

Follow the link or scan the QR Code below:

Explore Scotland with our app, Scotland-by-the-Book,
a new tool for readers at home and around the globe with
an interest in Scotland. Find out more on our website.

https://birlinn.co.uk/scotland-by-the-book/

Follow the link or scan the QR Code below: